THE DEVELOPMENT

A Cora Baxter Mystery

Jackie Kabler

ACKNOWLEDGEMENTS

As always, there are so many people I want to thank as another Cora Baxter novel heads out into the world. I have been so thrilled by the response to the series, not just from readers and those who follow me on social media but also from the book blogging and reviewing community. Thank you all so much for your love and support for Cora and her antics over the past couple of years – it means more than you know.

This time round I particularly want to thank my friend Sarah McKinnon for her advice on architects and property developers when I was creating the Randall Greythorpe character in *The Development*; Aaron Cupboard who responded to this childfree writer's plea on Twitter and suggested Lego Batman as a suitable toy for Harry; my family and friends, who never stop enthusiastically promoting the Cora books to others and encouraging me to keep going when I'm struggling to fit writing in around my full-time job (and especially my sister Loraine for the "robot baby" story); and of course my incredibly supportive (and extremely tolerant) husband, who puts up with me writing on every day off and every holiday and never complains (well, not very often).

And finally, my agent Robin Wade and the people who bring my books to life - the fabulous team at Accent Press, especially my editor Greg Rees and publishing assistant Katrin Lloyd. Your hard work is hugely appreciated. Thank you so much.

1

'Well, at least it's getting you out of the Brussels sprouts story. Be thankful for that, at least.'

The producer's voice sounded like that of a slightly manic Scottish robot as it crackled out of the Audi's speakers, and Cora Baxter smiled despite her anxiety.

'I think sprouts would have been a joy tomorrow actually, Sam, compared with the story we're on. But fair enough. Nathan hates cramming his floppy mane into a hairnet when we do food factory stories anyway, so at least he'll be pleased.'

She braked as a car slowed in front of her on the dark road, its left indicator flashing.

'Well, happy cameraman, happy life, eh? Anyway, stop worrying, OK? Go home, get some sleep, and I'll speak to you in the morning.'

'I'll try. That's if I get home at all, this traffic is murder. Speak tomorrow, Sam.'

'Night, Cora.'

Cora hit the button on her steering wheel to end the call and sighed, wishing heartily that the events of the past few days hadn't happened and that all she had to think about tonight was a straightforward story about Brussels sprouts. The warm summer had promised a bumper crop this year, but heavy rain through much of October had caused so much water damage that now, in early November, farmers had started issuing dire warnings about a Christmas sprout shortage across the UK. It was the perfect story for a Friday morning at this time of year for TV breakfast show *Morning Live*, on which Cora had worked as a reporter and newsreader for the past four years. After what had happened this week, though, the sprout story had tonight been given to another reporter, with Cora and her crew assigned to a live broadcast from Bristol for the third time this week.

As her mind drifted back to the past few days, she shivered despite the heat pumping out of the car's powerful air conditioning system, then groaned and braked again as red taillights suddenly glowed in front of her once more. She was still in south Bristol, at least an hour's drive from her home in Cheltenham even *without* congested roads, and her alarm would be going off at three tomorrow morning. She was used to the early starts, but even so…Cora glanced at the clock on the instrument display and made a sudden decision. It was after six o'clock, and she was exhausted. Time to forget attempting to reach the M5 motorway and try wiggling northwards along the back roads. She looked swiftly left and right, checking her exact location. She knew this area quite well, and suddenly remembered a right turn up ahead that should, she thought, take her onto a winding country lanes route she'd used once or twice before after seeing a taxi driver take it as he drove her to Bristol airport during rush hour. It was definitely a *longer* way home on paper, but with this congestion…

Five minutes later Cora was navigating the dark twists and turns of a narrow road that was single-track but blissfully free of traffic. She took a deep breath and rolled her head towards one shoulder and then the other, trying to release some of the tension. She'd get home, run a deep, fragrant bath, have one glass of wine – *just* one – and then collapse into bed. She might get five hours' sleep, if she was lucky. Not bad for a work night. And, hopefully, after tomorrow this horrible story would be over and she and the boys could get back to having some fun.

Cora stopped at a T-junction, checked the road signs and drove straight across. This was definitely the right way. There was a bridge a mile or so up ahead, she remembered, then a left turn, and then it should be an easy drive home on familiar roads. She breathed deeply again, relaxing a little, and reached over to turn the radio on. It was tuned to a classical music station, one she'd started listening to recently when she was feeling particularly stressed. It was a new habit which had resulted in much gentle mocking by her camera crew, and questions about whether she was "channelling Inspector Morse". Cora cheerfully ignored the jibes and now, as the reassuring strains of Grieg's *Piano Concerto in A minor* filled the car, she felt a sense of calm descend. She really must stop getting so anxious about work, she thought. It was just a job, after all; just a news story, as her boyfriend Adam repeatedly told her. As a London-based police officer, he had his share of difficult work days too, but over the years he'd learned to take them in his stride, generally getting a little less agitated about work than Cora tended to, and encouraging her to take a slightly less uptight approach too. Yes - as her friends never stopped reminding her, Detective Chief Inspector Adam Bradberry was good for her, very good indeed, in so many ways. They'd been together for about a year and a half now, since they'd met on a murder investigation Adam was leading, and Cora couldn't remember a time she'd been happier in a relationship. She wouldn't be seeing him this coming weekend because he was on duty, but she'd call him as soon as she got home, she thought. Tell him the latest news from Bristol, offload it before attempting to sleep. He'd know what to say to make her feel better. He always did.

The story had seemed fairly straightforward at first, if pretty nasty. Last weekend, the seventy-year-old Iraqi owner of a small north Bristol corner shop had been the victim of a vicious attack which had left him in intensive care in Southmead Hospital; not content with beating the man, the perpetrator had also smashed his shop windows, looted his shelves and daubed racist slogans across his walls. A strong story for the local press, it wouldn't normally have made the national news, but the victim, Ahmed Alwan, had recently been awarded an "Unsung Hero" award by the *Daily Mail* for his work in the community. The man, it seemed, never stopped - as well as keeping his shop open for fifteen hours a day he also managed to run a youth group, manage a children's football team and provide a home delivery service for local pensioners. The outrage which followed the attack drew the attention of the national media, and on Monday morning Cora and her crew had duly been despatched to cover the story.

So far, so simple. But on Tuesday, when Cora had been making some follow-up calls to the hospital, and to the police press office to check on the investigation's progress, she had received an email to her *Morning Live* account which had turned everything on its head. The anonymous tipster - giving his name simply as "Paul" - said that he had watched Cora's report from outside the hospital and wanted her to know that despite the police saying that attempts to find the attacker had so far failed, he was being named locally as Alan Gregory, a thirty-something man who'd appeared in court several times on minor assault charges, and who'd been warned by fed-up magistrates that his next offence would most likely land him in prison.

"He's very well known in this neighbourhood for his

racist views", the email continued. "*Many of us have seen him standing on street corners, shouting abuse at anyone whom he considers to look* 'foreign' *– Muslim ladies in headscarves, Sikhs in turbans. He's a nasty piece of work.*"

"Paul" went on to say that at least two witnesses had seen and recognised Gregory running from the scene of the crime, and had informed police, but that officers had failed to act. And then he dropped the bombshell – the fact that residents believed that Alan Gregory was the younger brother of Detective Chief Inspector Gordon Gregory of Avon police.

'What? Gordon Gregory? DCI Gregory, who's leading the investigation into the attack on Ahmed Alwan? Are you *sure*, Cora?'

Senior producer and Cora's close friend Samantha Tindall had been astounded when Cora had forwarded the email to her on the news desk in London and then called her to discuss it.

'Yep. I did some Googling and it appears that DCI Gregory does indeed have a younger brother called Alan – there's a photo of them together at a police open day event last year on Avon's website. And then I checked the *Bristol Evening Post* website for court stories about Alan, and several come up, all assaults, two on Pakistani shopkeepers, although nothing nearly as serious as this latest one. And a couple of the articles have photos – it's definitely the same guy. Right little thug, by the look of it.'

'Blimey.'

There was a pause as Sam digested the news.

'And these witnesses, they've told the police they saw Alan Gregory running from the scene of this latest crime? And the cops have done nothing? Seriously?'

'Yep,' said Cora again. 'I emailed this Paul guy back, and asked him a few questions. He says the shop doesn't have CCTV, and there aren't any cameras on that particular street either, so there won't be any footage unfortunately, just the eye-witness reports. But the two witnesses who saw Gregory running off are absolutely positive it was him, apparently. They went straight to the police who said they'd look into it, but according to Paul, they've done nothing. He says the guy's still wandering the streets, being abusive to everyone as usual and looking smug. There are mutterings locally that the cops are unwilling to arrest him because he's Gordon Gregory's brother, especially as an assault this serious will definitely result in him being banged up.'

'Gosh.'

The line went quiet again.

'I know.'

Cora, who had been calling from her car, parked in a quiet side street near the scene of the crime, pulled down the driver's mirror, ran her fingers through her dark brown bob and frowned at her reflection. She looked a mess, she decided. Those dark shadows under her eyes…an early night was *badly* needed.

'OK, so you're due to interview DCI Gregory on tomorrow's show, aren't you? When we do an update on Mr Alwan's condition, and film his kids' footie club bringing that massive card they've made for him to the hospital?'

'Yes. Gregory said he'll come up to Southmead and do a slot on the eight o'clock news, update us on the enquiry. Why?'

'Well…' Sam hesitated. 'I hope I won't regret suggesting this – but how do you feel about confronting him about it live on air?'

6

It was Cora's turn to hesitate. She thought for a moment, unsure.

'Really? Flipping heck, Sam. Isn't that a bit risky? I mean, I have no problem with it in principle – I can say the man is being extensively named locally as Alan Gregory, a man known for his racist views and with a history of assault charges. But to accuse him of covering up for his brother, on national TV...?'

'I know, I know. He'll probably walk off, but oh Cora – what great TV it will make! And if you're sure of your facts...just think carefully about how you word it. Are you up for it?'

Cora had thought for a moment again, then nodded slowly.

'OK. Let's do it.'

The following morning there'd been a knot of apprehension in her stomach as she'd greeted DCI Gordon Gregory, a tall, brusque, ruddy-cheeked man in his late forties, ahead of their 8 a.m. interview. As the camera rolled, and the interview was beamed live to the nation, she had taken a deep breath and calmly informed the police officer that the attacker was being named locally as Alan Gregory.

'And I also believe, DCI Gregory, that this man is your younger brother. Is there any truth in the rumours flying around this neighbourhood that *that* is the reason he has not been arrested for this horrendous attack?'

DCI Gregory's face had flushed a deep red, his eyes narrowing. For a long moment he stared at Cora, then swallowed hard.

'I cannot comment on that. And if that's all you've got to say, I have work to do,' he had growled, in his strong Liverpudlian accent. Cora had swiftly ended the interview, the police officer glowering at her. As soon as the camera had been switched off, DCI Gregory stepped menacingly towards her, standing so close she could smell the stale coffee on his breath.

'How dare you try to embarrass me like that on live television?' he hissed. 'How *dare* you? Consider the relationship between Avon police and your breakfast show well and truly over. And I'll be making a formal complaint to your editor, Miss Baxter, mark my words.'

Now, Cora drove wearily through the darkness, music still playing softly, her headlights illuminating the sharp edges of the old stone walls that bordered the narrow road, their outlines intermittently softened by hedgerows, bare now as winter took hold. There was already a shimmer of frost on the tarmac, the promise of another freezing cold night ahead. Cora shivered again. She knew that as a news reporter, confronting Gregory about what she'd learned had been the right thing to do, but the confrontation had unnerved her. True to his word, the DCI had made a formal complaint to Betsy Allan, editor of *Morning Live*. Betsy had reassured him that the matter would be looked into, and then immediately called Cora, telling her not to worry, that she had done the right thing and that 'it would all blow over, in time.' Sam too had been straight on the phone, telling her friend and colleague not to get stressed about it all.

'It was bloody awesome, Cora. Well done. Great TV.'

Then this afternoon, Thursday, two pieces of news had reached the news desk – one, that Alan Gregory had been arrested and charged with the attack on Ahmed Alwan. And two, that DCI Gordon Gregory had been temporarily suspended from duty while a misconduct investigation was carried out. Tomorrow, Cora and her crew would be reporting on these facts, on location outside Avon's south Bristol police headquarters, and she wasn't looking forward to it, knowing that their welcome from Gregory's colleagues was unlikely to be a warm one. Police officers, like journalists, were fiercely protective of their own.

'I have well and truly had enough of this story now,' she announced, as she rounded a corner and saw the silhouette of a bridge a few hundred yards ahead. She braked, remembering that the road became single track again where the bridge crossed it, then slowed the car to a halt as another vehicle approached, deciding to let it pass before she navigated the narrow way. As she waited, she admired the curves of the old bridge, rising high above the road, its graceful arch crowned with decorative ironwork, the detail blurred in the darkness but, Cora remembered, by daylight a striking example of Victorian craftsmanship, with fleur-de-lis topping elaborate scrollwork. There was a car parked on the bridge now, headlights on, the light casting a golden glow on one ornate section of the hundred and fifty-year-old structure.

'Clarton Bridge, I think it's called. Beautiful,' Cora thought, as she moved off again. As she drew closer to the bridge, a sudden movement high above caught her eye. Confused, she glanced upwards for a moment then braked sharply, snapping her eyes back to the road in front of her, aware that it was about to narrow significantly. And then, in what she would later describe as a series of events that appeared to happen in slow motion, but which in reality took mere seconds, there was a scream, a whooshing sound, and a terrible, violent thud as something crashed into Cora's car. She stamped her foot on the brake and then recoiled in horror, skull slamming into the headrest.

'Oh my GOD. What the…what the HELL?'

Heart pounding violently, breathing in ragged gasps, she shrank back in her seat as far as she could, trying desperately to get away from what was now just inches away on the other side of the windscreen. Because something hadn't crashed *into* her car. It had crashed *onto* it. Onto it from above. And not some*thing*. Some*one*. Lying on the Audi's bonnet, face pressed grotesquely against the cracked glass, blank eyes staring straight at Cora, neck at an unnatural angle, was a young woman. A young, and clearly very dead, woman.

2

'Recovery truck will be here in a few minutes. I'd stay in there and keep warm until then if I were you. It's perishing out here.'

The female police officer shut the rear door of the car and wandered off, back towards the cluster of emergency service vehicles parked near the bridge, their blue lights flashing. In the midst of them, Cora's Audi looked small and broken: windscreen shattered, bonnet buckled and bloodstained. She shuddered and dragged her gaze away from the scene, hearing again the sickening thud, and seeing in her mind's eye the hideous image of the dead woman's face pressed against the window. She had stopped shaking now, but it had taken a while, the combined effects of shock and cold making her tremble uncontrollably until one of the first police officers on the scene had ushered her into the back of his marked car, kindly leaving the engine on and turning the heating up high. When the paramedics arrived, one had tried to check her over but she'd told him she was fine. It wasn't entirely true – she felt dizzy and queasy – but she knew she hadn't been physically hurt. The shivering and sick feeling in her stomach were simply a reaction to what she had just witnessed, and they would pass.

But that poor woman…

Cora had leapt out of her car in horror as soon as she'd managed to bring it to a halt and switch the engine off. By then, the young woman who'd slammed into the bonnet had slid to the ground, a slumped tangle of limbs in denim

11

jeans and a dark coat, and it had taken just a moment for Cora to confirm her first thought – that this was most definitely a dead body, the neck clearly broken, blood streaking dark highlights through long red-brown hair, soulless eyes still wide open. Hands shaking violently, she had called 999, and then waited, trembling, on the dark road for what seemed like hours, gaze drawn repeatedly and helplessly to the face of the dead woman, a white blur in the darkness. With the Audi blocking passage under the bridge, there was soon a small queue of vehicles on either side, impatient drivers getting out of their cars to see what was causing the obstruction and then withdrawing with shocked expressions. It had taken around twenty minutes for the police and ambulance service vehicles to fight their way through the evening rush hour, Cora gabbling her way through the events of the past half an hour as a tall, serious-faced policeman took hasty notes.

Now, as she sat in the warm car, her body slowly calming down, her mind finally clear enough for logical thought, she remembered the conversation she'd overheard through the then slightly ajar door as two of the police officers had stood near the vehicle a few minutes earlier, confirming what Cora had already assumed.

'Suicide by the looks of it, then,' the younger of the two, a wiry looking man with a red goatee beard had said.

'Aye. Broke her neck in the fall so it woulda been quick, at least. Poor kid.' The older officer was shorter and stocky, with a Geordie burr.

'Mmm. Didn't look much older than eighteen, nineteen, did she? Shit. Don't envy whoever gets to tell the family. Any ID on her, did you hear?'

'Don't know. Paul found what's probably her handbag up on the bridge though. Not much in it except a laptop and purse. Ange is going through it now…'

There'd been a yell from the bridge where the ambulance was preparing to leave, and the two officers had marched swiftly back to the scene, leaping into their own vehicles to move them out of the way. Now, waiting for the recovery truck to take her car away – and, hopefully, to drop her home - Cora shook her head sadly and rubbed her eyes, feeling her mascara smearing on her cheeks and not caring. Suicide. How utterly, utterly dreadful. What was going on in that poor woman's world that had driven her to take her own life, leaping from a road bridge in such a deserted area on a cold November night? Lost in thought, Cora jumped as there was a sudden sharp tap on the car window.

'He's here.'

The officer Cora had seen earlier gestured with her thumb to where a recovery truck was now moving slowly towards the bridge, a revolving amber beacon flashing on its roof.

'Oh, great, thank you.'

Suddenly feeling overwhelmed with tiredness, Cora climbed slowly out of the car and headed towards the bridge. The ambulance had left, and just two police vehicles remained at the scene, the Geordie officer now issuing instructions to the recovery driver. The man, plump and grey-haired and wearing a luminous yellow jacket, nodded vigorously.

'Right you are. And I'm to take the driver – this young lady – 'ome too?'

He gestured at Cora, and she smiled weakly.

'Yes, please. If that would be OK?'

The officer nodded at Cora and she smiled again.

'Thanks. That would be great. It's been kind of a long day.'

'Right you are,' the recovery truck man said again, his

13

Bristol brogue drawing out the 'are' in what Cora's cameraman Nathan always described as 'pirate style'.

'If you want to grab all your personal items from the vehicle, my love, I'll get the truck ready. Won't take long.'

'OK. Thank you. There's not much, just my handbag and some bits of kit in the back seat and the boot.'

'Plenty of space, no worries, love.'

The man rubbed his hands together and marched off. Suddenly shivering again as she approached her battered car, and carefully averting her eyes from the spot where the woman's body had lain, Cora gingerly opened the driver's door and lowered herself onto the seat. Her bag had flown off its normal perch on the passenger seat when she'd slammed on the brakes, and her belongings were scattered across the footwell. As she leaned down and began to gather them up, the lights of the departing police cars illuminated the Audi's interior for a few moments, aiding her task. Confident that she'd found everything, she sat up just as the vehicles moved slowly off down the road, blue lights still flashing. She watched them for a moment in the rear-view mirror, then climbed out of the car again. As she did, something caught her eye. What was that, on the windscreen? Something seemed to be caught under one of the wipers. She leaned closer, wondering if it was just a piece of debris from the accident, then frowned. That wasn't debris. It looked like...but how would that have got there?

She reached out and carefully retrieved the small, oblong-shaped object, gently lifting the windscreen wiper to release it. It was, as she had first thought, a computer memory stick. Or a 'flash drive' as Adam calls them, she thought, although she wasn't entirely sure whether that was the same thing or not. How weird. Cora shrugged her bag onto her shoulder as she stared at her find, wondering why the police hadn't noticed it. It wasn't hers, she knew that. So did that mean it was the victim's? Had it fallen from the bridge with her, or fallen out of her clothing when she landed? Maybe.

Cora looked around, but the police had definitely gone. Unsure what to do, she shrugged again and popped the little stick into her bag. She'd hand it in tomorrow, after their live broadcast outside police HQ, she decided. Desperate now to get home, she headed round to the boot to collect the rest of her things.

3

Nathan Nesbit placed his camera carefully into its padded box in the boot of his car, pushed his dark floppy hair back out of his eyes and turned to Cora, a half smile playing on his lips.

'You haven't had much luck with that fancy new car of yours, have you? First that little drama on the day you got it, and now this. Car of doom, that one is.'

Cora scowled at her cameraman.

'Oh shut up, Nathan. Wish I'd never told you about that now. And anyway, you can't possibly compare the two... the two *incidents*. What happened the day I bought the car was down to me being a numpty as usual. What happened yesterday was... well, it was horrific.'

Nathan's smile faded and, suddenly looking rather shamefaced, he slammed the boot shut and turned back to face her.

'I'm so sorry, Cora, I didn't mean...yes, it was terrible. That poor woman. I'm really sorry, honestly. Don't think before I speak sometimes.'

'It's OK, and I'm sorry too, I didn't mean to snap at you. I didn't sleep much last night, kept seeing her...'

Cora shuddered. 'But to change the subject, can we just forget now about the "little drama" on the day I bought the car, as you so subtly put it? It's been *weeks*.'

'Maybe. Eventually. It's too much fun ribbing you about it to stop just yet.'

Cora rolled her eyes as Nathan's face creased into a broad grin. Soundman Rodney Woodhall, who was

16

leaning against the cameraman's car, polishing his little round glasses with the hem of his bright yellow fleece, sniggered.

'I still don't know how you managed it, Cora. I mean, who gets stuck in the back of their own car? Lucky that salesman came along, eh?'

Cora sighed. It *had* been slightly ridiculous, even for her. She'd picked up her new car, a sleek black Audi TT, just three weeks ago, to replace the BMW she'd driven since she started at *Morning Live*. As a roving reporter most of the time, unless she was covering on the newsreader's desk in London, she was on the road five or six days a week, and the job was tough on cars – she'd clocked up well over two hundred thousand miles in less than four years. She'd been thrilled with the new Audi, and with her surprisingly good trade-in deal, but it was when she'd been transferring her belongings from the old vehicle to the new one on the garage forecourt that things had gone slightly awry. For reasons even *she* wasn't completely sure about in retrospect, she'd clambered right into the rear of her new two-door car to stash her de-icer, car blanket and other bits and pieces in the storage compartments and on the back seat. But when she was satisfied that all was neatly arranged, and attempted to exit the cramped space, she'd found herself well and truly trapped, unable to reach the mechanism that slid the front seats forward. She'd struggled for several minutes, then decided to attempt to squeeze through the narrow gap between the two front seats instead. It was at this point that a bemused salesman had cautiously opened the car door, to find a red-faced Cora in a semi-horizontal position, feet on the rear seat and head hovering over the gear stick as she endeavoured to make her escape. He'd obligingly hauled her out of the car, politely asking if she was alright, but a mortified Cora could see that he was struggling to suppress his laughter.

'Bet he absolutely pissed himself when you'd gone,' Rodney added now.

'Yes, yes, OK, I'm an idiot. Now, if you've both finished packing up, can we go and find some breakfast? I'm starving.'

'Me too.'

Nathan slammed his boot shut and turned to look at his colleagues.

'There's a little greasy spoon place just on the corner - we can walk and leave the cars here. Rodney, do you want to help Scott finish up and then meet me and Cora there in two minutes? Oh – and nice look today, by the way. I hear giant banana is very in for spring/summer.'

Cora snorted. She adored Rodney, but he was notorious for his rather eccentric dress sense, and Nathan never missed an opportunity to comment on it. Today, the soundman had teamed the luminous yellow fleece with green khaki combat trousers and gold trainers, a fairly eye-catching combination on a grey November morning. Fortunately, easy-going Rodney was so used to the daily, light-hearted digs from his colleagues that he rarely got offended.

'Bananas are good for you, and yellow is a happy colour, so shut up, Nathan,' he said cheerfully over his shoulder, as he stomped off to the satellite truck where engineer Scott Edson was winding cable onto a big drum and whistling loudly.

'Yes, shut up, Nathan. Come on, let's go. We can order for everyone as soon as we get there to save time. We all have pretty much the same thing every day anyway.'

Cora shivered and pulled the zip of her padded jacket a

little higher under her chin. It was barely above zero this morning, and they'd been broadcasting from outside Avon police headquarters since 6 a.m., reporting live for the show's half-hourly news bulletins. As predicted, their welcome hadn't been a warm one. The police couldn't stop them from broadcasting outside the building – it was a public road, after all – but there'd been no niceties today, no offers of coffee or access to toilets, things which were usually commonplace. Today they hadn't been reporting on a crime which the police required public assistance to solve, but on alleged misconduct by the police themselves, so the lack of pleasantries had come as no surprise. It was 9.30 now and, despite her warm attire, Cora was freezing. A steaming cup of tea and some poached eggs would go down very nicely, she thought, as she and Nathan headed towards the café.

Forty minutes later she wiped the last of the yolk from her plate with a piece of wholemeal bread, swallowed and leaned back in her seat with a satisfied sigh. The "greasy spoon" had actually turned out to be a cosy little café with American diner-style booths, colourful prints of old movie posters on the walls and an extensive breakfast menu. The poached eggs, hash browns and crispy bacon Cora had ordered had been delicious, and she was suddenly feeling rather content, despite the horror of last night. Friday morning, a nice weekend ahead and - hopefully, she thought, mentally crossing her fingers – the end of the DCI Gregory story. With him suspended from duty and his brother in custody for the assault on the shopkeeper, *Morning Live* editor Betsy had earlier declared her interest in the case to be at an end.

'Wonder how he persuaded all of his colleagues not to arrest his brother though? Even though more than one witness saw him running away from the scene of the crime?' she mused aloud.

'DCI Gregory?'

Nathan plonked his ketchup-covered knife and fork onto his empty plate and pushed it aside.

'Yes. Do you think he gave Alan an alibi or something?'

Nathan nodded. 'Must have been something like that. Maybe claimed it was a case of mistaken identity. Or maybe he just bullied all his colleagues into keeping quiet. Wouldn't surprise me. He's a pretty unpleasant bugger.'

'True. Maybe. Anyway, I suppose it doesn't really matter now. We'll be on to something new for Monday's show, thankfully.'

Cora picked up her second mug of Earl Grey tea and took a sip.

'Oh I dunno, I've quite liked being so close to home this week. *Way* more sleep than usual,' said Rodney, picking at a brown sauce stain on his fleece.

Rodney lived in Bristol with his girlfriend Jodie, so it had been a delightfully easy week for him – not bad for any of them, in fact. Cora's Cheltenham flat was only an hour or so away, the Gloucestershire cottage where Nathan lived with his partner Gareth and a menagerie of chickens, ducks and geese was a similar distance, and Scott's home with his wife Elaine and two daughters was in Worcester, a short hop up the M5. It hadn't been a particularly enjoyable week, but it had been a nice change from their usual routine. The quartet had been on the road together for most of Cora's four years on the breakfast show, and were normally in a different part of the country every morning, on call for breaking news stories twenty-four hours a day and spending long hours driving from location to location, often through the night. They frequently survived on three or four hours' sleep a night during the week, desperately trying to catch up on Saturdays, their only full day off.

'Yes, not bad I suppose,' said Cora. 'I certainly don't feel as knackered today as I usually do on a Friday. And thanks again for making such a big diversion to pick me up this morning, Scott. It was very kind. I'm collecting a hire car straight after this so I'll be fine for Monday.'

'No problem. What goes around bums around, you'll pay me back one day.'

Scott, who was still chomping his way through the last of the four sausages he'd ordered with his full English, waved his fork at her. The burly engineer, six feet tall with a shiny shaved head, had lived down south for years, but had never lost his broad Bolton accent, or his tendency to mangle the English language with frequent and always amusing malapropisms.

'Err – what goes around *comes* around, not *bums*, Scott. You're hilarious.'

Cora giggled, and Nathan and Rodney grinned. Scott shrugged, shovelling another forkful of sausage into his mouth.

'Whatever,' he said, mouth full, then chewed and swallowed. 'Anyway, what's happening with your lovely new car? A write-off or what?'

'Not sure. Garage said they'd let me know later today. I don't think I want it back though, to be honest. Not after someone's…well, someone's *died* on it.'

She shuddered, the image of the dead woman's face against the windscreen flashing into her mind for the umpteenth time since last night.

'Bloody hell, I don't blame you. I wouldn't want it back either. Sorry again, for being so insensitive earlier.'

Nathan, who was sitting next to Cora on the bench seat, slipped an arm round her shoulders and gave her a

21

squeeze.

'It's fine, forget it.'

She smiled at him, then gasped.

'Oh shit! I totally forgot!'

'What?'

Nathan jerked his arm away from her in surprise at the sudden outburst, and all three looked at her questioningly.

'Last night. I forgot – I found something, after the police had left. On my car, stuck under the windscreen wiper. Hang on…'

She groped under the table for her handbag and rummaged in it.

'Here, look!'

She finally located the memory stick and slapped it down on the table. Scott reached out and picked it up carefully.

'A flash drive? Where did you say you found it?'

'It was stuck under one of my wipers. I noticed it when I was collecting my stuff from the car before it was taken away. It's obviously not mine, so I'm thinking it might be the woman's…the woman who jumped off the bridge. Maybe fell out of her pocket or something? The police obviously didn't notice it – well, I suppose they were more concerned with getting her body into the ambulance and reopening the road. I was going to hand it in to somebody at police HQ today but I totally forgot.'

'You can do it now, when we go back to collect the cars,' said Nathan. 'But I wonder why she was carrying a flash drive? Shall we be naughty and have a peek, see what's on it? I've got my laptop in my bag.'

Cora hesitated. 'I'm not sure. Seems a bit – I don't know, a bit intrusive?'

She looked across the table at Scott and Rodney, who both shrugged.

'Might be nothing but photos and music on it. But, on the other hand, it might give us some clue as to why she jumped,' said Nathan. 'You did say earlier that you'd love to know why she did it, what drove her to do something so extreme. Might give you some closure.'

Cora nodded slowly. She had slept badly last night, thoughts of the young woman swirling around her mind. What had happened in her life that was so terrible she felt she couldn't go on? Had she been ill, maybe? Why had she travelled to a lonely bridge on a quiet country road and flung herself off it on a cold, wintry night? There would be an inquest, of course – there always was in the case of a suspected suicide – but Cora knew that the reasons behind such tragic deaths weren't always revealed. A quick look at the contents of the memory stick wouldn't hurt, would it? Nobody would know, after all. She thought for a moment, swinging wildly between feelings of guilt and curiosity, then made up her mind.

'Let's do it,' she said, and Nathan nodded and pulled his laptop out of his bag. A minute later, the laptop quietly whirring, he inserted the little drive into one of the ports on the side.

'OK, here we go…oh. Just one document, by the look of it. Just called "INFO". Right, let's see… hang on…'

He put the laptop on the outer edge of the table and angled the screen to face inwards towards the wall, giving all four of them a decent view but ensuring that nobody else in the café could see what they were looking at. The place had filled up now, a cluster of harassed-looking mums with toddlers and pushchairs chattering away at the window table, a scattering of chilled out student types drinking coffee and eating toast in the nearby booths. Cora peered at the screen.

'OK, so it's a picture. Or a map, or plan of some sort?

It says "Elmsley Park". Where's that?'

Nathan shook his head.

'Dunno. Looks like an architect's drawing to me. Of a housing estate, maybe? Look – houses, some green space, a few roads linking different bits together... a kids' play area there too, look.'

He jabbed at the screen with his finger.

'The houses are funny-shaped though,' said Scott, tipping his head to one side to get a better view. 'Space-age, almost. Look at those weird round roofs and those spiky turret bits. Odd, isn't it? And look – there's a big X marked on that street to the right. Wonder what that is?'

'Buried treasure?' said Nathan, and grinned.

'Elmsley Park!'

Rodney suddenly banged his hand on the table, making them all jump.

'I knew that name was familiar. I remember now. It's here, in Bristol, I read an article about it in the weekend papers a while back.'

'What is it, then? A housing estate?' Cora was puzzled.

'Yes. Well, a *proposed* housing estate, more accurately. It's not built yet. Not even sure how far along it is with planning permission and so on, to be honest. It's been in the news a bit, because this whizz kid housing developer – I can't think of his name right now, but it'll come to me – wants to build this new, really funky development on an old factory site, right next to a residential area. There've been protests about it for some reason, can't remember why. But could be due to the design. *Architecturally daring*, I think the article said. Wonder why this girl had a copy of the plans on her though?'

'Maybe she was into architecture?' Scott frowned.

'What's it say there, though? There's a few words scribbled alongside the picture. Can you zoom in, Nathan?'

Nathan nodded.

'OK, let's take a look. Handwritten, she's obviously written on a hard copy of the map and then scanned it,' he said, and squinted at the screen.

'I think it says "*M Diamonds*" at the top? And under that, "*U18*", with a question mark. And the word "*Manchester*", underlined a few times. No idea what that's all about.'

They were all quiet for a moment, staring at the drawing and its scribbled annotations. Then Rodney yawned.

'Nope, no clue. And we still don't know why she jumped either, which is a shame. Poor woman. Anyway, I'm off. You lot coming?'

'Suppose so.'

Scott yawned too, and Nathan looked questioningly at Cora.

'Finished with this, then?'

She stared at the laptop's screen for a long moment, then nodded.

'Thanks, Nathan.'

But as they all gathered their belongings and stood up to leave, Nathan handing the memory stick back to her, Cora suddenly felt a strange reluctance to hand her find over to the police. There was something a little bit odd about what they had just seen – what did those notes on the map mean, and why was the woman carrying it with her, if indeed it *was* hers? The journalist in Cora was intrigued.

'I'll take it home, make a copy, and then hand it in next week,' she thought as she and her crew left the café and headed back down the road to where they'd left their cars. After all, nobody would know. What harm would it do?

4

'Have either of you ever heard of Randall Greythorpe?'

Cora plonked herself down on one end of the chocolate brown suede sofa in her living room and looked at her friends in turn.

Nicole Latimer, who was curled up on the other end of the big couch, put her wine glass carefully down on the little Perspex table next to her and shook her head.

'Sounds like a posh accountancy firm or something,' she said.

'No, no, it's not an accountant's. I've heard of him, yes.'

On the sofa opposite, Rosie Gregg was frowning as she tried to place the name.

'Isn't he that housing developer, making a bit of a name for himself with his wacky architecture? He's working on something down in Bristol. Alastair was telling me about him.'

'Ah, of course! I should have thought of asking Alistair,' said Cora, and reached for her own wine glass. Rosie's husband was a furniture designer, becoming quite well known himself and always knowledgeable about the latest movers and shakers in the property and interiors worlds.

'Why are you interested? Not moving to Bristol, are you?'

There was a note of alarm in Nicole's voice, and Cora gave her a reassuring poke in the arm.

'Course not. Wouldn't leave you two, would I?'

Cora and Rosie had been friends since they were twelve years old, and had met Nicole at a party more than eight years ago. The three of them had been inseparable ever since, or certainly as inseparable as their busy jobs and families allowed, living within a couple of miles of each other in Cheltenham and getting together as often as they possibly could. Cora's fifth-floor apartment in one of the smartest parts of town was one of her favourite places in the world, and it was always a joy to have Rosie and Nicole there with her, sipping wine and eating pizza, and catching up on their latest news. Rosie, a mum of three young children, ran a successful floristry business, while Nicole was a small-animal vet and had one young son with her science teacher husband Will. Cora was on the road for work much of the week, and often spent weekends in London with Adam, so a Friday evening at home in Gloucestershire with her friends was a rare treat, and they were making the most of it tonight. There was plenty of chilled white wine in the fridge, and a huge curry was tonight's fast food of choice, already on order from their favourite Indian restaurant. For now, 'just in case we might pass out with hunger before the food arrives,' as Cora had explained, she had filled bowls with spicy mixed nuts and cheddar and red onion crisps, and she leaned over to grab a handful of nuts, popping one in her mouth with a satisfied sigh. Friday nights in were the *best*, she thought.

'Well, phew,' said Nicole. 'Can't have you breaking up our little gang by moving to some swanky pad down there. We see you little enough as it is. Why the interest in this Randall bloke, then?'

Cora swallowed, and washed the nut down with another gulp of wine. Her friends already knew about the horrible death of the young woman who'd jumped from the bridge, so she quickly filled them in about the USB stick and what she and the boys had seen when they'd viewed its contents on Nathan's laptop.

'Randall Greythorpe is the housing developer who's building Elmsley Park, the new estate on the drawing we found,' she explained. 'I looked it up when I got home from work earlier. In his pictures he looks like one of those suave, wide-boy estate agents, all sharp suit and quiffy hair, but he's quite impressive. He's an architect by trade, so quite unusually he does the lot, the designing as well as the developing. He's only in his late thirties but he's made a real splash in the business already. He's done a few really high-end, quirky developments in Essex and Surrey and now wants to move west and north, hence Bristol.'

'So why's a young woman carrying a plan of his new housing development around with her?'

Rosie pushed a strand of red-blonde hair back from her forehead, looking puzzled.

Cora shrugged.

'I'm not entirely sure, as we don't even know her name yet. I think the inquest will probably happen early next week though, so hopefully we'll find out more then. But after reading up on it today I'm wondering if she might have been one of the protesters. There's a small group of locals who've been extremely vocal in their opposition to it all. That could be why she was carrying the plan around with her, I suppose, although I guess that could have been for any number of reasons…'

Nicole leaned forwards to stretch her long arms, clad as always in black, out in front of her, then sank back in her seat again.

'Yep. Maybe it was the opposite. Maybe she *loved* the place, and wanted to buy one of the new houses or something. Or maybe she was an architecture student and was studying the designs. And anyway, Cora, why does it matter? I'm slightly shocked that you and the boys even looked at the contents of that memory stick, actually. You're not getting... well, *involved* in something again, are you?'

'Oh, Cora! Please don't. We're only just getting over the last thing. Can't we just have a nice quiet winter?' Rosie's tone was pleading.

Cora shook her head. 'I'm not getting involved in anything, don't worry. I don't even think there's anything to get involved *in*, just a few unanswered questions, that's all. Yes, I know we probably shouldn't have been so nosy, Nicole, and I do feel a bit guilty. But the plan, map, whatever you want to call it, is kind of interesting, you know? Those odd scribbled notes, and the big X marks the spot thing.'

'Hmmm. Well, it's done now. And it's an awful tragedy, granted. And dreadful that it happened right in front of you. But we know you too well, Baxter. You've got that look in your eye,' said Nicole dubiously.

Cora grimaced. They had, admittedly, had quite a difficult few months earlier in the year, when she had enlisted the help of all her friends to try to find a woman connected to a murder which had happened a little too close to home. It had been an extremely stressful period, and she could totally understand why Rosie and Nicole might not want her to get tangled up in anything else so soon, especially with Christmas looming.

'No look in my eye, honestly, except a hungry one – wish the curry would hurry up! But...well, that poor girl *died* on my car. Died right in front of me. It was horrific, you know? And I'd just like to know why she jumped, that's all. I feel sort of – well sort of personally involved, even though I didn't know her. I can't stop thinking about her, and knowing why it happened might, I don't know, help me to move on from it. Nothing more than that, I promise.'

Nicole and Rosie exchanged looks of exaggerated scepticism, rolling their eyes theatrically, and Cora laughed.

'Stop it! I'm serious. Come on, let's change the subject. Chuck the remote over, Rosie. That Benedict Cumberbatch thing is on in a minute and the food shouldn't be long. More wine, anyone?'

'Ridiculous question,' said Rosie, throwing the TV remote control at Cora, who caught it deftly. 'When have we *ever* said no to more wine?'

5

'Cora, that can't be his real name. It just can't. Seriously, have you checked it's not a joke?'

Nathan was wide-eyed as he scanned the call sheet which had been emailed to his phone. It was just before 5 a.m. on Monday morning, and Cora and the crew were setting up their kit in a dimly lit and rather fusty office at a car parts factory in Birmingham, ahead of an interview with its managing director. The factory had last night announced its imminent closure after forty years of business, putting two hundred people out of work with Christmas just weeks away.

'I mean, *Randy Person*? Come on, really? That is *not* a real name. And we're going to need more lights in here, it's like trying to shoot an interview down a coal mine. Rodney, can you ask Scott if he's got any extras? Shame you're not wearing that hideous bright yellow fleece today. Might have helped.'

'Yeah, yeah, whatever. I'll go and ask Scott. See you in a mo.'

Rodney rolled his eyes at Cora and headed for the door, and she smiled and turned to her cameraman.

'He's American. Randy Person, I mean. Randy doesn't mean the same thing over there, does it? And yes, I've checked, I Googled him last night when I got the job email through. It's his real name, alright. In fact, there are loads of Randy Persons, if you look – Facebook, LinkedIn, everywhere. There's even a police chief in the States called Randy Person. Can you imagine – Chief

Randy Person?'

'Bloody hell. Hey guys, I'm not just a Randy Person, I'm the *chief* Randy Person…that is *insane!*'

Nathan let out a loud cackle, then stopped abruptly as the door opened and the secretary who had let them in earlier reappeared, balancing a tray of mugs.

'Tea!' she said brightly. 'Anything else you need? Mr Person will be down very shortly.'

Nathan snorted, tried rather unsuccessfully to turn the noise into a cough, and turned quickly away to rummage in his camera bag, shoulders shaking.

Cora glared at him, then smiled at the woman, who had put the tray down on the office desk and now had a rather confused look on her face.

'Very kind of you. And no, we're OK I think,' she said, suddenly suppressing a violent urge to giggle herself. She desperately hoped she'd be able to keep a straight face when Randy introduced himself. Clearly, Nathan was going to be of no help whatsoever this morning.

'I mean, it might be fine over in the States. But if that was me, and I moved to the UK, I'd have changed my name sharpish.'

Nathan picked up a slice of toast and took a large bite, shaking his head in wonderment. Three hours later, the cameraman was clearly still enchanted by the extraordinary name of that day's interviewee, and across the breakfast table Scott groaned loudly.

'Give it a rest, Nath. Can we not just eat in peace? It's Monday morning, we've got a long week ahead of us and I need to digest. Quit banging on about randy people, will you?'

Cora and Rodney laughed.

'You two are like an old married couple sometimes,'

33

Rodney said. 'Let's just change the subject, OK? It's probably short for something anyway – Randy, I mean. I bet he wasn't christened that. More likely to be Randolph or Randall or something…'

Rodney's voice tailed off as he speared a baked bean with his fork, and they all chewed in silence for a minute. As they did most days, the crew had retired to a local eatery once their live broadcasts were over. Today's was a cheerful little place just off the Hagley Road, a café they'd visited before and liked. Scott kept a list of good breakfast spots they'd found on their travels pinned to the corkboard in his truck - it saved time for subsequent visits to the same town. Cora swallowed the last of her bacon and egg butty with a satisfied sigh.

'Yes, could be Randall I suppose. As in Randall Greythorpe, the man behind Elmsley Park. The inquest is today, you know – the inquest into the death of the woman who jumped? We might get to find out her name, at least. I'd like to send flowers to her family or something. Which reminds me, I told you what I'd found out about Mr Greythorpe earlier but I forgot to tell you about what the police said when I rang on Saturday to tell them about finding the USB stick.'

'Oh yeah? Go on then,' said Nathan, and shovelled another mound of scrambled egg thickly covered with brown sauce into his mouth.

'Well, put it this way, they weren't very interested,' said Cora.

She'd phoned Avon police headquarters on Saturday afternoon, planning to tell somebody about the memory stick and offer to drop it in at some point during the week when work allowed. After being kept on hold for several minutes, she'd eventually been put through to a friendly-sounding officer who introduced himself as Detective

Constable James Jordan and asked how he could help. When she had given her name, however, the man's tone had suddenly changed.

'Baxter? As in the breakfast TV reporter? The one who interviewed DCI Gregory last week? And was outside here again on Friday morning?'

'Errrm…yes, that's me.'

'Right. Well, what do you want now?'

Slightly taken aback by the brusqueness of the question, Cora had quickly explained.

'So, I wondered if you wanted me to drop it in? So it can be returned to her family, maybe? I did have a quick look at the contents, I'm afraid – well, I just wanted to check that it wasn't one of mine, that had somehow got flung out of the car during…during the accident.'

Cora paused, feeling guilty about the lie, then continued.

'There's nothing on it really, just one document, a drawing of a new housing estate in Bristol. But I just thought I should give it back…'

'Just a drawing? Nothing else?'

The DC's tone was sharp, his voice suddenly raised.

'Err…positive, yes. Just the one document. Nothing else. Why…why do you ask?'

There was a pause on the line, then DC Jordan spoke again.

'No reason. Just bin it, Miss Baxter. I doubt very much that the family would be interested in a memory stick when they're grieving for their daughter. It's not exactly important, in the grand scheme of things, is it? Thanks for your call. Goodbye.'

'And then he just slammed down the phone,' Cora said, as she recounted the story to the boys now.

'Rude. Guess they really don't like us very much at the

moment, do they?' said Nathan. 'But hey, it saves you a trip back down there.'

'I suppose so. I'm not going to bin it though. I want to have another look at it. I was going to make a copy of the contents anyway – there's something about it that's bugging me a bit. I'd love to know why she had it on her. What's the significance of that plan, and what were her notes about? The big X and everything? It's kind of intriguing, isn't it?'

Nathan nodded.

'Kind of. What else did it say again?'

'"*M Diamonds*", "*U18*" with a question mark after it, and the word "*Manchester*", heavily underlined. Makes no sense to me...'

Cora's voice tailed off as Rodney suddenly dropped his cutlery on the table with a clatter.

'Damn, thanks for reminding me!' he said.

They all looked at him.

'Can you stop doing that? Reminding you about what?' said Scott grumpily. 'I'm just not going to get a peaceful breakfast today, am I?'

'Oh hush, Scott. Listen, guys – I popped to the DIY store on Saturday morning and the road was closed, gasworks or something, so there was a diversion. Anyway, I ended up driving down a road I'd never been on before – funny isn't it, how you can live in a city for years and still come across things you didn't know were there? We've lived in Bristol for yonks and I'd never even heard of this street. Rotunda Street it was called. Anyway, the traffic was crawling along, you know what it's like on Saturdays, so I was just gazing out of the window, people watching, and that's when I saw it.'

He paused to scoop up the last few beans from his plate and popped them into his mouth.

'Saw what? Bloody hell Rodders, you do know how to spin out a story.'

Nathan shook his head as they all waited for the soundman to swallow.

'Sorry. Too good to leave,' said Rodney. 'OK, so I saw this sign, over a shop front. Well, I say a shop front, but it was more a blacked-out window. But the name caught my eye. It was all done in fancy lettering, with sparkly, glittery bits – and it said *Midnight Diamonds*. Midnight Diamonds, as in "*M Diamonds*", maybe? From the notes on the plan? I mean, it could just be a coincidence, but what do you think?'

'Midnight Diamonds? Gosh, it could be, couldn't it?'

Cora sat forward in her chair, suddenly feeling excited.

'What was it, Rodney? The shop? Was it a jeweller's or something? Why was the window blacked out?'

'Well, that's what was a bit odd. I'm not sure why it would have been scribbled on a young woman's map of a housing estate. It was a club, Cora. Well, sort of a club, but kind of a sleazy-looking one, in a fairly grotty-looking back street. Midnight Diamonds is a lap-dancing club.'

6

It was the time of day in the *Morning Live* newsroom that Cora loved the most – just after 9 a.m., when the show had finished and the programme's overnight staff were winding down, de-briefing, breakfasting and chatting, before handing over to the dayshift and heading off for some much-needed rest. Cora had been called by the news desk last night to cover today's news-reading shift. Regular newsreader Alice Lomas, a single mum, had phoned Cora before the desk had, frantic because her eleven-month-old daughter Claudia was poorly and she didn't want to leave her so early the next morning. Cora had reassured her friend that it was fine, that she was delighted to drive to London to cover, and happily told the duty editor the same thing when he phoned her to confirm a few minutes later. And it was true – although she loved her life on the road with the boys, an unexpected mid-week trip to the studio was always nice. It meant she could catch up with her London-based work pals and, *his* work permitting, snatch a few bonus hours with Adam too. She hadn't seen enough of him over the past few months, and she missed him. Until August, Cora had been temporarily job-sharing with Alice, spending three days a week in London. But since Alice had come back to work full-time, leaving baby Claudia with a nanny, Cora was back to full-time reporter duty. Breakfast TV was tough no matter what job you did, the hours long and anti-social, but it was widely accepted that the roving reporter role was among the most gruelling. Being on call twenty-four hours a day during the week was tough, Cora never knowing when her phone would ring with a breaking news story, rousing her from her bed to drive to some far-flung location for the breakfast show's live broadcasts. A 4 a.m. start at the studio for a news-reading shift almost felt like a day off, especially as she would probably be free by mid-morning. She'd already been asked to cover tomorrow morning for Alice too, and she was planning a little Covent Garden shopping trip later before heading to Adam's Shepherd's Bush apartment.

'That is a truly enormous pain au chocolat. Is it…is it *two* stuck together?'

The soft Scottish lilt heralded the arrival of senior programme producer Samantha Tindall, who plonked herself down in the empty chair next to Cora's desk with a weary sigh and ran her fingers through her wavy, caramel-coloured bob.

'Errrm… yes. I was hungry. One didn't seem quite big enough,' said Cora, looking at her friend a little shamefacedly. She might have to squeeze in a run later, after the shopping, she thought. There was a nice park near Adam's place – she could burn off a few calories there before dinner.

'Fair enough. I'm not judging you – I'm always starving at this time of day too. How are you anyway? Haven't seen you in the flesh for weeks. Oh – and did you see that press release I emailed you? The one about the inquest of that poor girl? So bloody sad.'

'Oh, is it here? No, I haven't seen it yet. Much detail…?'

'Woooo! Cora!'

Cora's question was interrupted by the sudden arrival of a small, busty redhead with a strong Dublin accent.

'Girls, girls, girls! What's the gossip? Fabulous to see

39

you, you big lanky giraffe!'

Graphics designer Wendy Heggerty, Cora's other closest work friend, leaned down to peck her on the cheek, carefully balancing a large mug of steaming coffee and a paper plate bearing a blackberry and apple flapjack. She put the mug and plate on the desk and looked around for another chair, wild auburn curls swinging around her pretty face.

'Great to see you too, dwarfy!' Cora grinned at her friend. 'There's a chair over there on the runner's desk, Wend, grab that one, she's in a meeting. And no gossip really. The press release about the inquest is in though. We can all look at it together.'

Cora tapped her keyboard, found the email and clicked on it.

'OK, let's see. *"A Bristol student who had been suffering from long-term depression wrote a suicide note to her family before leaping to her death from a bridge on an isolated country road, an inquest heard. It is believed Leanne Brimley, 17, drank several glasses of wine and consumed a number of sleeping pills before travelling to Clarton Bridge on a secluded stretch of the B1539..."'*

Cora stopped reading, aghast.

'Only seventeen. Gosh, *seventeen*. I knew she looked young, but I didn't think she was *that* young. That's just dreadful.'

She glanced from Sam to Wendy, who both shook their heads sadly.

'What a horrible waste,' said Sam. 'That poor, poor girl.'

Cora turned back to the press release, and stared for a moment at the accompanying photo, taken aback by how different Leanne looked in the image compared with her appearance that dreadful night at the bridge, when death had robbed her skin of its glow and stolen the light from her eyes. She was pretty in a quiet, unusual way, with perfectly shaped lips and a long straight nose, her eyes sharp and intelligent. Cora swallowed hard, then scanned the email, looking for the pertinent details.

'OK. Leanne Brimley. Student from Bristol. Had suffered emotional stress, anxiety and depression for some time. Suicide note found on the body, no details of contents revealed. Toxicology report showed she'd taken sleeping pills and that her blood alcohol level was approximately twice the drink-drive limit. Multiple internal and external injuries, consistent with a substantial fall from height. Family declined to make any statement to the press. Coroner's verdict, suicide.'

She sat very still for a moment, staring at the screen, remembering again the sickening thud as the girl's body had made contact with her car, the twisted limbs, the tangle of red-brown hair, the white face, the unseeing eyes. Leanne. Leanne Brimley. Seventeen years old. A young life, surely full of promise like all young lives were, blighted by mental health problems, and brought to such a gruesome end, her tragic death reduced to a few clinical lines in a press release. Cora knew that this was standard practice, but suddenly something inside her raged at the way the dead girl had somehow been depersonalised, reduced to yet another teen suicide statistic. Leanne Brimley had died right in front of her, and she knew that was affecting her perception of this case, but suddenly her decision to send flowers to the girl's family once her name had been made public just didn't seem enough.

'I'm going to visit them. Her family.'

Sam and Wendy both looked at Cora in surprise.

'Really? I mean, sending flowers or a card would be

lovely, and I'm sure they'd appreciate that. But – visiting? They're strangers Cora, grieving strangers at that. Are you sure?'

Sam looked doubtful.

'I'm sure. I just feel like I need to meet them. I was there when she died... for a short while on that awful night, it was me and Leanne on that dark cold road, just the two of us, and I feel responsible for her somehow. I know her death was nothing to do with me, but all the same... And, as I told you earlier, I'm puzzled about that plan of the housing estate, Sam, and those strange things she wrote on it. The lap-dancing club, for example, if that *is* what the note refers to. It's a bit odd, isn't it? It probably has no relevance whatsoever to her death, but she was carrying it, so it must have been important to her. I'll go and see them, just once, and then leave it, and try to forget about her. Fair enough?'

Sam shrugged.

'Up to you, my darling. If it will help you to move on, do it. Want me to track down the family address in Bristol? Brimley's not a common name, shouldn't be too hard. Electoral roll will probably have it.'

'Thanks, Sam, that would be great.' Cora smiled at her friend gratefully.

Wendy reached for her coffee.

'Well, I think it's a really nice thing to do. Let us know how it goes, Cora. Poor girl. Her family must be in bits,' she said.

At Avon police headquarters, Detective Constable James Jordan had been sipping coffee and skimming through the pages of the *Western Daily Press* when he had come across the article about Leanne Brimley's inquest. Now, coffee forgotten, he was re-reading the piece for the third

42

time. *Leanne Brimley*. He'd known it was her who had died a couple of days ago, when the guys who'd been at the scene at Clarton Bridge were chatting about it by the coffee machine and he'd overheard the name, but he'd been busy on another case that day and the significance of it hadn't really struck him. He'd only realised how important it could be when that annoying cow of a TV reporter had rung, harping on about some memory stick of Leanne's she'd found. Luckily, the stick had only contained a plan of some housing estate, not relevant to anything, so he'd sort of forgotten about it again. But now, reading the report about the inquest, he suddenly wondered if his currently suspended DCI, Gordon Gregory, had seen the article. Did he get the morning paper? Maybe he should call him, tell him to check out the story online? Or email it to him? Yes, maybe that would be safer. It probably wouldn't be sensible to call the disgraced officer, not from police premises anyway.

He wondered if the DCI would be back at work any time soon. He really hoped so. Gordon Gregory had been good to him since he joined the team, even covered for him a couple of times when he'd slept in and arrived late for his shift. James was on his way up the ladder, and being on the right side of the DCI was definitely helping him with the climb. He was actually alright, a decent enough bloke in many ways, underneath all the bluster. They'd become friends, of a sort. He could be a right bastard too, mind. If he didn't like you, he made your life hell, but for some reason he liked James, and that made James' life a whole lot easier. It was why he, along with several of his colleagues, had turned a blind eye to the witness reports that Alan Gregory, Gordon's brother, had been seen running away from the scene of the assault on that old shopkeeper. Gordon told them all it was rubbish, that Alan had been with him that evening, and although some of them didn't *completely* believe him, it was easier just to accept what the DCI was saying than to go against him. Easier, and better for their careers too, because who knew where they might end up if they accused Gordon Gregory of lying? He *was* lying, of course. That TV reporter had caught him out, pretty much accused him of lying on live TV. Some of his colleagues had silently applauded her for that, James knew. Many of them had been delighted that Gregory had been suspended, those who weren't part of his in-crowd, those who had been waiting for a long time for the DCI to fall from grace. Not James though. Yes, what Gregory had done was wrong. Yes, he deserved to be punished for it. But to be humiliated on television like that? That hadn't been nice at all. No need for it. He read the news article once more. Leanne Brimley. He should really have told DCI Gregory about this sooner. He would be interested in this, very interested indeed. It would probably make his day, in fact, awful though that sounded. James reached for his computer keyboard and started to type an email.

7

Cora stretched luxuriously, snuggled deeper into the sofa cushions, and sighed happily.

'That was an excellent foot massage, DCI Bradberry,' she said. 'If you ever want to move on from being a top murder detective, I suggest foot masseuse as your next career. You'd make a fortune.'

Adam grinned at his girlfriend, then flipped her feet off his knee and leaned forward to top up their glasses from the red wine bottle on the coffee table. He'd whipped up a quick carbonara pasta while Cora had been showering after her run in the park and now, dinner eaten, they'd retired to the sofa to catch up both on some TV and on the recent happenings in each other's lives – they hadn't been together in over a week. The flat – a modern, two-bedroom apartment in the heart of Shepherd's Bush – felt deliciously cosy on this chilly evening, candles flickering on the bookshelves along one wall, the big grey sofa piled with soft, colourful cushions and faux fur throws. The candles and throws had recently been added by Cora, who'd complained that while clean and tidy, the place had lacked warmth in the winter months, and Adam had had to agree that she was right. He loved his home even more now, looked forward to retreating here after a tough day, and it was even better when Cora was in town. She drove him mad at times, with her impetuous nature and stubbornness, but he loved her with all his heart, and he knew she felt the same about him. They'd only been together for eighteen months or so, but Adam couldn't imagine being without Cora Baxter. She'd become a vital part of his world, and fortunately the other most important person in his life loved her almost as much as he did.

As Cora flicked idly through the TV channels, Adam's eyes rested on the big photo of his son Harrison, known as Harry, on the wall next to the television. The child had just turned seven, and was a miniature version of Adam, a cheeky-faced little boy with messy dark blond hair and striking green eyes. Adam's hair was close-cropped and a slightly lighter shade of blond, but otherwise they looked remarkably alike. Harry lived with Adam's ex-wife Laura in Swindon, but there was no animosity in the former couple's relationship, and Adam had his son with him as often as he could, generally at weekends. Cora had from the start been very open about the fact that she had no desire to have any children of her own, but she and Harry had liked each other immediately and now were the best of friends. Laura too had liked Cora from the first time they had met, and had no issues with the part she played in Harry's life. It was, thought Adam, pretty damn perfect.

'*Silent Witness* or *The Tunnel*?' asked Cora, interrupting his contented musing.

'I don't mind, you choose,' he replied, pulling her feet back onto his lap again. 'But you were going to finish telling me about going to see this girl's family first. When are you going, Friday?'

'That's the plan, yes. Depending on where my story is on Friday morning I should be home by early afternoon, so I thought I'd zoom down to Bristol then. I'll be back in plenty of time - you and Harry won't be in Cheltenham much before eight, will you?'

'No, between seven thirty and eight I reckon, depending on traffic out of London. Laura's going to drive him down to that garage near the Swindon junction of the M4 and meet me there, which is good of her. It'll save a lot of time if I don't have to navigate town centre traffic in Swindon as well as whatever's on the motorway. He can't wait, by the way. He loves going to your place. He's excited about seeing Rosie and Nicole's kids again too.'

'Well, they can't wait to see him! Ava's a little besotted, I think.'

Ava was Rosie's oldest child, a bright and beautiful little girl with soft red hair like her mum's, and a winning smile. The same age as Harry, the two had hit it off at once on Harry's first visit to Cheltenham, and Ava had been pestering Cora for months to bring her little 'boyfriend' back again.

'I think the feeling is mutual. We'll have to watch those two,' said Adam, with mock sternness. 'Anyway – the Brimley family? Did you speak to them earlier?'

Cora nodded. 'I did. Sam tracked down their address and phone number for me, and I gave Mrs Brimley a call. She was pleasant enough on the phone, seemed OK about me coming round, which was a relief. I half thought she might blame me in some way for her daughter's death, which I know is ridiculous, but anyway… it's just her and her teenage son, as far as I could tell. I'll pick up some flowers on the way. The funeral's being arranged for the end of next week I think - I probably won't be able to go because of work, but at least I can sort of pay my respects to her family this Friday instead.'

'It's more than a lot of people would do, Cora. I wouldn't feel guilty about the funeral. What's happening about your car, by the way?'

'It's definitely being scrapped. I've got the hire car for now, and the insurance company stuff should all be sorted out by the weekend. I'm going to get another Audi, I think. I loved that car, no point in getting something different just because I had a bad experience in it, right?'

'Right. Maybe we could go and find you one on Saturday in Cheltenham? Harry loves cars, he won't mind tagging along.'

'Great, I'd like that. Right – *The Tunnel* it is. Pass my wine?'

'Certainly, ma'am.'

They grinned at each other. A Tuesday evening together. What an unexpected treat.

8

It was nearly 4 p.m., the sky already a forbidding dark grey, when Cora knocked on the door of the Brimley home that Friday afternoon. When she'd arrived on Flower Street, a neat road of terraced houses on the southern outskirts of Bristol, she'd been surprised to see the large sign at one end: *Elmsley Park – a Randall Greythorpe Development.*

'It's right here, then, on Leanne Brimley's street,' she thought, as she peered through a gap in the fence surrounding the building site. Work on the housing estate had clearly already started, some sort of heavy machinery throbbing not far away, bright yellow diggers and cement mixers lined up in the yard. The Brimley home was right next door, a small patch of grass at the front and a blue bicycle chained to the drain pipe. Clutching a bouquet of ivory roses, silvery eucalyptus and berried ivy, Cora shivered as she waited for somebody to appear at the door, half dreading the forthcoming encounter. The mother had sounded fine on the phone, but what if the family *did* blame her in some way for Leanne's death? It was her car the poor girl had slammed into, after all. But it wasn't her fault, was it? And Leanne had been dead as soon as she hit the ground, there was nothing Cora could have done to save her... was there? She had already decided not to tell the family about finding the USB stick. How could she explain that she had found it *and* looked at the contents? It was awful really, she shouldn't have done it, what on earth had she been thinking...

Cora jumped as the door suddenly opened. Standing there was a petite woman who looked to be in her mid forties, dark red hair pulled back off her make-up free face in a severe bun, light blue eyes red rimmed.

'Hello,' she said quietly.

'Mrs Brimley? Hello, thank you so much for agreeing to see me. I'm Cora, Cora Baxter. I…I brought you some flowers.'

Cora held the bouquet out awkwardly and the woman smiled weakly and took it from her.

'That was kind of you. Please come in. And I'm Lisa. Always did hate being called Mrs, makes me feel old.'

Her accent was slight, a hint of West Country.

'Thanks, Mrs… I mean Lisa.' Cora stepped into the hallway, closing the door behind her as Lisa headed down the corridor.

'First on the right, make yourself at home,' she said over her shoulder. 'I'll stick these in the sink for now and put the kettle on. Tea or coffee?'

'Oh, tea please. Black, no sugar. Thanks.'

'Right you are. Back in a mo.'

Cora stepped into the room Lisa had indicated. It was a small, tidy lounge, a real log fire glowing in the fireplace. Across the mantelpiece and on every available flat surface were lines of cards, the words 'sympathy', 'condolences' and 'so sorry' emblazoned on their fronts. An oversized black leather sofa took up most of one wall, opposite a large flat-screen television which was tuned to MTV, the volume low. A teenaged boy who was slouched on a red beanbag on the floor turned to look at Cora with a blank stare.

'Err… hi. I'm Cora. I've just popped in to visit your mum, sorry to interrupt,' she said, feeling self-conscious.

The boy, pale and skinny with messy red hair the same

shade as his mother's, was silent for a moment, then suddenly pushed himself into a sitting position.

'Oh, right. The reporter? My sister hit your car, right? I'm Liam.'

'Liam, hi.' Cora edged further into the room and sat down on the big sofa. 'How... how are you doing? It must be a very difficult time, I'm so sorry for your loss.'

The boy shrugged and rubbed his freckled nose.

'Yeah, it's shit,' he said, matter-of-factly, then slumped back down onto the beanbag again, eyes back on the TV screen.

Cora sat uncomfortably in silence, relieved when there were footsteps in the uncarpeted hallway and Lisa Brimley reappeared, carrying two mugs. She handed one to Cora, lowering herself onto the sofa too as she did so.

'Tea. Hope it's not too strong.'

'It's fine, thank you so much.'

For the next few minutes, Lisa and Cora made small talk, Liam still spread-eagled on his beanbag but listening intently, eyes on his mother's face. To Cora's great relief, she wasn't asked for any additional details about Leanne's fall from the bridge, the family clearly having been given enough information by the police and seemingly aware that it must have been a traumatic event for Cora too; Lisa, to Cora's intense mortification, even apologised for the damage her daughter had caused to the Audi, batting off Cora's protestations with a wave of her hand.

'Nobody should have to face that when they're driving home from work, Cora. It was an awful thing to happen to you too. I'm so sorry.'

'Please, it's *so* not important. Tell me about Leanne. What was... what was she like? I'd like to know.'

Cora clutched her cooling mug, heart twisting in sympathy as Lisa talked, the grieving woman's eyes

51

frequently filling with tears which she wiped away
fiercely with the back of her hand. Leanne was, it
emerged, a grade A student, studying five subjects at sixth
form college and hoping to go on to study English
Literature at university.

'She was brilliant. Well, Liam is too, to be fair. Just as
clever as his sister, if he'd spend more time doing his
homework and less time out on that bike of his.'

Lisa glanced fondly at her son and he rolled his eyes
and then grinned, the smile lighting up his face.

'Shouldn't have bought me the bike then, Mum. Your
fault.'

She shook her head and turned back to Cora.

'They got it from their dad, the brains I mean. I'm not
stupid – I'm an accounts assistant, I do payroll and office
admin for a stationery company in the city centre. I'll
never be a millionaire, but I manage. But Graham, that's
my late husband, he was the clever one. He... he died
three years ago. It was the same... the same way...'

Her voice cracked and she covered her eyes with her
free hand, a loud sob wracking her small frame.

'Oh Lisa, I'm so sorry. You don't have to tell me any
more, I understand how painful it must be...'

Cora reached out and patted the woman's knee. She
nodded, hand still over her face.

'She means he killed himself too.'

Liam's voice was quiet but calm. Cora turned to look
at him.

'Your dad did? Oh Liam, that's dreadful. I'm so
sorry.'

'S'OK. He had a drink problem, and depression. All
got too much for him.'

Lisa gulped and straightened up, eyes wet, carefully
placing her tea mug on the carpet before she spoke again.

'Same as Leanne, he was. Or she was the same as him, I suppose. Too alike, those too were. Too bloody alike. She suffered anxiety and depression too, you see. Started after her dad died. I took her to the doctor, tried to get it fixed, but… well, clearly that didn't work, did it? It was my worst fear for her, the very worst. And it happened, didn't it? She did it, did away with herself, same as him… when I heard, I wasn't even surprised, you know? I'd half expected it to end like that, half expected it for years…'

Her voice tailed off.

'Oh Lisa, I'm so desperately sorry. The inquest said… well, the inquest said she'd been drinking, the night it happened, before she went to the bridge? So you didn't realise, didn't know how bad things were that night?'

Even as she spoke, Cora suddenly wondered if this was a question too far. Was she being too intrusive? Should she just leave it now, and go? Lisa looked sharply at her, then looked at her son as a little gasp came from the beanbag. Liam's mouth was open, as if he was about to say something. Then he shut it again and looked down at his hands, shaking his head.

'I wasn't here,' Lisa said quickly. 'I was… I was out that night. I didn't know anything about it 'til I got home. The police were here, waiting.'

A shudder ran through her, as if she was reliving the terrible moment, then she took a deep breath and spoke again.

'It was that development that did it, tipped her over the edge. If she hadn't been so anxious about that…' she said, and started to cry again, making no effort to conceal it this time, fat tears snaking down her pale cheeks. Cora leaned forward, reaching for the woman's hand.

53

'The – the development? What do you mean, Lisa?'

Lisa shook her head. 'Liam will tell you. Sorry, I think I need to lie down. Thank you for coming, and for the flowers, Cora. It was very good of you. Goodbye.'

She squeezed Cora's hand then stood up shakily and left the room, her footsteps echoing down the hall. Moments later there was a clinking noise from the kitchen, and Liam glanced towards the door, a sudden stricken look on his face. Was Lisa pouring herself a drink, Cora wondered? Something a little stronger than tea? Cora wouldn't blame her if she was – what an absolutely dreadful time the poor woman was going through. She heard footsteps on the stairs, then a door closed and the house was quiet again, the only sound the low murmur of the MTV host on the television. Cora looked at Liam, whose face was blank again as he stared at the screen. She knew she should leave now, and not sit here questioning a teenage boy, but she had to ask. What did Lisa mean about the development? Did it have some connection to Leanne carrying the drawing of Elmsley Park on the USB stick?

'Liam? I'm sorry to interrupt, and I'll go in a minute, but can I just ask - what did your mum mean? When she said the development tipped Leanne over the edge? Does she mean Elmsley Park, the development next door?'

The boy turned his head and stared at her for a long moment. Then he took a deep breath.

'You're a proper reporter, right? A news reporter? You investigate stuff? I've seen you on the telly in the mornings when I'm getting ready for school. You got that dodgy cop suspended for lying about his brother. That was you, right?'

Cora nodded. 'Well, yes… why?'

Liam rolled off his beanbag and crossed the room on

his hands and knees until he was in front of the sofa, then sat up straight and looked her directly in the eye.

'Because I have something for you to investigate. My mum's just accepted what's happened, because she thinks Leanne was like Dad. But I don't think that's true. I don't think my sister committed suicide at all.'

9

'Shhh. Don't want Mum to hear us up here. Although she's probably fallen asleep already, she hasn't slept much at night since Leanne… well, since what happened. Hang on, give me a minute to find them.'

They were in Leanne's bedroom now, Liam having urged Cora to follow him upstairs saying he wanted to show her something, and he was speaking in an urgent whisper. He turned and started rifling through a stack of papers on a small desk in the corner of the room and Cora, still reeling from what the boy had said to her down in the lounge, looked around. The small single bedroom was cluttered with the usual teenage girl junk – piles of clothing, a wicker basket filled with make-up on top of a chest of drawers, a couple of boy band posters tacked to the walls. On the bedside table a framed photograph caught Cora's eye, and she moved closer to take a better look. It was Leanne, looking a little younger, standing next to a smiling man, his arm looped around her shoulders, their faces strikingly similar. Her dad, Cora assumed. The dad who had suffered depression and alcohol problems and taken his own life. Why on earth did Liam think *Leanne's* death wasn't suicide, when the coroner had seemed in no doubt? How could it not be suicide? She'd been there, after all, seen her falling from the bridge, hadn't she? And there was the suicide note, for goodness' sake…

There was a satisfied 'Hah!', and she turned to see Liam pull a sheaf of papers from the pile.

'Here they are. Look.'

He peeled the top sheet from the bundle in his hand and thrust it at Cora.

"NO TO ELMSLEY PARK!"

The headline was large and in red ink. Below it was a map that Cora instantly recognised as the plans for Randall Greythorpe's new development, and under that, *"Please voice your objections to the plans to increase the size of this new development! A larger Elmsley Park will:"* followed by a column of bullet points:

- *Adversely affect the intrinsic character of the local area in terms of style and design*
- *Bring increased traffic, noise and pollution to an already heavily populated area and overload local services and amenities*
- *Damage and divide our precious community.*

Cora looked up at Liam, confused.

'So – Leanne was opposed to this new development? What's the bit about increasing the size of it? I don't really understand, Liam. Why? Why was it so important to her? I mean, I know it's right next door – was that it? All the noise and everything? Or did she object to the design?'

She kept her voice low, conscious of Lisa being in the next room.

Liam sighed. 'No, nothing like that. It's kind of a long story, but I'll try and summarise it for you. OK, so Elmsley Park is based on an old factory site – it was a tobacco factory once, made cigarettes. It closed in the nineties, and it's just been a big rundown heap ever since. Not very nice really, living next door to it – druggies would sometimes break in and use it as a place to shoot up, and there were loads of rats too – they used to come into our garden sometimes, Mum used to freak out. So when this Randall, this cool developer guy from London, when he came along, and announced his plans for this wicked new estate right at the end of Flower Street, everyone round here was quite excited, at first. Specially as the plans included a kids' playground and a skate park, 'cos we'd be able to use them too, being locals, see?'

Cora nodded. 'Sounds pretty good, yes. So, what went wrong?'

Liam sighed again, and sat down on the single bed with its pink floral duvet cover. Cora hesitated for a moment and then sat down next to him.

'Well, one day this letter came through the door. Turns out this factory site wasn't quite big enough for all of this Randall bloke's plans. The letter said he'd applied for planning permission for two different sizes of development, one quite a bit bigger than the other. But for the bigger development, he needed extra land. Some of it was more waste land on the opposite side from here, so not really a problem. But the rest was the land our house was on. So he offered to buy it, for good money, so he could knock it down. Not just our house – half the street, this end, nearest to the factory site. Eight houses, in total. He wanted to buy them all and demolish them, and he wanted to do it quickly. We were all given three months to decide if we'd sell.'

'Wow. So what happened then?'

'Well, of course some of the neighbours were thrilled. He was offering thousands of pounds over the market value for the houses, and we had a community meeting to discuss it and a few people said they were going to say yes straight away, no problem at all. But it was all or nothing you see – the developer wanted all eight houses, or none, so it was something we all needed to agree on. Mum was half and half, she likes it round here but said moving out would be a fresh start for us all, you know, after dad and everything. One or two of the older residents weren't so keen to leave – some have lived here for fifty, sixty years, you know? But even they were tempted by the cash. And that's when Leanne stood up, and said she absolutely refused to go.'

'Why?' Cora was gripped by the story now, eyes fixed to the teenager's face.

'Because of Dad. When he... when he did what he did, it was in the shed, in the back garden. He... he hanged himself. Mum got rid of the shed after, but when he was cremated Leanne said she wanted something to remember him by, something here, at the house. They were close, you see, Dad and Leanne. So we scattered his ashes in the back garden, and planted a tree on the spot. It's a Japanese maple, I think. I'm not very good on trees, but I think that's what it's called. And that's why Leanne said she would never leave, never let them knock the house down. She didn't want to leave that tree, and Dad's ashes. Me and Mum, we just said we could dig up the tree and replant it in our new garden, if we moved. But Leanne said no. She said it wouldn't be the same.'

He looked down at the leaflets he was still clutching in his hands.

'She knew that pretty much everyone in the eight houses would probably cave in and sell eventually, even Mum. Mum knew how anxious Leanne was about it all, but she doesn't like to antagonise people, and the money probably was really too good to turn down. She thought Leanne would get over it, in time. We could have bought a much nicer house somewhere else with the money too, but Leanne didn't care about that. She wanted to stay here, and that was that. So she decided to do something about it, all on her own. She used her wages to get these printed.'

He waved the leaflets at Cora.

'She had a Saturday job, at M&S in town. She knew a tree in our back garden wasn't a valid reason for everyone else to stay put, so she widened it out, looked at all the negatives of increasing the size of the estate, trying to get as many locals as possible on board, to get them to object to the planning application. Randall had already applied for permission for both the smaller and the bigger one, you see, but there was still time for locals to object. If he didn't get permission for the big one, he couldn't build it, even if we did all decide to sell. Leanne was very persuasive, and she got a few people, especially the older ones, on her side pretty quickly, and that really pissed off some of the others, the ones who wanted to sell up. They got mad, told her she had to stop, that she and the old guys were ruining it for everyone else. It got pretty bad, actually. She got abuse in the street, we had angry letters through the door, threats against her and stuff if she didn't stop her campaign. Mum knew what she was up to, but not about how nasty it had all got. Leanne showed *me* the threatening letters, but not Mum, didn't want to frighten her – Mum works hard, she had enough to worry about. Some of the elderly neighbours were intimidated too, told if they didn't agree to move that they'd get hurt. It was pretty horrible actually. But Leanne wouldn't give up. She was determined not to move, and she knew that if she refused to budge, and got enough people to object, Randall wouldn't get permission for his bigger estate and would have to just build the smaller one instead.'

'How old are you, Liam?' Cora was suddenly very impressed at how well this young boy was explaining the story.

'I'm fifteen. Why?' He frowned at her.

She smiled. 'No reason. You're just clearly very bright. Go on. Did the police get involved, with all this harassment and intimidation?'

He flushed, obviously pleased by the compliment, then continued.

'Leanne didn't call them, no, said it was all talk and that she could handle it, and that it would all be worth it when she won. It was affecting her though. She'd suffered from anxiety and depression on and off ever since Dad died, and I started to think it might be coming back. She just kept trying to fight it though, she said she'd be fine once it was all over, this Elmsley Park thing. I'm fairly sure she persuaded the other neighbours who were being bullied not to involve the police either. She thought it would all escalate, get even worse, if people started getting arrested. Anyway, all of a sudden the weirdest thing happened. She got a call from the developers next door, and they just told her they'd changed their minds about building the bigger development. Out of the blue, just like that. They said that planning permission had actually just been granted for the smaller one, as there'd been no objections about that one, so work would be starting immediately, but our homes were safe. Leanne was absolutely thrilled, said it had all been worth it. Didn't go down too well with everyone, though.'

'I'm sure. I can imagine your neighbours who'd been hoping for a big pay-out for their houses weren't happy at all,' said Cora quietly. 'Wow. There must have been some angry people out there. Did the developers say why they'd changed their minds so suddenly?'

Liam shook his head. 'Nope. Or if they did, Leanne didn't tell me. But she did say, a few weeks before that, that she was onto something, something that she thought might help her win her case. Didn't tell me what though.

Seems like she was right.'

Cora sat still for a moment, thinking.

'And when was this, Liam? When did Leanne hear her fight was over?'

Liam tipped his head back, staring at the ceiling, then blinked hard and turned to face her.

'It was last Wednesday. The day before she died.'

10

'Daddy, you don't understand. It's *good* for children to stay up late. I mean, we'll have to do it when we're older, won't we? So it makes sense for us to start practising now, doesn't it? Otherwise we might not be able to do it when we're grown-ups. Tell him, Cora!'

Adam turned to Cora, eyebrows raised. 'Cora?'

Cora shrugged. 'Well, it's a logical argument, to be fair. However, Harry, I think tonight may not be the night to practise. We're meeting your Cheltenham friends in the park first thing in the morning, remember? It's eight thirty already. If you stay up any later tonight, you might sleep in and miss it...'

'OK! Goodnight!' Harry, who'd been sitting cross-legged on the bed in Cora's spare room, abruptly uncrossed his legs and burrowed under the duvet, giggling as Adam leapt on top of him, making monster noises.

'Daddy! Get off!'

Adam rolled sideways and clambered off the bed again, grinning.

'OK, trouble. And the light only stays on for ten minutes, remember? Finish that chapter of your book and then SLEEP,' he said sternly.

'Yeah, yeah, whatever.'

'Don't you whatever me. Ten minutes!'

Adam bent down to ruffle his son's untidy mop of hair and dropped a kiss on his forehead.

'Goodnight, Harry.'

'Night, Daddy. Night, Cora.'

Cora leant over to kiss him too. 'Sleep well, my darling.'

Harry smiled then grabbed his book from the bedside table, opened it and nestled into his pillows, instantly engrossed. Back in the lounge, Adam closed the door and headed for the dining table, where a bottle of Pinot Grigio was cooling in an ice bucket.

'I'm so glad he's reading more these days, instead of being obsessed with Minecraft and all that rubbish. Wine?' he asked.

'Yes, it's great. And yes, please.'

Cora flung herself onto the sofa with a happy sigh. It had been such a nice day. She, along with Adam and Harry who'd arrived in Cheltenham last night, had gone out to her favourite café in Montpellier for breakfast, then for a wander and to feed the ducks in Pittville Park, before heading for the out-of-town car showrooms. Less than an hour later, to Cora's delight, she'd shaken hands on an excellent deal for a smart Audi TT, blue this time, with just two thousand miles on the clock. It should be hers by midweek, if all the paperwork came together in time.

'Hopefully there'll be no horrible accidents this time – with my new car, I mean,' she said, as Adam handed her a glass of wine and sat down beside her.

'Hopefully not,' he agreed. 'And speaking of which...how long have we got before they arrive? Was it nine they were coming? You were going to finish telling me about yesterday once we got Harry to bed, remember? After we got a bit... well, *distracted*, last night...'

He grinned lasciviously, and Cora punched him gently on the arm.

'Oh, shush!'

Once Harry had fallen asleep last night Cora had started to tell Adam about her visit to the Brimleys, but

64

his fingers gently running up her thigh as they lay wrapped around each other on the sofa had indeed become a *distraction*, as he had so coyly put it. Today had been so busy she'd almost forgotten about it all but now, as they waited for Rosie and Nicole and their husbands to arrive for drinks and a good old gossip, Cora decided it would indeed be a good time to finish the story.

She took a sip of her drink, put the glass down on the coffee table and turned to Adam.

'Right, where did I get to? I told you about the campaign Leanne Brimley led, and the angry letters and intimidation and so on, and then how the developers suddenly decided not to go with the bigger development after all, didn't I? And that the day they announced that was the day before Leanne died?'

Adam nodded. 'And you said Liam was about to dig around for the threatening letters to show you when you heard his mum moving around in the room next door.'

'Yes. He rushed me downstairs and out then. He didn't want his mum to know we'd been up there, poking about. But he said he'd find the letters this weekend, photocopy them at school on Monday and post them to me. I scribbled down my address before I left. I really want to see those letters, Adam. There's something a little bit odd about all this.'

Adam frowned. 'Go on.'

'Well, it's like Liam said to me, before we heard his mum getting up. Leanne spent months campaigning so she could stay in their home. And then she told Liam she was onto something, something which might help her win, but wouldn't say what. Not long after that, the developer suddenly caves in, and her fight is over. And then, the very next day, she jumps off a bridge? I know there was a suicide note, which does make it seem fairly clear cut. But isn't it a bit strange that she'd do it *then*, the very day after her fight ended in such a positive way for her? The day after she'd been celebrating the fact that her home was finally safe? Liam said she was ecstatic, totally overjoyed. It doesn't make huge amounts of sense, does it?'

'Well…' Adam paused. 'Well, think about the report from the inquest. She had alcohol and drugs in her system. Maybe she got drunk and didn't really know what she was doing? And she'd been suffering from mental health problems, remember? Maybe she slumped back into a depression that day? Maybe the campaign had been keeping her going, and once it was over life suddenly seemed really flat again? You know how you can feel a bit low after a really big occasion, because all the excitement is over? Maybe it was like that for Leanne – maybe she felt she didn't have any real purpose anymore. Or maybe there was no real reason at all. There's often no reason for depression to strike – it's an illness, it just happens. The coroner didn't seem to think there was anything suspicious, did he? I mean, surely Liam's not suggesting that somebody killed her? Threw her off that bridge? You were there, did *you* see anyone?'

'No, I didn't.' Cora sat thinking for a minute. 'I know, you're probably right. It's just that there are a few things the coroner didn't know about. The threatening letters, for example. They weren't mentioned at the inquest because nobody told anyone in authority about them - Liam and Leanne had kept it all from their mother, remember? And Lisa herself found it easy to simply accept Leanne's death as suicide because of her mental health history, and because the kids' dad had taken his own life too, a few years previously. Lisa just didn't question it.'

'What else, then? What else wasn't the coroner told?'

Cora pointed to her wine glass.

'Well, the fact that the sleeping pills and wine were totally out of character. Liam told me that Leanne hated the idea of pills – she'd been offered them by her doctor, after her dad died, when she wasn't sleeping well, but she refused. There weren't any in the house, as far as he knew. Lisa didn't take them either. And he also said Leanne didn't drink, not ever. She'd seen what it had done to her father, and she just wasn't interested in it. He can't understand why the tox report showed her as being twice the drink-drive limit. How much wine would that be, roughly, do you know?'

'Tricky question. It's different for everyone, depends on your age, sex, weight, metabolism…very roughly, four to six small glasses of wine, maybe? She clearly *did* drink it though, if it was found in her system, no matter what Liam says. Maybe she *was* a drinker, and hid it from him? He's only fifteen, after all.'

Cora sighed. 'I suppose so. It's just that he was so adamant that she never drank. He did admit that there *was* wine in the house though. It had been Lisa's birthday a few days before and she'd had friends round. There were still several bottles on the kitchen counter, so Lisa told the police Leanne must have taken one of them, drunk it and then stuck it out in the recycling bin before she headed to the bridge to jump, according to Liam. And that maybe she got the pills from a friend. Nobody seems to know how she got to the bridge though – they're assuming she walked. Liam doubts that too, he said she wasn't big into exercise, never walked anywhere if she could help it. And it's several miles… she would have been pretty unsteady on her feet, wouldn't she, after that much wine and pills on top? He says he just doesn't believe any of it.'

'What does he think, then? That somebody forced the wine and pills down her? And then what? Dragged her to the bridge and threw her off? Bit unlikely, isn't it?' Adam was frowning again.

'He doesn't know what to think. He just says it's all wrong, that it wouldn't have happened like they said. He's not sure if he thinks someone actually killed her, or if somebody took her there and forced her to jump, or even if somebody threatened her and scared her so much that she *did* decide to take her own life to get away from them. All he says is that she wouldn't voluntarily have done it without someone else being involved. I know he's only a kid, Adam, but he's very persuasive.'

Adam leaned back in his seat and stared at the ceiling for a moment.

'Why hasn't he told someone about these concerns of his then? Other than you, I mean?'

'I think he just didn't know who to tell. I did ask him, especially about why he didn't say anything about the threatening letters to the police, if not to his mum. He said everyone just seemed so certain that it was a suicide, and as you say, he's only fifteen. He thought the police wouldn't take him seriously, that they'd just assume he was a grief-stricken kid not wanting to accept that his sister killed herself. He said he decided to tell *me* because I'm a reporter, because I "investigate" things. He saw me expose that lying DCI on TV and thinks I might be able to help him too. Bless him, Adam. He's a really sweet, bright, kid. My heart goes out to him.'

Adam raised his eyebrows. 'You're getting involved again, aren't you? And I have no objection to that, in principle. You've been right before, about crimes that seemed cut and dried and turned out to be something else entirely. But this one... I don't think so, Cora. The poor girl had a history of mental health problems, she'd just been through a highly stressful time, she'd been drinking heavily, and she plunged from a bridge and killed herself. It's a terrible tragedy, and I can understand why you feel personally involved – it happened right in front of you, for goodness' sake. But I'm not sure there's any more to this one, honestly. There's the little matter of the suicide note, remember? Typed on her own laptop, didn't Liam say?'

Cora leaned back on the sofa and rubbed her eyes. She felt desperately sorry for Liam, but she knew Adam was talking sense.

'Yes. The police found it in her coat pocket at the scene, and also a copy on her laptop. She'd obviously typed it and then printed it out. And yes, that's pretty impossible to explain away. Liam said he doesn't understand that bit, and he can't explain it either. He just kept saying that in his heart of hearts he doesn't believe she would have killed herself. She'd gone through it with her dad, she knew what a devastating affect it had had on everyone. But yes, you're probably right, Adam. It's just that there are a few things still bugging me. What were those notes on her drawing of the development about? Why the name of a lap-dancing club, if we're right about that? What was this something she was onto, something she'd found out, that she wouldn't tell Liam about? And I want to see those threatening letters. And her suicide note. Liam said he'll copy that for me too. I'll just take a little look, it won't hurt, will it?'

'Well, it's up to you. Just don't read too much into anything, OK?'

She smiled. 'OK, DCI Bradberry...oh, doorbell, here we go!'

And she leapt from the sofa and went to greet her friends.

11

'Ugh. I hate fancy dress parties. I wouldn't go if I were you, Rodders. Pretend you're ill or something. Why do people enjoy dressing up so much? I don't get it. Now, do we need that second light for this next hit or not, what do we think? These bloody dark mornings do my head in.'

Nathan finished adjusting his tripod and stood back, brow furrowing as he assessed the light levels. It was just before 8 a.m. and Cora and the crew were in the Peak District in Derbyshire, after being called from their beds in the early hours when reports of a woman missing on the moors had reached the news desk in London. They'd arrived on location at around 5 a.m., Cora finding the three-hour drive even more tiring than she normally would after her busy weekend. As soon as she was at the scene, though, the adrenaline had kicked in. There was nothing quite like a breaking news story, even one with a potentially grim ending. As they'd set up on the edge of the high moorland plateau of the northernmost Dark Peak, waiting for news from the overnight mountain rescue team, Cora had scribbled notes for her first live broadcast, stomach flipping with nervous tension. Would she be reporting on a positive outcome this morning, or on yet another tragedy?

The missing woman, a 27-year-old walker from Huddersfield, had gone out alone yesterday, telling her family she fancied a Sunday afternoon ramble and roughly where she was heading for, and saying she'd be home before it got dark. When she wasn't back by 7 p.m., her anxious husband had raised the alarm. Cora knew this area, had covered stories here numerous times, and she knew the terrain could be treacherous, especially in winter, the weather changing quickly. There had been heavy rain yesterday, and it wasn't unknown for lone hikers to get trapped in waterlogged boggy areas out on the wild moorland and die of exposure. It was with a sense of relief then, that a few minutes ago, and just in time for *Morning Live*'s eight o'clock bulletin, Cora had received news that the woman had been found, hypothermic and with a broken ankle, but otherwise fine and on her way to hospital. Now, as they got ready to give the nation the good news, Cora turned to Nathan.

'Second light please. Need all the help I can get, today, I'm knackered. And I agree with you about fancy dress parties. Do you *have* to go, Rodney?'

Rodney, who'd just been telling them about a party he was being forced to attend in the run-up to Christmas, and bemoaning the dress code, groaned.

'Yes, I do. It's Jodie's mum's sixty-fifth birthday and she's *obsessed* with fancy dress. I mean, what on earth do I go as? I'm rubbish at this sort of thing but Jodie's insisting I make my own flipping costume. She wants us to *surprise* each other.'

Nathan shivered and pulled the zip of his heavyweight fleece higher under his chin.

'Well, you could go in what you're wearing today. That would surprise her. Just tell everyone you've come as a Mad Soundman.'

Cora, who'd been stomping up and down the road behind the camera to keep warm, stopped for a moment and snorted with laughter. Rodney's outfit of choice today was, as usual, remarkable: a pair of red flannel trousers which looked suspiciously like pyjama bottoms, chestnut coloured UGG boots and a calf-length military-style coat, complete with some realistic-looking medals pinned to the left lapel. A pale blue knitted hat topped with an enormous fluffy pompom completed the look.

'That's not very helpful, Nathan,' the soundman said. 'Come on, give me some ideas. Or maybe I'll ring my mum and ask her. She always made us enter fancy dress competitions as kids because she loved making the costumes. Yes, why didn't I think of that before?'

'Good idea, Rodney,' said Cora, rubbing her hands together. Her thermal gloves just weren't cutting it today – she doubted the temperature was much above zero, even now that the sun was slowly rising, and a bitter wind wasn't helping.

'What sort of things did she dress you in as a kid? Maybe you could just recreate one of those outfits?'

Rodney nodded slowly, adjusting the sound mixer strap around his neck.

'OK, let me think. It might be a bit tricky because she used to pair me and my brother Chris up. One year he went as a paramedic, and I went as a road accident victim, all covered in bandages. And the next, Chris was a sort of Indiana Jones adventurer, and I was a mummy, all covered in bandages…'

He paused, frowning, as Nathan and Cora burst out laughing, then grinned.

'Guys, do you think my mother was trying to tell me something…?'

Later, as they huddled around a small table in a café in Edale, refuelling and warming up before the drive home, Cora told the story of her Friday visit to Lisa and Liam Brimley's.

'Wow, interesting,' said Nathan. 'Couldn't the

developer, this Randall Greythorpe bloke, have used a compulsory purchase order to get those houses he wanted, then? Or doesn't it work like that?'

'No.' Cora shook her head and took a sip of tea. 'I studied compulsory purchase for a story a while ago. It's really only used if the development is in the public interest, like a motorway, or if a council wants to develop a run-down town centre, things like that. Not just for a funky new housing development. They can't make people move out if they don't want to, not for something like that.'

Nathan nodded his understanding, and then raised his eyebrows, gesturing at Scott with his fork. The engineer, who was the only one who hadn't been frozen to the bone this morning, having been locked in his cosy truck for most of it, was stripping off his thick blue jumper, his shiny shaved head gleaming.

'Sweating,' he explained. 'It's friggin' boiling in here.'

'Well some of us are only just starting to feel our feet again,' Cora retorted. 'So don't complain.'

'Fair enough.' Scott grinned at her, dumped the jumper on the floor beside his chair and then asked:

'So, these threatening letters to Leanne Brimley? What's in them?'

'I don't know. Haven't seen them yet. Liam didn't want his mum to know he was showing me stuff in Leanne's room, so he's making copies and posting them to me. It seems there were a lot of people who weren't happy with what she was doing though. And not just the neighbours who wanted to sell up and were trying to get her to stop campaigning either - apparently she had a run-in with the developers too, at least once. Liam mentioned that she went to visit the site office one day, to try to persuade them in person to drop their plans for the bigger development. He said she tried to appeal to their better nature by explaining about her dad's ashes in the garden, but it didn't go too well. They pretty much turfed her out, according to Liam.'

Rodney, who had removed his military coat to reveal a red flannel shirt which matched his trousers (definitely pyjamas, Cora thought, but decided not to comment), screwed up his nose.

'OK, but even so. You don't really think there was any sort of foul play, do you, despite what her little brother says? I mean, she sounds like a pretty impressive kid, to take on a big developer like that. But doesn't everything point to suicide, with the note and everything? If somebody chucked her off that bridge, you'd have seen them, wouldn't you? Or *somebody* would have? Surely her brother can't actually think somebody would go that far, just because she was campaigning against a housing development?'

Cora ran her hands through her brown bob, trying to restore it to some semblance of normality after its hours crammed into a woolly hat earlier, then gave up.

'He's not saying that, necessarily. It's like I said to Adam at the weekend when he asked the same question - from what Liam said, I think he's thinking more along the lines of somebody maybe getting her drunk so she didn't know what she was doing, or somebody bullying her into jumping, something like that. He just doesn't believe it was as straightforward as the police and coroner think it was. But yes, I know, the suicide note…'

She sighed. She was starting to wish she'd never gone to visit the Brimleys now. Why hadn't she just sent them some flowers with a note of condolence? It would have been so much easier to forget about it all if she hadn't spoken to Liam, and learned of his doubts about what had happened. But now she couldn't unhear what he'd told her, couldn't unsee the pain in his eyes. She was involved, whether she liked it or not.

'So what does Adam think?' asked Nathan. 'I assume he's telling you to leave it alone?'

'Yes, more or less. He's pretty sceptical. And honestly, I am too. I'm not saying there's anything dodgy about it, the poor girl probably did just take her own life. But... I don't know. Liam was pretty convincing, and there are definitely a few odd things about it all.'

She stretched her arms over her head and yawned.

'Oh, guys, I don't know. I'm too knackered to think straight right now. Forget it for today. Everyone done? Let's hit the road.'

It was at eleven o'clock that night when it came to her. After a long, exhausting day which had included a detour to West Midland Safari park on the way home from the Peak District to shoot a VT about an escaped water buffalo, Cora had finally collapsed into bed, groaning as she set her alarm for 4 a.m. She loved her job, but sometimes the hours were an absolute killer.

As she drifted off to sleep, half thinking and half dreaming, she began to relive again in her mind's eye the drive to Clarton Bridge that night, the night Leanne Brimley had died. She could see the road now, as if it was right there in front of her, feel the steering wheel in her hands and hear the classical music playing on the radio as she drove towards the towering Victorian structure, admiring again its graceful arch and ornate ironwork high above the road, one section of its elaborate scrollwork lit up by a car's headlights...

Cora sat bolt upright in bed. She was suddenly wide

awake. That *wasn't* a dream, was it? It had just come back to her, something she'd totally forgotten, something she'd only barely been aware of even at the time, but something which suddenly seemed hugely, massively important. A car. There had been a *car*. Just before Leanne Brimley plunged to her death. A car parked on Clarton Bridge.

12

It was one of those afternoons that Scottish Sam would have described as 'dreich', Cora thought as she gazed out of the satellite truck - a cold, dreary, bleak November day with, on and off, torrential showers. Another one had just started, the rain hammering on the truck's roof, the deluge of water pouring down the side window blurring Cora's view of the car park outside. Despite the weather, she was in a good mood – she'd picked up her new car first thing this morning, and had thoroughly enjoyed putting it through its paces on her drive from Cheltenham to Reading, where she and the boys had just finished filming at a school which had hit the headlines after a row about its toilet facilities was made public.

Rodburn High was a secondary school at which parents were objecting to a recent building revamp which had abolished single-sex toilets, girls and boys now having to share a communal bathroom block. The seemingly minor row had been picked up by the newspapers and become something of a national talking point during what was proving to be a fairly quiet news week, with increasingly vociferous arguments on both sides. The "fors" pointed out that siblings of opposite sexes shared toilet facilities in their own homes, so why should things be any different at school, while the "againsts" argued that the cubicles did not offer enough privacy during the tricky teenage years, and that both girls and boys were concerned about classmates "looking under or over the doors".

After an afternoon filming with teachers, parents and students, the crew had just packed up their kit, and were now sitting in the truck nursing mugs of tea as Scott fed the pictures and Cora's voiceover to the studio in London. Nathan generally had to edit their news packages himself, but as yesterday had been an eighteen-hour day – they'd started with live broadcasts in Worcester and ending up on an evening shoot in Yorkshire – the news desk was, for once, being lenient and allowing them a relatively easy shift today.

'So, this car on the bridge thing. We didn't really have time to talk about it with all that tearing about yesterday, Cora. Do you really think it could be important?'

Nathan looked quizzically at Cora, then back at the monitor where the last of his pictures were playing as they were fed to the *Morning Live* hub, where camera feeds were constantly arriving from all over the world before being edited into sequences and news VTs for the show.

Cora sipped her Earl Grey and thought for a moment.

'I'm not sure. I mean, I didn't see any people or anything, nobody at all except poor Leanne. But I *do* wonder if that car might be significant, yes. I mean, it was there just seconds before she fell off the bridge. So, at the very least, whoever was in it was a witness. And at worst... well, who knows? So how come they never made themselves known to the police? If I was sitting in a parked car and saw a girl about to jump off a bridge, and then *actually* jump, I'd have been out of it like a shot. I wouldn't just sit there watching and then calmly drive away and not mention it to anyone in authority. Would you, any of you?'

She looked from face to face, and Nathan, Scott and Rodney all shook their heads.

'It is a bit weird, agreed,' said Nathan. 'And it adds to

the list of little oddities we've already talked about, I suppose. So, what are you thinking? Should we take a closer look, investigate this a bit like Liam asked you to, Cora?'

She was silent for a moment, thinking. Then she nodded.

'I honestly think I'm going to have to. I can't stop thinking about it, especially since I remembered the car. But you don't have to get involved, honestly. I can do it myself.'

Rodney raised a hand, like a little boy at school trying to get his teacher's attention.

'Errrm... no way, count me in. I'm definitely on board. That lap-dance club thing has been bugging me, to be honest - that Midnight Diamonds place I saw in Bristol? I'd love to know the connection between that and the housing development, and why Leanne had it written on her drawing. If that *is* what "*M Diamonds*" stands for, of course.'

Scott nodded.

'I'm up for it too. I know it's bugging the heck out of you Cora, so the sooner we do a bit of poking around the sooner you might start to chill out again. And it's been a bit dull recently, hasn't it? It's been months since we've had something like this to get our teeth into. When we've got downtime over the next couple of weeks, no harm in doing a bit of investigating, is there? Ah, good, that's the last of it gone.'

He leaned towards the microphone on the desk in front of him and flicked the switch so he could speak to the hub technician.

'That's your lot from SNG2 in Reading. All look OK your end?'

'Give me a minute, SNG2, I'll just give it a quick

check, stand by.'

Scott flicked the switch to the off position again and leaned back in his seat.

'Well? Shall we do a bit of enquiring?'

'I'm in,' said Nathan. 'We might as well. As you said Scott, it's been a bit boring recently. It'll be good to have a bit of an investigation to sink our teeth into again, even if I'm not so sure how far we'll get with this one. It's a funny one, isn't it? But yeah, go on Cora. We're all up for it.'

'Oh, guys, thank you so much.' Cora beamed at her friends. 'It would be brilliant to have some help. I mean, yes, it may well be a waste of time, but if you look at what we have so far...'

'Yes, go on, summarise it for us, so we all have it clear in our minds,' said Nathan. 'But speak up, this bloody rain's ridiculous. Sounds like we've got a troupe of tap dancers on the roof.'

'OK.'

Cora cleared her throat, and held up a hand, preparing to count off the points she was making on her fingers.

'Well, we have a police team on the scene who assumed immediately it was suicide. I know that, because I was there and heard them talking about it. Then we have a coroner who's *officially* ruled the death a suicide. And we can all see why – a young girl with a history of mental health problems, a suicide note typed on her own laptop, a high level of alcohol and pills in her blood and a leap from a bridge with no witnesses other than me – well none who've come forward, anyway.'

She held up her other hand.

'But then, on the other hand we also have a girl who's just won her fight against a big housing developer, who was absolutely thrilled by it, in a really happy place, just the day before. So it does make the timing of her death a little odd. And she's a girl who's made a lot of people very angry over the previous few months, angry enough to send her threatening letters. Then there's a brother who says there's absolutely no way his sister would take her own life. A brother who also says Leanne told him she'd discovered something that might help her case, but didn't say what. And then that car, parked on the bridge, moments before she died. Who was in it that, and what connection do they have to all this? My biggest problem is the suicide note, but still...when you weigh it all up, it's probably worth a look, eh?'

Scott frowned. 'Do you think you should tell the cops, Cora? About that car?'

Cora shook her head. 'I did wonder that myself, and I mentioned it to Adam when I spoke to him last night. He's not sure how seriously they'd take it, or how interested they'd be, and I tend to agree. I mean, they're not treating Leanne's death as suspicious, are they? The case is closed as far as they're concerned. And, as Adam pointed out, there's no real evidence that a car was there at all, just my hazy recollection, although I'm pretty certain I'm not imagining it. And the police weren't remotely interested when I told them about finding the USB stick, so I doubt they'd care much about the mysterious car either. So no, I honestly don't think there's any point.'

'Fair enough.' Scott shrugged. 'So, how do we start? What do you want us to do?'

'Well, I suppose one of the first things we need to do is try to talk to some of these angry local residents, the ones who wanted to sell up and who were hassling Leanne. Maybe we can work out who might have sent her the threatening letters. I'll get hold of Liam again, get him to send us a list of names and addresses of everyone involved. And we also need to try to work out what those notes on Leanne's drawing mean, and if we might be right about the lap-dancing club. That would be interesting... we'd need to see what, if any, link it could have to the Elmsley Park development... oh, hang on, it's Sam.'

Cora's phone had started ringing, and she put her mug on the floor and hit the button to accept the call.

'Sam, hi! Please don't say you're sending us to Wales or Cornwall or something now...'

Cora pressed the speaker button so the boys could hear, anxiety suddenly flashing across all of their faces. Not another long drive, not now, surely?

'No, no, don't panic! Think you're clear for today, soon as your school VT's in. I was calling about the Leanne Brimley thing, actually.'

There were four simultaneous sighs of relief in the satellite truck.

'Oh, OK, thank goodness! We were just talking about that, actually. We really want to check it out a bit, Sam. You're on speaker, by the way. The guys and I think there are enough... well enough *irregularities* to warrant a little investigative journalism. We won't spend vast amounts of time on it, and it won't get in the way of our day to day work, I promise. Is that OK with you?'

'Definitely,' said Sam. 'I've actually mentioned it to Betsy, hope that's alright? After what you told me yesterday about the car on the bridge, and all the stuff Liam Brimley told you about his sister. We agree with you that the suicide note is a little hard to explain away, but still. Betsy's pretty keen on building up our investigative reporting side, so she's actually agreed to give you a bit of time out to look into this one. And she's had quite a good idea.'

'Oh – well, great! Betsy's ace, isn't she? What's her idea?'

Cora winked at the boys, who were nodding approvingly.

'Well, this Randall Greythorpe guy has become quite a big shot in the housing world, as we know,' said Sam.

'He's young, but he's made a name for himself and a lot of money pretty quickly - the property magazines love him, and he's apparently being lined up for a major TV show too, a sort of BBC version of *Grand Designs*. But he also has a reputation for being pretty ruthless – I have some articles I can email you and you'll see what I mean. Anyway, so our programme editor's idea is that you guys go and *interview* him, and I'm doing air quotes around the word interview at this end. I mean, he's not the sort of person we'd feature on *Morning Live*, we don't really *do* profile pieces, but he won't know that. Go and flatter him a bit, record an interview, bring up the Elmsley Park development story and the controversy with the locals and see what you can get out of him. You only really have what you got from Liam so it would be good to hear another side of the story. And then we'll also have him on tape talking about it too, should we need it in the future. We might get a decent story out of this, you never know. What do you think?'

Cora looked at Nathan, who was nodding vigorously.

'Let's do it,' she said. 'I'll call his office tomorrow and get it set up. Thank you, Sam. And thank Betsy for me too, will you? It's really good of her to let us do this, even if it does come to nothing.'

'I will. Now go home and get some rest. Speak soon. Bye Cora…bye, boys!'

'Bye, Sam,' they all chorused, and Cora ended the call.

'Wow. Good old Betsy,' she said.

'Dead right,' agreed Rodney. 'Old Jeanette would never have let us do something like that. She'd just have seen it as a waste of time. Betsy rocks.'

Cora grinned. Betsy Allan had taken over as programme editor over a year ago, and was getting more and more popular the longer she was in the job, in stark contrast to the show's previous boss Jeanette Kendrick, who'd been murdered some months before Betsy's arrival. Rodney was right – they'd been very lucky to get such a good replacement. Jeanette had *not* been popular, and was missed by very few of her former staff. Cora still remembered the time she had managed to trap her finger in the truck door minutes before a live hit, ripping the nail and a chunk of skin clean off it. Her hand dripping with blood, and throbbing with pain, she had called the newsroom, asking if she could skip the broadcast to rush to the nearest GP surgery or accident and emergency department to get it looked at. Jeanette had simply refused, insisting that the hit go ahead as planned.

'Just keep your hand out of shot. We don't want viewers being put off their breakfasts,' she had snapped down the phone.

Cora had done as she was told, gritting her teeth against the pain and apologising profusely to the rather horrified interviewee who had to rush to get a mop and bucket as soon as their slot was over, the mangled finger having produced a substantial puddle of blood on the floor by their feet. Cora very much doubted that Betsy would be quite so tough if the same thing were to happen under *her* reign.

'All clear, SNG2. Thank you.'

They all jumped as the London tech's voice rumbled out of the speakers.

'Yay! Does that mean we can go home, Cora?' Scott

rubbed his big hands together in anticipation.

'Certainly does,' she said. 'Let's all get a good night's sleep. We can make a plan of action tomorrow, divide up who does what, OK? And thanks guys, so much, for agreeing to do this. It means a lot. I feel I owe this girl, strange as it may sound. There's probably nothing at all suspicious about her actual death, but there definitely seem to be a few strange things surrounding it. And I know I never met her, not when she was alive. But she's become important to me, for some reason. Does that sound mad?'

Nathan grinned.

'It sounds very...very *Cora*. And no need to thank us. We get it, totally. All for one and one for all, and all that jazz. We're a team, you know that. Now go home and relax. Goodnight, love.'

He pulled her in for a quick hug, and she returned the embrace gratefully. They all said their goodbyes and, as Cora manoeuvred her new TT out onto the main road, and turned her classical music station on to start the relaxation process, she made a silent vow. We *are* a team. We're a *top* team, Leanne Brimley. An unbeatable team. And if there is anything suspicious about your death, we're bloody well going to find out what it is. Then she put her foot down and headed for home.

13

It was raining softly as Leanne Brimley's coffin was lowered slowly into the grave, the light, steady kind of rain which appears innocuous at first but then seems to make you far, far wetter and colder than the pounding, driving kind ever does, seeping into your pores and chilling your very bones. A leaden sky glowered at the few dozen mourners who'd gathered at South Bristol Cemetery, the scattering of school friends – released from lessons early for the occasion on this Thursday afternoon – neighbours and relatives standing now with lowered heads as the vicar said his final prayers in a low monotone. Detective Constable James Jordan and Detective Chief Inspector Gordon Gregory stood at a respectful distance, watching as the committal service came to a close and the dead girl's mother and brother, so like her with their red hair and pale skin, were led away, the mother sobbing quietly, the boy's face tight and white despite the thick covering of freckles. As the graveyard emptied, Gregory turned to Jordan.

'Thanks for coming, mate. I needed to see that. Things are shit at the moment – that little bitch being put in the ground has been the one bright spot in the past couple of weeks. Sorry if that sounds nasty, but it's true.'

Jordan flinched a little, but nodded. 'No problem, boss. I'm not on shift today anyway, so it was something to do. Fancy a pint, on the way home?'

Gregory smiled. 'Definitely. I want to talk to you anyway. Something I need to tell you. Just give me a minute. I'll meet you by the gate.'

He stood still for a moment as Jordan headed off across the muddy grass, then walked slowly to the graveside, where a cemetery worker was laying the last of the floral tributes on the mound of soil that now covered Leanne Brimley's coffin. The man touched his forehead deferentially and moved away as Gregory approached, and the DCI gave him a nod, then stood in silence for a full minute, staring at the freshly piled earth. What a relief, he thought. What a bloody great relief. And when he finally turned away and went to join James Jordan, he was smiling.

'I feel really bad that I couldn't get to the funeral. I hope Liam and Lisa coped alright. It must have been the most awful day for them.'

Cora unzipped her knee-length brown leather boots and shoved them under her chair, then curled her feet under her with a sigh. She, along with Nathan and Rodney, was in a small country house hotel near Exeter, where they'd spent the afternoon filming with a woman who claimed to have Britain's biggest collection of Tom Jones memorabilia. Tomorrow morning they'd be doing a live broadcast, with Scott and his satellite truck joining them as the famous Welsh singer himself surprised his devotee on her doorstep. After a delicious dinner of peppered steak, dauphinoise potatoes and some good red wine, the crew were now comfortably ensconced in the cosy little residents' lounge, an open fire blazing in the Victorian hearth.

'Horrible, yes,' agreed Nathan. 'Even more horrible than watching that mad woman caress that half-rotten sausage today. And that's pretty hard to beat.'

Rodney, who was sprawled next to the cameraman on

a large, faded leather Chesterfield sofa, groaned theatrically.

'Ugh. Don't remind me, Nath, or I might throw up my dinner. That was one of the most disturbing things I've seen in ages. Or maybe in my entire life. What on earth is wrong with these people, and why is it always us who gets sent to film them?'

Cora sniggered. The woman, whose entire home was full to bursting point with pictures, items of the singer's clothing acquired at charity auctions, and endless souvenirs including a life-sized cardboard cut-out in the front porch, had proudly showed them her 'pièce de résistance' – a rotting sausage, with a chunk missing, which she claimed had slipped unnoticed from a sandwich Tom had been eating as he left a hotel one evening three months ago while on tour. The super-fan, who'd been camped out in the hotel reception area waiting for a glimpse of her idol, had failed to grab his attention but succeeded in grabbing the sausage, which now sat in pride of place under a glass dome on her mantelpiece.

'I mean,' continued Rodney, 'she doesn't even seem to care that it's got mould all over it and looks like a severed penis. Imagine sitting there in front of your telly with that thing looking at you. MENTAL.'

Cora laughed again.

'Well, we'll have to see it again in the morning. Bet none of us will want sausages for breakfast after that, eh? Anyway, before we all start to crash, and seeing as we have this lovely room to ourselves, can we have a quick chat about this Leanne thing? I've fixed the interview with Randall Greythorpe for Monday morning, Nathan. I'll tell you more about that in a minute. And I've got those letters finally, the ones from Liam – I managed to grab the post before I drove down here this morning. I've glanced at them, but we can look at them properly now. He's putting together a list of locals' names and addresses for me too and he's going to email that as soon as he can. But first – Rodney, you said you were going to make a detour to Clarton Bridge on the way home last night. I forgot to ask – did you have time?'

The soundman nodded, pushing his little round glasses further up his nose.

'I did. It was dark by then, of course. But I drove up there and parked on it, and had a quick wander round. It's a very quiet road, the one that goes over the bridge – I got there just after six, so peak traffic time, and a similar time to when you were there, Cora, the night Leanne died. But I was there about five minutes, and only three cars passed me. So if you were going to jump, or *help* somebody to jump, there'd be plenty of time between passing vehicles, I reckon. There aren't any houses nearby, certainly not with a line of sight of the bridge. And I didn't see any CCTV cameras anywhere. No streetlights either. It's very dark. Bit spooky, actually.'

'Hmmm.'

Cora thought for a minute, remembering again the lights she had seen illuminating a section of the old bridge just before she'd driven under it. Last night as she'd lain in bed, trying to get the memory to sharpen in her mind's eye, she'd wondered if maybe the light had come from a torch – that of a passing dog walker or jogger, or even Leanne's own? But she'd instantly dismissed the thought. It had been car headlights, she was convinced of it.

'Thanks, Rodney. OK, so as I said Nathan, we're going to see Mr Greythorpe on Monday morning. I spoke to his assistant – his name is John Smith, excellent name, clearly has imaginative parents – and he seemed quite keen, so that was good. I have some articles about Greythorpe that Sam sent through. I'll show you those on Monday before we speak to him, but Sam was right – he sounds pretty ruthless. Not a very endearing character, certainly not when it comes to business matters. Eleven o'clock OK?'

'Perfect. Gets us out of Monday morning lives too, which is a bonus,' said Nathan happily.

'That's what I thought,' said Cora with a grin. 'There are definite plus points about this investigative reporting project. Betsy wouldn't let us take you though, Rodney, sorry. We have to one-man-band it. Hope you don't end up somewhere awful.'

The soundman shrugged.

'Don't worry about it. I'm more interested in seeing these letters right now – come on, show!'

'OK, hang on.'

Cora reached down into her handbag, which had been resting against the leg of her chair, and pulled out a large brown envelope. Tipping it upside down, she shook it and a collection of papers fluttered out onto the low table between her seat and the boys' sofa.

'He's photocopied them all for me, so these are copies we can keep,' she said, sorting through the pages. 'Apparently there were one or two more of these anonymous letters, which Leanne destroyed as soon as she received them, but Liam said they were very similar to these two, look.'

She selected two letters, both typed in large block capitals, and pushed them across the polished wood. Nathan picked them up, angling them so Rodney could see them too.

'STOP CAMPAIGNING AGAINST ELMSLEY PARK. LOCAL FEELING IS VERY STRONG – WE WANT OUR MONEY! YOU HAVE BEEN WARNED.

BACK OFF OR YOU WILL REGRET IT.'

Nathan read the first letter out loud.

'Short and not so sweet,' he said, putting the sheet back on the table and turning to the second letter. Again, he read it aloud.

'WHY WON'T YOU LISTEN? WE'VE WARNED YOU MORE THAN ONCE. STOP YOUR CAMPAIGN AND BACK OFF, YOU STUPID LITTLE BITCH. BACK OFF OR PAY THE PRICE.'

'Wow. Pretty nasty. Bit scary too, especially for a young kid like Leanne,' said Rodney.

'I know. Pretty impressive that she didn't just quit,' said Cora. 'I might have, in her position.'

'You, quit? No, you wouldn't. Come on, what else have we got here?'

Cora smiled, knowing that Nathan was probably right. Once she set her mind to something, she rarely gave up.

'OK, well this one's just the initial letter Greythorpe's office sent out, outlining the plans for the development, both the original smaller one and the bigger one - the one he'd have built if everyone agreed to sell their houses so he could demolish them. Then there's another one, saying he was aware that Leanne had started a campaign and saying that if she wanted to discuss her concerns with him, she could come in to the site office for a chat. Perfectly polite letter, look.'

'So, was that when she was "turfed out", as Liam put it? When she went in for that chat in the site office?' asked Nathan.

'Must have been, yes. Things must have taken a bit of a bad turn.'

'Right. So there's just one more letter then... is that what I think it is?'

Nathan pointed at the remaining sheet of paper. Cora

reached for her almost-empty wine glass and drained it.

'Yes. That's… that's the suicide note.'

They all stared at the letter, which was lying face-down on the table. After a long moment, Cora reached out a hand that was suddenly shaking a little, and carefully turned the page over. Centred on the page were a few lines of typed script.

'Read it to us, will you?'

Nathan's voice was soft, his eyes watching Cora's face.

She nodded and took a deep breath.

'To my family and friends. I'm so sorry. It's been a long few months and I can't take it anymore. It's too hard. I apolojise for what I'm about to do. I know this is going to come as a terrible shock, but I want you to know that I know what I'm doing. This is my decission and it's the right one for me. I love you. I will always love you. But I can't stay with you any longer. Please try to understand. Leanne xx'

She looked up. Nathan and Rodney were silent, sombre-faced.

'Well? What do you think? Do you think it sounds like a genuine suicide note?'

Rodney nodded slowly.

'Sounds real enough to me. Can I see it?'

Cora handed the piece of paper to him and he read the note and then passed it to Nathan.

'Couple of spelling mistakes – but if the toxicology report's right she was probably drunk when she wrote it, so that makes sense. And very stressed too, if she was about to do something so drastic,' the cameraman said. 'I agree with Rodney. It looks like the real thing, Cora. Maybe we're wasting our time here.'

Cora sank back into the squishy armchair and rubbed

her eyes.

'Oh guys, I don't know. When I saw that letter this morning, I thought the same as you at first. But...'

She sighed heavily.

'Look, can we just do this interview on Monday and then see how we feel? Maybe you're right. It's just that Liam...well, he seemed so sure his sister wouldn't have done this. But as we've said before, he's young, and grieving...'

'Of course, let's do the interview. We're all too tired now to think about this properly,' said Nathan soothingly. 'We can think about it over the weekend, do the interview on Monday and take stock then, OK?'

'Good idea. Thanks, Nathan. Sleep now, then?'

'YES,' said Nathan and Rodney, vehemently and simultaneously.

And wearily, they helped Cora scoop the letters back into the envelope and headed upstairs to bed.

14

After a wet, cold week, Saturday afternoon was so bright and sunny that when Rosie and Nicole popped in for a coffee and a catch-up, the decision to sit outside on Cora's terrace was unanimous. Bundled up in coats and hats, but with sunglasses on, the three of them cradled steaming mugs and nibbled on the iced madeira cake Rosie had picked up at the local bakery on the way.

'Sitting outside in November – must be a first,' said Nicole, wiping a blob of icing off her bottom lip. Her long dark hair was pulled back in a neat chignon today, and with her black coat and scarf and big black sunglasses she looked a little like a fifties Hollywood movie star, Cora thought.

'I know. What a beautiful day. And aren't my pots looking nice?'

'Gorgeous,' said Rosie. 'I'm very impressed.'

'Well, from a top florist, that's a massive compliment, thank you.'

Cora sipped her Earl Grey – she couldn't stand coffee – and gazed with satisfaction at the large aluminium planters that lined the front of her fifth-floor terrace, affording her some privacy from the occupants of the apartments opposite. She'd splashed out on new pots and furniture for her beloved outdoor space during the summer, and she'd been delighted with its updated look. They were sitting at a Scandinavian-style rectangular table, a combination of metal and pale wood, with matching chairs softened by striped grey and ivory cushions. The tall planters were now filled with ivy and winter flowering heathers for some seasonal colour, and dotted around the terrace were some of Cora's favourite garden accessories, collected over the years. A group of elegant steel candle holders occupied the corner nearest to the seating area; across the terrace, a low table with a heavy white-painted terracotta wine cooler sat between two sun loungers; and hanging from a bracket on the back wall, an avocado-coloured ceramic birdhouse swayed gently in the breeze. It was rarely inhabited, partly due to its slightly perilous location and partly, Cora thought, thanks to the regular visits to the balcony of Oliver and Pebbles, her neighbour's cats. She didn't mind, though – the birdhouse made a nice ornament regardless, and she was rather fond of the cats.

They'd been sitting there for a good forty-five minutes, had refilled their mugs twice and thoroughly discussed the latest goings-on in Rosie's florist's shop and Nicole's veterinary practice before Cora finally brought up Leanne Brimley. She'd tried to put the girl out of her mind for a while yesterday, returning from Exeter to enjoy a quiet Friday night in front of the TV with a glass of wine, and giving herself a much-needed manicure and pedicure. Adam was working, and although she'd chatted to him on the phone before bed, she'd deliberately kept the conversation light and general and away from work matters, not wanting anything to spoil the relaxed mood she'd lulled herself into.

Now though, after a rare nine hours' sleep, she was feeling clear-headed and fired up again. OK, so there was a suicide note, which appeared to have been typed by Leanne on her own laptop. That didn't mean nobody else was involved in her death, though, did it? Maybe she was hounded so much by those angry residents, or by somebody else, that she felt she had no choice. Maybe one of them got

95

her drunk, then drove her up to Clarton Bridge and urged her to jump. Or maybe not. But for some reason, Cora didn't feel that this story was over, no matter what the police and coroner thought. It wouldn't hurt to keep on checking things out, just for a little while…

'Cora? CORA! Have you drifted off behind those sunglasses? Jason Momoa or Kit Harington?'

'Huh? Who are they? What was the question?'

Cora straightened up in her chair, looking from Nicole to Rosie with a puzzled expression.

Nicole sighed. 'Oh, I forgot. You don't watch *Game of Thrones*, do you? Never mind. What were you thinking about? Let me guess – the girl who jumped from the bridge?'

Cora put her mug down on the table and picked up the last few cake crumbs from her plate, popping them into her mouth. She nodded and swallowed.

'Yes. Sorry. Nathan and I are going to see the property developer on Monday, just to see what he has to say about it all. But I've been thinking about that architect's plan – remember, it had some handwritten notes on it, presumably put there by Leanne?'

Nicole and Rosie exchanged looks, then both turned back to Cora.

'Oh, bloody hell. Go on, then. Get the flipping thing and let's look at it properly. You won't be happy until we've done a bit of brain-storming, will you?'

Nicole sounded resigned.

'Thank you. You guys ROCK.'

Cora jumped up from her chair and skipped into the lounge to retrieve her laptop. She'd now saved the contents of the memory stick onto her hard drive, popping the stick itself into the drawer of her bedside table for safe-keeping. Back on the terrace, she fired up the laptop and opened the file.

'OK, so this is the drawing of Elmsley Park. As you can see, there's a big letter X – there, look. I didn't know what that was, at first. But now I've realised it's marking the location of Leanne's house, which of course would have been demolished if plans for the larger estate had gone ahead. So that's cleared that up, she was just marking her home on the map. It's these notes at the side that have been puzzling us - "*M Diamonds*", "*U18?*" and "*Manchester*".'

Rosie and Nicole peered at the screen.

'Well, Rodney found that lap-dancing club called Midnight Diamonds, didn't he? Do you not think that's it? Because if it is, it might tie in with the next line, "*U18?*"', said Rosie thoughtfully.

'Gosh, maybe,' said Cora. 'Are you thinking under-eighteen girls working at the club? But why would Leanne care about that? I still can't see what connection that club has to the housing development plans…'

'Well, it must have some connection, or she wouldn't have written it on that map,' said Nicole.

'True.'

Cora thought for a moment, eyes glued to the screen of her laptop. Randall Greythorpe, a wealthy property developer… and a lap-dancing club. Could there be a link? Did he frequent the place, maybe?

'I wonder if Randall Greythorpe was a regular there or something, and Leanne found out about it?' she said slowly. 'If there *were* underage girls working there, and he'd had more than just a lap dance from them, and Leanne somehow knew that, maybe she was blackmailing him? OK, so I'm speculating wildly here, obviously. But it's a thought, isn't it? Liam did say Leanne was on to something – could it be something like that? Maybe that's why Greythorpe seemed to cave in so easily all of a sudden, and let her win her fight against the bigger development? He wouldn't want something like that getting out, would he? I mean, I don't really know how she'd find out about it...'

Nicole was frowning.

'Or maybe he *owns* the club,' she said. 'He owns it, and he's *employing* underage girls, and Leanne found out about that somehow. Again, wild speculation. But that wouldn't be good for his reputation either. Shall we see if the place is listed with Companies House, see if we can find out who owns it?' she said.

Cora was already typing, calling up the website. All UK limited companies had to register with Companies House, and it was a useful resource for journalists, with plenty of information freely available to the public online.

'Great idea. OK, here we go... Midnight Diamonds, Rotunda Street, Bristol. Licensed club. Hmmm, that's one way to describe it, I suppose. And if I click on "people"... oh, wow. Good call, Nicole! Bingo!'

She grinned widely and turned the laptop round so her friends could see the screen.

'Two officers,' read Rosie. 'Director, Randall John Greythorpe. Director, Douglas George Granley. Two of them, then – he has a partner.'

'How very interesting.'

Cora turned the computer back towards herself again.

'I've seen no mention of Greythorpe being involved in this sort of business in any of the news articles about him, so he clearly keeps it under wraps. It's obviously all legal and everything, but still, a little bit unexpected. Very interesting indeed. Who's this Douglas guy then? And the fact that Leanne wrote that *under-eighteen* comment is even more interesting now...I wonder how she even *discovered* the link between Greythorpe and the club?'

'Probably just looked up Randall Greythorpe to see what else he was involved in. It's all there online if you look, isn't it? Clever girl. Still, that *possibly* clears that up – wonder what the Manchester reference is?' Nicole asked.

'And why was she still carrying that memory stick around with her, even though the campaign was over?' said Rosie.

'Probably just backed up her file, stuck it in her pocket and forgot about it,' said Cora. 'I do that all the time. Find memory sticks in all sorts of random places. It's more what's on it that's interesting me, but we're definitely getting somewhere now...'

'Brrrr.'

Nicole pulled her scarf a little more tightly round her neck, and Cora suddenly realised she was feeling rather chilly too. It was three thirty, and the sun had gone in now, the afternoon sky already darkening.

'OK, you've helped me enough for now and it's getting cold. Let's go in. Thanks so much guys. I'll keep you posted.'

'Oh, *good*.'

Nicole and Rosie spoke simultaneously and in identically sarcastic tones, making them all laugh. As they gathered up the plates and mugs and made their way back into the warm apartment, Cora felt a wave of love and gratitude. She really did have wonderful friends. It wasn't the first time they'd reluctantly but stoically helped her to investigate something she felt needed looking into, and she hoped they knew how much she appreciated it. Smiling, she locked the terrace doors and retreated into the cosy lounge.

15

Elmsley Park – a Randall Greythorpe Development

Cora had seen the sign before, the day she'd visited Lisa and Liam Brimley, but now, on this chilly Monday morning, she stood back and read it properly.

Award-winning design, from a team passionate about improving local communities

Traditional craftsmanship in harmony with cutting edge technology for sustainable modern living

The board was striking, with dark purple lettering on a cream background. Below it, a smaller notice directed visitors to the site office. Further along the expanse of wooden fence which marked the edge of the development, two men on ladders were stringing up coloured lights, one whistling 'Jingle Bells' as he worked.

'A month today is Christmas Day,' remarked Nathan, as he hoisted his tripod on his shoulder. 'Blimey. This year's gone quickly, hasn't it?'

'It has. I haven't even thought about Christmas shopping yet either. Well, I've done a few bits online but I still have loads to get. Anyway, hurry up, Nath, we need to get in there. This way, look.'

Cora led the way through a gate in the fence and across a concreted parking area, at the far end of which sat a squat, pre-fabricated building with another cream and purple sign telling them that this was the site office, where they were due to meet Randall Greythorpe in exactly one minute from now at 10 a.m. It was another cold, bright day, the rat-tat-tat of a pneumatic drill and the steady engine rumble of some sort of building machinery filling the crisp air. Cora knocked on the office door, and seconds later it was opened by a smiling young man with cropped dark hair and a small, neat goatee beard. He was wearing a close-fitting emerald green sweater, which showed off his muscular torso.

'Mr Nesbit? And Miss Baxton? Hello, I'm John Smith, Randall's assistant, I spoke to you on the phone. Good to meet you, come on in out of the cold!'

His voice was pleasant, soft with a hint of a Welsh burr. Cora smiled.

'It's actually Baxter, not Baxton. But don't worry, I've been called worse!'

John laughed.

'Ah, my fault, can't read my own handwriting half the time! Come in, come in!'

He ushered them inside, into what was a surprisingly pleasant space, painted white and dominated by a large glass and chrome desk, empty apart from a sleek, expensive-looking laptop and a telephone. To the left of the desk was a seating area with two plush, deep purple sofas, a scattering of tub chairs, and side tables piled with glossy brochures; to the right, a wooden partition had been erected, another large desk just visible behind it.

'Randall will be with us in a minute, he's just signing some papers back there. Would you like to set up here, in the guest area? And can I get you some tea or coffee? Anything else you need?'

John gestured towards the purple sofas, and Cora and Nathan smiled their agreement and accepted the offer of a hot drink.

'Great. Won't be a minute.'

John bustled off and disappeared through a door at the far end of the room, through which more desks were visible, a few people tapping away on keyboards, and

Cora and Nathan started setting up for the interview. They'd met up in a café round the corner for breakfast an hour ago, so Cora could brief Nathan on what she'd discovered about Midnight Diamonds and on what, to all intents and purposes, would be a 'normal' chat, other than the fact that it wouldn't actually be broadcast. The articles Sam had forwarded to Cora made interesting reading over their tea and toast – Randall Greythorpe had, it seemed, a spectacular success rate in getting planning permission for housing on greenfield sites and other 'sensitive' areas, and in persuading locals to sell up to allow his developments to grow, his predatory applications leading to a number of protests similar to the one led by Leanne Brimley in Bristol.

'He seems to win nine times out of ten,' Cora said, as Nathan speed-read a newspaper piece about a controversial development in Essex.

'Which makes it even more interesting that he caved in so easily here. It's out of character. As Liam said, everyone would probably have agreed to sell in the end, even Lisa, despite Leanne's best efforts, so all he had to do was wait a bit longer and he could have built the big development he wanted to. Odd, eh?'

'It is,' said Nathan. 'But don't go jumping to conclusions, Cora. Let's just see how this goes.'

Now, as Nathan declared himself happy with the camera shot, and John re-appeared clutching a tea tray, Cora turned to see a tall, extremely attractive man emerge from behind the wooden partition and stride towards them, hand outstretched.

'Randall Greythorpe. Very nice to meet you,' he said with a smile.

His voice was deep and educated, his teeth flashing white, dark hair slightly ruffled as though he'd just got out of bed, the casual look belied by the fact that he was wearing an extremely smart grey checked jacket over a crisp, collarless shirt as white as his teeth. He had light grey eyes too (not quite fifty, but several shades of grey here, Cora thought with mild amusement, remembering that his name had the word 'Grey' in it too) and, like his assistant John, sported a neatly trimmed goatee beard.

'Clearly the *in* look for those in the property business,' she thought, as she shook hands and returned the greeting.

'Cora Baxter,' she said. 'And this is Nathan Nesbit, my cameraman. Thanks so much for doing this at such short notice, we really appreciate it.'

Nathan settled the man in his seat, attached the microphone to his lapel, adjusted the lighting and turned to John, who was hovering anxiously nearby.

'Would you mind just staying out of Mr Greythorpe's eyeline when we start?' he asked politely. 'It's just that it can be a bit off-putting for the interviewee.'

'Oh, of course, sorry! I'll be over at my desk if you need anything. All OK, Randall?' The man rushed off, hands flapping a little.

'Fine, thanks, John.' Randall Greythorpe looked amused.

'He worries,' he whispered conspiratorially to Cora and Nathan, who both smiled. Nathan turned to Cora.

'Ready when you are,' he said.

Cora started with some standard interview questions, asking Randall how he got started in the property business (he had inherited some money from his grandfather, who died not long after Randall graduated from university, and used the cash to fund his first development); his design inspiration ('I like to find architectural solutions to modern-day problems – lack of space for new housing, the need for sustainability. But I like drama too. There's

103

no reason not to combine the two approaches.'); and his plans for the future ('I like this part of the country – its proximity to London, but with beautiful countryside on the doorstep. But I want to go north too – land and property is cheaper, and there's more space. Scotland, for example – imagine what I could do there, with those views!').

His passion for his chosen profession was clear and Cora, who was fond of modern interior design, quickly found herself transfixed, drawn in by the man's descriptions of clean, contemporary architecture and the challenges of combining style with function. After ten minutes had passed though, she carefully brought the conversation back to the Elmsley Park development, asking first about the idea behind the unusual design. Then she casually said:

'It's been a little controversial though, hasn't it? A bit of a protest, locally?'

Randall shrugged.

'Happens to me a lot. It wasn't a big deal here – I've lived through worse. It's the environmentalists who don't want me to build on greenfield sites who tend to get the most heated. This one was relatively minor – I had two plans for this site, one a little bigger than the other. I offered to buy some local properties so I could demolish them and go for the bigger development, but some locals didn't want to sell up. I tried to persuade them, but a campaign had been started, and one or two were pretty adamant about staying put, so in the end I let it go and plumped for the smaller development. No biggie, as I said.'

Cora nodded, and glanced at Nathan. His eyes were fixed on his viewfinder but the faintest twitch of an eyebrow gave her the signal. *Go for it.*

'From what I've heard, one family in particular didn't want to move - the Brimleys?' she said. 'The dad's ashes were scattered in their garden as far as I understand. Did you have much contact with them?'

There was a clatter from the desk to their right.

'Oh gosh, sorry. Knocked my mug over. Lucky it was empty!'

John righted the mug and looked anxiously at his boss, who gave him a reassuring smile.

'Don't worry, John. We're nearly done here now anyway.'

Randall turned back to Cora.

'You were asking about the Brimleys?'

His voice was calm, but Cora suddenly noticed a tenseness in his face, in the set of his jaw. Was she imagining it? She wasn't sure.

'I came across them, yes. Well, one of them. The daughter was the driving force behind the protest. She came to see us here once, actually. It was all very amicable... well, more or less. She did get a little... well, emotional, during our meeting. I tried to impress upon her how much my larger scheme would benefit the wider community, but she didn't really want to listen. I had to ask her to leave eventually, if I remember correctly. There were other people here, you see, potential buyers, and she was causing a bit of a scene. But we're used to this sort of opposition, as I said earlier. People are resistant to change, especially if they've lived in a place for a long time and have an emotional attachment to it. We understand that. It was one of the reasons I decided to abandon plans for the bigger development. Sometimes, it's just not worth the fight. Negative publicity and all that.'

He smiled.

'Sure.' Cora thought for a moment, then decided to go

for it.

'Are you aware that Leanne Brimley is dead, Mr Greythorpe? That she died in a fall from a bridge, just outside the city, the day after she'd been told that you'd abandoned plans for the bigger development?'

Randall Greythorpe glanced sideways at John, but at his desk his assistant's head was down, gaze fixed on some papers on the desk in front of him. He didn't turn to look at his boss, and after a couple of seconds Randall turned back to Cora.

'Errrm, yes. I did hear about that. It was tragic. I think the papers said she'd been depressed? Frighteningly common among young people nowadays. Very sad. I'm not sure why you're asking me about it, though?'

He smiled again, but there was a definite lack of warmth in his eyes now. Cora decided to ask one more question.

'Oh, just because you'd met her, that's all. No real reason. One final thing, Mr Greythorpe – obviously your property empire is your main interest, but it's come to my attention that you have fingers in other pies too. Well, one pie in particular, and a local one at that. Midnight Diamonds?'

Randall's eyes opened wide in surprise, and over at his desk John abruptly stood up, pushing his paperwork to one side. He took a step towards the seating area and then stopped.

'Randall, we need to finish up,' he said. He sounded slightly frantic.

'We have that… that meeting via Skype in five minutes. Guys, can we end the interview now?'

Cora looked at Nathan, who gave her the slightest raise of an eyebrow again.

'This *was* the last question – could we just finish this

one, then we'll be out of your hair?' she said, smiling at both John and Randall.

There was a moment's silence, the two men locking eyes. Then Greythorpe spoke.

'Of course. It's OK, John. The Skype meeting can wait. We're almost done here.'

He turned back to the camera.

'Yes, I am part-owner of another business here in Bristol. And yes, it's slightly different to my main business, but it's all above board. I have nothing to hide. I'm mostly a sleeping partner, to be honest. An old school friend of mine, Dougie Granley, wanted to open a gentlemen's club but didn't have enough capital. I stepped in to help. I rarely set foot in the place, he runs it day to day. He returned the favour though – he's the reason I'm here in Bristol. He spotted this old factory site and knew it would be perfect for me, and so it was. I have no other businesses locally though, and no plans to open any – Randall Greythorpe Developments keeps me busy enough. Any other questions?'

There was definitely a hint of steel in the grey eyes now, and Cora shook her head.

'No more. Thank you so much, that was incredibly interesting. We'll get out of your way, and we'll give you a call John, as soon as we have a transmission date for the interview.'

John nodded, a look of relief on his face now, the friendly smile back. As Randall said his goodbyes and disappeared behind the partition again, his assistant buzzed around, helping the crew to pack up their kit.

'Sorry – I get a bit anxious when he's doing interviews. He can be a bit of a loose cannon, and he gets enough bad publicity with all the controversial developments he insists on starting. And when you mentioned Midnight Diamonds...well, he doesn't really like to talk about it. I thought he might kick off. Quite well-behaved today, though,' he whispered to Cora as he showed her and Nathan to the door.

She smiled. 'Don't worry. We probably won't use the stuff about the club anyway,' she said. 'Not really relevant.'

'Oh, phew!' John grinned. 'As he said, it really is all above board, there's nothing shady about it or anything. It's just that some people are a bit funny about places like that, aren't they? And he really did get involved mainly to help out his mate. He's got a good heart underneath it all, has Randall. But still, it doesn't really fit with the image, does it? So if you could leave it out, I'd be ever so grateful. We have a PR company we work with to publicise big projects, but they leave the day-to-day stuff like this to me, and I'm not sure how happy they'd be about him talking about his lap-dancing club on morning TV...'

'Don't worry, honestly.' Cora held out a hand. 'Nice to meet you. I'll be in touch.'

'Thanks ever so. Lovely to meet you both. If there's anything else you need, let me know.'

He beamed again and disappeared back into the office, the door closing gently behind him. As they headed for the gate, Nathan turned to Cora.

'So – what do you think?'

'I think...' said Cora slowly, 'that they both acted a little oddly when I mentioned Leanne Brimley. And definitely oddly when the club came up. You?'

'Agreed,' said Nathan. They'd reached the gate in the wooden fence, and he pushed it open, gesturing to Cora to go first.

'So what now?'

Cora thought for a minute.

'I think we definitely need to check out the club somehow, and as soon as possible. See if there *is* anything dodgy going on there. The fact that Leanne had noted the name on her plan, alongside the under-eighteen thing… there must be something in that. We need to try and find out what that is. See if whatever she discovered was enough to make Randall Greythorpe give up on his bigger development, if she confronted him with it. Or…'

She paused. Nathan dumped his camera and tripod on the ground next to his car and turned to look at her.

'Or enough to make someone want her dead?' he said.

'I don't know, Nathan. Maybe there's nothing in any of this at all. Let's do a bit more investigating first, before we jump to any crazy conclusions.'

'OK. Have you run all this latest stuff past Adam, by the way?'

'A bit. I'll talk to him again tonight, see what he thinks. You know what he's like though…doesn't always like me getting involved in things like this!'

Nathan grinned.

'I'd like to see him try to stop you. Come on, let's get out of here.'

Inside the site office, Randall Greythorpe was sitting at his desk, flicking a silver pen between his fingers and staring into space.

'Can I get you anything, boss? And there are a few more papers for you to sign, I'm afraid.'

John appeared at his side, and slid a sheaf of documents onto the desk. Randall put the pen down and turned to his assistant.

'Nothing for now, thanks John. Except…'

He paused, and John waited expectantly.

'Except… keep that Baxter woman away from me, OK? She's done her interview. If she calls again, don't give her any more information. About anything. Right?'

'Err… yes, alright. Of course I can do that. No problem at all. Don't worry, Randall. Can I get you a cup of tea now?'

Randall nodded.

'Actually – make it a coffee. A strong one. Thanks, John. Don't know what I'd do without you.'

John smiled, a warm glow creeping over him as he headed off. Randall could be a tad difficult at times, and a little demanding, but he was a good boss. John was lucky to have this job, and he knew it. It was interesting, and well-paid, and he needed a job with a decent salary, with *his* responsibilities. He had liked Cora Baxter, and her cameraman too, but if they rang again he'd just have to put them off, politely but firmly. That was what the boss wanted, and what Randall Greythorpe wanted, Randall Greythorpe got. That was just how it was. John picked up his boss's favourite mug and started making the coffee.

16

'I can't believe I agreed to do this, Cora. Hope you appreciate the huge sacrifice I'm making. A *lap-dancing* club – a *straight* lap-dancing club, at that – on our precious Friday night off? Gareth was in hysterics at the very idea.'

Nathan rolled his eyes as he got out of the back of Scott's car to join Rodney, who was already shivering on the pavement. Cora, who was sitting in the front next to the engineer, grinned and rolled down the window a few inches so she could speak to them through the gap. It was after eleven o'clock and freezing, the cold air licking at her face. Across the road, neon lights around the Midnight Diamonds sign flashed silver and white, illuminating what was otherwise a dark, quiet street. They'd pulled up outside two minutes ago, but so far hadn't seen anyone enter or leave.

'I do appreciate it, really I do.' She did. Friday night was the only night of the week when the crew could actually let their hair down, knowing they had a full day off the next day. They frequently had to work on Sundays, filming or travelling to a far-flung location for Monday morning's show, so Saturday nights weren't always quite so relaxing.

'And I'm sorry it's not a gay club, but you'll just have to fake interest in those half-naked women for a few hours,' Cora continued. 'Come on, Nathan, it's work. Put your finest investigative photo-journalist cap on and go for it.'

'Yeah, come on Nathan. I'm mortified at the very idea, and Jodie's not too happy about it either. But we all agreed to help Cora out with this, and if I can do it without moaning, you can too. Do you think what I'm wearing is OK, Cora? I didn't really know what was appropriate, you know, for a club like this? I've only been to one once before, on a stag night years ago...'

Rodney looked dubiously down at his outfit.

'Errrm... yes, it's absolutely fine, Rodney.'

Cora and Nathan exchanged amused glances. The soundman was wearing deep burgundy coloured trousers with silver thread running through the fabric, teamed with an emerald green velvet jacket, over which he'd thrown some sort of Apache Indian style poncho with multi-coloured beads woven into its copious fringing. Try as she might, Cora could not think of a single occasion in life when this outfit would be remotely appropriate, but it was probably best not to say that right now.

'And you have the hidden camera, Nath?' she asked instead.

'I have. It's working perfectly, checked it earlier.'

Nathan, who was smartly dressed in shirt and jacket, gestured to his tie. He had a number of discreet cameras for use on their very occasional undercover filming jobs, and the tie-cam was one of his favourites. The tiny, pin-hole camera was undetectable in the knot of the patterned tie, and was operated by a wireless remote control which fitted in the palm of his hand and could easily be hidden in his trouser pocket. The camera could record up to three hours of video and audio if necessary, and had proved invaluable on several previous occasions. Cora still wasn't sure if tonight would be a total wild goose chase, but she'd asked Nathan to come prepared to record the evidence, just in case.

'Brilliant. Well, good luck, you two – enjoy! Keep an eye on your phones - if Scott and I see anything unusual out here, or you have anything to report, we'll communicate by text, OK?'

'OK. See you in a bit.'

Nathan and Rodney crossed the road, and moments later disappeared through the doorway of Midnight Diamonds. Cora closed the window and sat back in her seat with a sigh.

'And now, we wait,' she said.

'Yep. Toffee?'

Scott reached into the storage compartment between the two seats and pulled out a bag of sweets. Cora took one and they chewed quietly for a couple of minutes. The street was deserted, the only sound a faint thud-thud of music drifting from the club. Finally, Scott spoke again.

'Still not exactly sure what you're hoping to get out of this little evening out, Cora. I mean, even if there *are* under-age girls working in there, how do we prove it? You know what girls are like nowadays, all make-up and boob jobs and hair extensions and the like. It's bloody hard to tell if they're fifteen or twenty-five sometimes.'

His deep voice reverberated in the quiet car, the strong Bolton accent sounding even broader than usual.

Cora sighed.

'I know. I'm not sure either, really. But it's pretty clear that Leanne had some sort of concern about this place. You're right though, I don't know how we'd prove anything. Unless Nathan and Rodney spot anyone who's very obviously underage, and maybe we can speak to her to confirm it? If she'd agree to speak to us, of course... which she probably wouldn't, if it meant losing her job... oh heck, Scott, I'm going round and round in circles here. This is going to be a complete waste of time,

113

isn't it?'

The engineer reached across and patted her on the arm.

'Maybe. But we're here now, and as you say, Leanne wrote the name of this place down, and that under-eighteen thing. And it's owned by the same man she was having run-ins with about the housing development. It's worth looking at, even if we end up with nothing. Don't fret. Here, have another toffee. The mint ones are good.'

'Thanks.' Cora took another sweet then pointed out of the window.

'Look, a couple of guys coming down the street – punters?'

They watched as two middle-aged men in heavy overcoats approached on the club side of the road, one a little unsteady on his feet. They paused outside the door, looking up at the sign and appearing to discuss whether or not to enter, before the taller of the two slapped his friend on the shoulder and pushed the door open. A moment later the street was quiet again.

'Least it'll be warm in there, and there'll be beer,' Scott muttered, and shivered. Cora nodded, blowing on her fingers to warm them. Scott had turned the car engine off when Nathan and Rodney had left, not wanting to draw attention to the vehicle, but the temperature inside had dropped rapidly in the past few minutes. He turned the ignition key and cranked up the air conditioning to its warmest setting.

'Let's just get a blast of heat for a minute,' he said. 'And have you got those articles Sam emailed, the ones about this Greythorpe bloke? I haven't seen them yet. Might have a look now, pass the time.'

'Sure. I printed them out.' Cora rooted in her handbag and pulled out a cardboard file. Scott took it and, using the torch app on his phone for light, started to read. Cora stared out of the window, bored. She'd done many stake-outs like this during her years as a reporter, and they never got any easier. Hours of dull nothingness, legs and backs getting stiffer and stiffer, eyes drooping with tiredness and nowhere to go to the loo, the tedium only slightly eased by whatever food and drink they'd brought with them. It was, of course, all worth it if you got the picture or interview you'd been waiting for, if the persistence paid off and you beat every other journalist or TV show to the story. But all too often, it was all for nothing. Would tonight be one of those nights? Cora had a horrible feeling it might be. She stared down the street, watching listlessly as every few minutes another customer arrived at the club, sometimes a man alone, looking furtively over his shoulder as he approached, sometimes a small group, laughing and shoving each other through the door. No women, not so far, anyway, she noted.

'Hey, Cora.' Scott's voice broke into her thoughts, and she turned to look at him.

'Leanne's notes, on the map of the estate. As well as *"M Diamonds"* and the under-18 thing, she wrote the word *"Manchester"*, right?'

'She did. Why?'

'Well, it's probably not significant, but I've just read in one of these articles that Randall Greythorpe went to uni in Manchester. Studied at Manchester School of Architecture. Probably just a coincidence though, can't imagine why Leanne would care where he did his training, can you?'

'I don't know. And I didn't know he studied in Manchester.' Cora straightened up in her seat. 'I must have missed that – although to be fair, I didn't read all of the articles, just skimmed a few before we interviewed him. I wonder if that could be it? What else does it say?'

'Not much. It's just mentioned in this *Telegraph* piece about careers in the property business. They say, and I quote: *"Manchester School of Architecture is one of the UK's largest architecture schools and is considered to be one of the best of its kind in the world. Founded in 1996, it's a collaboration between Manchester Metropolitan University and the University of Manchester. A notable alumnus is Randall Greythorpe, the architect and property developer known for his controversial residential developments."* That's it, really.'

'Hmmm.'

Cora leaned back in her seat again, watching as another figure turned into the street and started walking briskly in the direction of the club, this time on the side of the road they were parked on.

'It could mean something, I suppose. No idea what though...hang on...'

Her voice tailed off. There was something very familiar about the figure – the man, she could see now – who was approaching. Was that... could it be...?

'Scott! Is that Gordon Gregory?'

'Huh? Who?'

'Gordon Gregory! You know, the DCI from Avon Police. The one who got suspended after we confronted him on air about covering up for his thuggish brother. Look, it *is* him, isn't it?'

The man was almost level with their car now, and as he passed he glanced into the vehicle, catching Cora's eye. He paused for a second, a flash of recognition crossing his face, then pulled up the collar of his long dark coat and hurried past, crossing the road just behind the car. Outside the door of Midnight Diamonds he hesitated again, looking back towards Cora and Scott. Then he pushed the door of the club open and vanished inside.

'Bloody hell, that was definitely him,' Cora said. 'It was, wasn't it? And he recognised me too, when he looked into the car, I'm sure he did!'

'I think it was, yes. Can't mistake that ugly mug. What's he doing hanging out in a place like that, then? Dirty bastard!'

Scott scratched his shiny, shaved head and scowled.

'Well, exactly. I mean, there's nothing illegal about going to a club like this, of course. But in his position? Not going to help him get back to active duty any time soon, is it, especially if his superiors find out how he's spending his time off... and even more especially if there are underage girls working in there. Shit, Scott. This could be another story we've stumbled onto here. I'm going to text Nathan and Rodney, get them to find him in there and keep an eye on him.'

She tapped out a message on her phone. Maybe tonight wouldn't be a complete waste of time after all.

Inside the club, Nathan and Rodney were sitting on a low, padded bench seat, upholstered in red velvet, a little way back from the long, central stage on which two young women were currently gyrating. The place had got busier over the past hour and was now about half full, waitresses in tight black sequinned dresses and extremely high heels weaving their way expertly between tables, drinks trays held aloft, wafts of perfume trailing in their wake. The spectator areas all around the stage were dimly lit, the walls draped with heavy black curtains, velvet like the seating. In contrast, the stage was brightly illuminated, colour-changing spotlights turning the dancers' skin by turns green, blue and red. Every now and again a girl would lead a male punter through a door at one side of the room, presumably the 'private dance' area, judging by the grins on the men's faces when they emerged some ten minutes later.

'I feel like such a lech, Nath,' said Rodney.

The music was so loud he was nearly shouting.

'I almost want to take my glasses off so I can't see them properly. I feel like I'm being unfaithful to Jodie. I mean, that girl up there now... I know she's got her pants on, but they're just... they're just so *small*.'

Nathan snorted into his beer glass.

'Oh, come on, Rodney, don't be such a prude. I think I'm enjoying this more than you are, and I'm *gay* for goodness' sake. The music's good, the beer's cold, if rather over-priced, and some of these women are bloody good dancers. It's not as seedy as I expected, actually. And I haven't seen anyone who looks obviously under-age yet, have you?'

Rodney shook his head. 'All look in their twenties or so to me. Hey, is that a message?'

On the table in front of them, the screen of Nathan's phone was flashing. He picked it up.

'Text from Cora,' he said. He clicked onto the message, read it and passed the phone to Rodney, scanning the room as he did so.

'She's right. Look, over there.'

He nudged Rodney, and the soundman followed his gaze. Sure enough, standing by the bar, shaking the hand of another, younger man, was DCI Gordon Gregory.

'Wow. Last place I'd expect to see a senior police officer, even if he is suspended from duty. Well, *especially* as he's suspended from duty,' said Rodney, leaning his head towards Nathan's ear so he didn't have to shout quite so loudly.

'I know,' Nathan yelled back. 'Hope he doesn't spot us. I'm turning the camera on.'

He groped in his pocket, found the remote control and hit record, making sure to angle his body, and hence his hidden tie camera, towards the police officer, who was now deep in conversation with his companion.

'You know, I think that's Douglas Granley. The owner of the place, the guy who's in partnership with Randall Greythorpe? Cora and I looked him up online after we did the fake interview with Greythorpe. Yep, definitely him.'

'Really? Gosh. So he's friendly with the dodgy copper?' Rodney shouted back.

They watched as the two men talked. Gregory, even from across the room and in this dim light, appeared to be somewhat flushed in the face, and irate about something, repeatedly gesturing towards the door of the club. Granley, who was smartly dressed in dark jeans and a jacket, broad-shouldered and good-looking in a boyish way, seemed to be trying to placate the older man, placing a hand on his shoulder and gesturing to the barman to bring drinks. Finally, Gregory nodded, took a drink and downed it, then reached out to shake hands with the club owner again. Granley slapped him on the back and headed off across the room, disappearing through a curtained alcove, and Gregory, carrying a fresh drink, sat down at a table on the opposite side of the stage to Nathan and Rodney, the dancers obscuring their view of him.

Nathan pressed his remote control again to switch the camera off and turned to the soundman.

'OK, well I don't know if that footage will ever be of any use, but I've got it. Shall we go, Rodders? It's bloody late and I don't think there's much more for us here.'

'Hang on.' Rodney was frowning, his eyes fixed on the stage.

'Look. That new girl who's just appeared up there. How old do you think she is?'

Nathan looked, then slowly nodded, reaching for his camera remote control.

'Yeah. She could be under eighteen. Very fresh-faced, even with all the make-up.'

The girl was right in front of them now, body firm and slim in a tiny, metallic silver bikini. She had long blonde hair in two plaits which, along with the dusting of freckles across her nose, made her look like a schoolgirl despite the heavily made-up eyes and glossy pink lips she was sporting. Nathan and Rodney looked at each other, both suddenly feeling deeply uncomfortable as the girl slipped off her bra top and flung it across the stage, wiggling her bottom and bouncing her small breasts to whoops and whistles from the boozy crowd.

'OK, I've got a few shots. I'm not enjoying this anymore. Let's get out of here,' Nathan said.

'Right behind you, mate.'

And they pushed their drinks aside, stood up and headed for the door.

Across the room, DCI Gordon Gregory sipped his drink and watched as the newest dancer swung expertly round a pole, thrusting her hips seductively back and forth, her silver bikini pants barely covering her pert rear, blonde plaits brushing the ground as she arched her back and swayed in time to the music. Normally, he enjoyed spending time at Midnight Diamonds, and he hadn't been here for a while so he'd been hoping for a good night. Suddenly though, he wasn't feeling like it this evening – seeing that little bitch of a TV reporter outside had ruined his night. And it *had* been her, he'd been sure of it, even though he'd only caught a glimpse of her in the dark, through the car window. He wouldn't forget that face in a hurry, not after what she'd done to him on live television.

Dougie had told him he must be mistaken, that he'd seen no sign of journalists hanging around. But it was her, he was positive. Shit. What was she doing here? He took another gulp of vodka and slammed his glass down on the table. Then he looked again at the girl writhing on the stage in front of him. Damn it. She looked like one of Dougie's young ones. Was *that* why the reporter was out there? Were there other journalists in here too? Some sort of sting? He scanned the room but didn't see anyone he recognised. Oh, to hell with it. He'd have another drink and call it a night. He wasn't in the mood now, and that cow being outside was making him anxious. Had she recognised him, when he'd passed her? He wasn't sure. He'd thought he was safe coming back here now, seeing as that other little bitch, Leanne, was no longer a problem. If this reporter dared to cause him any more trouble…

Gregory gestured to a passing waitress, waving his empty glass at her. Yes, if he had a single sniff that she was on his case… well, she'd be the one in trouble. He'd see to that.

17

The giant inflatable Santa, at least twenty feet tall, swayed gently in the early morning breeze from its precarious position on the ridge of the roof. Below it, a flashing 'Let it Snow!' sign lit up the gable, strings of multi-coloured fairy lights draped below it. Down on the ground, a row of almost-life-sized tin soldiers barred entry to the garage of the small semi-detached house, and a family of six animated gold reindeer filled the patch of front lawn, heads bobbing mechanically up and down. In every window of the house, giant illuminated snowflakes, stars and baubles glistened and twinkled. Next door, the similarly small square of front garden boasted, rather inexplicably, the entire cast of the seven dwarfs in light-up plastic form, a huge glowing snowman towering over them. Across the street, a ten-foot-tall green Shrek, dressed in a Santa outfit, was stationed by the front gate of another house, the roof of which was covered with fake snow. In every direction, coloured lights shimmered and inflatable characters bobbed as magical festive scenes were played out by every single home in this quiet Liverpool cul-de-sac.

'Bloody nutters,' said Nathan. He dumped his tripod on the ground with a groan and straightened up, rubbing the small of his back.

'Every bloody year, the same old bollocks. Who cares if a whole street decides to light itself up for Christmas? Massive waste of electricity in my book. Bonkers, all of them.'

Cora grinned. 'Well, it *is* for charity, remember. They raised over ten thousand pounds last year, so many people came to see them. And... well, it's certainly festive, isn't it? I wasn't feeling Christmassy at all until this morning, with everything that's been going on. Now I feel all warm and glowy. I'm going to put up a Christmas tree with Adam and Harry on Friday, can't wait. So don't be so bah, humbug, Nathan. Get into the festive spirit!'

She punched her cameraman gently on the arm and he sighed.

'Oh, alright. Plenty to shoot, anyway. A veritable feast for the eyes here, even eyes as knackered as mine. Shall we do the six thirty hit here, with the reindeer?'

'Fine by me.' Cora shivered. It was just after 5.30 a.m., and her car thermometer had shown a steady minus four degrees for the entire three-and-a-half-hour drive northwards. The decision to cover the 'most festive street in Britain' this morning had been a last-minute one by the news desk; a planned story about a group of junior school mothers who were outraged after a teacher told their six-year-olds that Santa wasn't real had fallen through, after a profuse apology and a promise to try to put things right from the teacher, and a quick scan of the news wires for a substitute story had resulted in the early hours call-out for Cora and her crew. At least, she thought now, it was Monday and she was feeling relatively well-rested, despite her late night sitting outside the club on Friday. It was the very early calls towards the *end* of a busy week that were the real killers.

'I'll go and find the owner, help her with the tea,' she said to Nathan. 'You OK out here?'

He nodded, rummaging in his kit bag for a camera lens.

'Fine. But see if you can get her to whack on some

toast too, will you? I'm starving.'

A few hours later it was time for breakfast number two, as they all huddled around a rather-too-small table in a rather-too-chilly but quite stylish little café a mile or so from their live location. Although it was only 9.45, they'd all actually chosen distinctly *non*-breakfast-style food from the all-day menu for a change, Cora spreading chicken liver paté on crusty bread, Rodney chomping on a goat's cheese and Mediterranean vegetable tart, and both Nathan and Scott enjoying braised beef on brioche topped with poached eggs, all the dishes accompanied by tall white mugs of steaming tea.

'We've been up for about eight hours, so it's lunchtime for us,' Nathan had explained to the slightly bemused-looking waiter, who clearly didn't expect quite such a drastic departure from the breakfast menu at this early hour. Earlier, as they'd drunk yet more tea in the truck in-between live hits, Nathan had played the tie-cam footage from Midnight Diamonds for them on his laptop, first showing the pictures of the young-looking dancer, with all of them agreeing that she may well indeed have been under-age, although they couldn't be sure. Then he scrolled backwards to the footage of DCI Gregory, in conversation with the man who was probably Douglas Granley, the club owner.

'Yep, that's definitely him. I recognise him from the Google images we looked at, Nath. And that's a hundred per cent DCI Gregory as well. Gosh. Although, as we've said before, there's nothing illegal about going to a strip club,' Cora said, as she leaned in to see the screen more clearly. 'But still, there's something a bit surprising about a senior cop doing it. And doing it regularly, maybe, as he seems to know Granley, doesn't he?'

'I would have said so, yes,' agreed Nathan. 'Looked like they were quite pally, and he definitely seemed to be getting free drinks. He seemed a bit irate about something when he first came in, then calmed down as you can see here, and settled down to watch the show.'

'So, if he's a friend of Granley's, maybe he's a friend of Randall Greythorpe too. Not that that means anything in particular,' said Cora. 'But if there *are* under-age girls there, surely he would notice, and do something about it? Wouldn't he?'

'You would have thought so,' said Scott. 'But hey, as we know he's not a very *good* cop, is he?' He put his mug down, picked up a damp cloth and started wiping down the narrow shelf which held the kettle and cups.

'You're so house-proud, Scott. Or *truck*-proud, I should say. And he's not a good cop, no.' Cora sighed. 'And there's probably not much point in trying to ask him about it either. He's hardly going to want to help me out, after what we did to him, is he? Bummer. I think we need to try to speak to one of the girls at the club somehow. I wonder if Leanne knew one of them, maybe? I might have to ask Liam about Midnight Diamonds, you know – I don't want to really, partly because he's so young to talk to about a place like that, but also because I'd have to somehow avoid telling him that we found out about it by snooping into his sister's memory stick, which he doesn't even know we have. Oh, I don't know. Leave it with me. I'll come up with something.'

'What about this Manchester connection then? Did you hear, Nathan and Rodney, that I read that Greythorpe went to uni there?'

Scott finished wiping and stepped back to admire his handiwork with a satisfied nod, standing on Rodney's fingers in the process. The soundman yelped.

'OW! Get your giant hoof off my hand! Holy crap, Scott. You know I always sit on the floor, be careful! This truck is too small to be doing housework when you have guests. Not going to be able to work my knob properly for the seven thirty now.'

He rubbed vigorously at his hand as Cora, Nathan and Scott all smirked. Rodney looked from one to the other and rolled his eyes.

'The knob on my *mixer*, as you well know, idiots,' he said, then grinned, and they all laughed.

'Anyway – the Manchester thing,' said Cora, and yawned, the early start now starting to take its toll. 'What do you…'

Her question was interrupted by a loud squawk from the speakers on Scott's control panel.

'THIS IS THE TD IN LONDON. WE NEED YOU UP IN TWO MINUTES. CHANGE OF RUNNING ORDER. CAN YOU DO IT? SAY YES, PLEASE.'

The technical director's voice boomed around the truck. Scott looked at Cora, eyebrows raised. She glanced out of the side window and nodded.

'Yep, we'll be OK, there are a few residents hanging around in the street over there, look. I'll run out and grab them, tell them we need them for a quick hit. They'll be fine, they're a chatty lot. Two minutes enough for you two?'

She stood up, zipping up her puffer coat.

'Sure,' said Nathan, reaching out a hand to help Rodney haul himself off the floor. 'Rodney might need some help with his knob though…'

'SHUT UP, NATHAN!' Rodney yelled, and the two of them tumbled out of the truck, pushing and shoving each other like excitable children. Cora followed, grinning and remembering a few months back when she had managed to say 'big knob' on live TV, much to the amusement of all her friends. She wondered if she, or any of them, would ever actually really grow up. She very much hoped not.

Now, as she swallowed another mouthful of deliciously creamy paté, she thought again about Leanne's "*Manchester*" note on the housing estate drawing. There must be something significant about the city, but what? Surely it couldn't just be because Randall Greythorpe studied his craft there?

'So – Manchester,' she said, wiping a crumb from her chin. 'We started discussing it earlier, just before you tried to break Rodney's hand and put his knob-twiddling in jeopardy, Scott. Any new ideas?'

They all shook their heads, still engrossed in their early lunch.

'Could be absolutely anything, Cora,' Nathan mumbled through a mouthful of brioche. 'I mean, we could try to check to see if Greythorpe has any links to Manchester other than having gone to uni there, I suppose, but still…'

Cora pushed her plate, now empty, away from her.

'I know, I know. Might be a big waste of time. It's a needle in a haystack, isn't it? Yes, we could give it a go, but, as you say, it could be absolutely anything. Rosie and Nicole said they didn't mind helping out, so maybe I'll get them on the case. Tell you what we *do* need to do as soon as possible though, as well as trying to talk to some of the girls at the club – we need to go and chat to some of those local residents. Will you come with me again, Nath? In case they get nasty?'

He nodded. 'Of course. One condition though.'

She raised her eyebrows. 'Go on?'

'You buy me a dessert. This is lunch. Can't have lunch

127

without pudding, can we?'

Cora smiled and reached for the menu again.

'No, we can't. Puddings all round?' she said.

18

'Got the names and addresses? We'll be there in a minute.'

Nathan gave Cora a sideways glance as he turned the car left down a side street. It was Wednesday, and they'd been on a story in Gloucestershire this morning, just a few miles north of Bristol. Now that they'd been cleared for the day by the news desk, it seemed an ideal time to go and visit some of Leanne's neighbours. They'd practically had to pass Nathan's front door on the way, so they'd decided it made sense for Cora to leave her car there and travel to Bristol together. After a planned short stopover at Nathan's so Cora could say hello to Gareth, who was on a day off, and have a cup of tea and a piece of Gareth's homemade lemon drizzle cake, the visit then became slightly longer than planned when she decided she needed to spend some time inspecting the cottage garden's menagerie of chickens, ducks, geese and a new arrival, one very cute quail. Nathan finally managed to drag her away, Cora bemoaning the fact that her Cheltenham flat only had a roof terrace which was wholly unsuitable for poultry-keeping, and they were now just around the corner from Flower Street. Cora waved a piece of paper at her cameraman.

'All here. Don't know how much we'll get out of these people, but let's just tick this box. Liam copied the list Leanne had made of all the neighbours for me – it says who was pro and who was anti the big development, which is handy. It seems to have been a fifty-fifty split. I think we should go and see one of the people who was on Leanne's side first, one of those who wasn't so sure about selling up. Just to see what they have to say about the general feeling in the community at the time. Then we'll try and talk to one of the people who wanted to move. It seems from Leanne's notes that a lot of the people in the street were older people, retired, or stay at home mums, so I'm hoping we'll find at least some at home at this hour. Sound like a plan?'

'Whatever you say, you're the boss. Ah, great, a parking space.'

Nathan manoeuvred the car into a vacant spot at the end of the terraced street and turned off the engine.

'Which one was Leanne's again?' he asked.

'The end one on this side. Number one. Right next door to the new estate site.'

Cora pointed. It was just after two o'clock and, aside from the throb of building machinery audible from behind the fence of the new development, the street was quiet, an elderly lady shuffling along on the opposite pavement and a small fluffy dog scurrying ahead of her the only signs of life.

'Ah yes, I remember. So, where do we start? And what are we going to say we're doing?'

Nathan reached into the back seat for his woolly hat and pulled it firmly down over his unruly mop of dark hair.

'I think we need to be vaguely honest. I was going to say I'm a reporter doing a story about the death of Leanne Brimley and the events that led up to it. And you're the photographer, of course – bring your stills camera in, will you? And we'll start with... Mr Arthur Everton, I think. From Leanne's notes he's eighty-five and has lived here all his life. He was very against selling up, certainly at first. He lives at number seven, which is just down there, look.'

Cora pointed down the street to a house with a red door. Two wheelie bins, one green and one black, stood against the wall and there was an empty window box, painted in cheerful blue and yellow, on the sill to the left of the door.

'OK. Let's do it.'

They walked down the street and, in the absence of a door bell, Cora rapped firmly on the red door. Moments later steps could be heard in the hallway, and the door was opened by a short, sprightly-looking elderly man with a shock of white hair and dark brown eyes. He looked at them with a mildly surprised expression.

'Oh. I thought you might be the Tesco delivery man. I don't see any bags though so I'm assuming not. Can I help you?'

Cora smiled. 'Sorry, no groceries here!'

She gave him the story about Leanne and the story she was doing, and his expression changed, his eyes suddenly sad.

'Ahh, Leanne. What a lovely girl. I still can't believe what happened. It shocked me, I don't mind telling you. Never saw that coming. Come in, come in...'

He stood back and gestured down the hallway, then shut the door and led them into a cosy little sitting room at the rear of the house, a gas fire glowing in the hearth and crammed bookshelves lining every wall. He lowered himself into an armchair and indicated that they should sit too.

'So, what can I do for you?' he said.

'We're just interested in the campaign Leanne was leading against the bigger housing development - the one which would have meant you and a number of others

131

selling your homes for demolition.'

Cora reached into her bag and pulled out the folder which held the copies of the threatening letters sent to Leanne.

'We believe it got a little bit nasty – neighbours falling out over it? Can you tell me anything about that? How bad did it get?'

The old man sighed.

'Pretty bad, actually. I've lived here all my life – I was born in this house, and my parents lived here for more than sixty years. So it has memories, you understand? And it was the same for Leanne, with her father – you know her story?'

'His ashes, in the garden? Yes.' Cora nodded.

'Indeed. She didn't want to move either. And a few others – Gladys Parker over at number four, for one. She reared seven children in that house. Has eighteen grandchildren now, and hers is where they all meet up year after year, family get-togethers, you know? And then there's Charlie Evans across at number two…'

He coughed, and rubbed his eyes.

'It was this end of the street he wanted, you see, that developer. And some people got all excited about that, saw a chance to make some easy cash. It split the neighbourhood down the middle, destroyed the community spirit we've always had here. Four of us wanted to stay, the other four families wanted to leave. Once money is involved, you see…'

He sighed again.

'Well, it's never been the same since. I mean, we *might* all have agreed to sell up, in the end, if we'd had more time to think about it. Probably would have, to be honest. The money would have made life a lot easier, that's for sure. But it would have been a very hard decision. And in

132

the end, we didn't have to make it because the developer changed his mind. All down to Leanne, I reckon. She did a good job, that little girl.'

Cora nodded, then opened her folder and flicked through it, before pulling out one of the anonymous letters. She glanced at it again herself, the words still disturbing even though she'd now read them a number of times.

"STOP CAMPAIGNING AGAINST ELMSLEY PARK. LOCAL FEELING IS VERY STRONG – WE WANT OUR MONEY! YOU HAVE BEEN WARNED. BACK OFF OR YOU WILL REGRET IT."

Cora handed the note to Arthur.

'Mr Everton, Leanne had received some... well, I suppose you could call it hate mail. Letters threatening her, warning her to drop her campaign. Did you know about these?' she said.

Arthur fumbled down the side of his armchair, pulled out a battered black spectacle case and put some reading glasses on. He took the letter, squinting as he read it, then looked back up at Cora and Nathan with a horrified expression.

'No! This is... this is dreadful. Who would do this? I mean, there was a bit of aggression, yes. When we had community meetings a couple of times, to discuss the developer's proposals, things got a bit heated. But I'm talking about a bit of shouting and arguing. Nothing like this. Nothing really threatening, you know? I mean, once or twice some of those who wanted to sell up would stop me in the street, tell me how the money would change my life, and why didn't I just take it and move into some nice little apartment somewhere, with all mod cons. I said I had no interest in that, that this was the only home I wanted...'

He gestured vaguely with one hand.

'They called me a stupid, stubborn old man. Even their wider families got involved, people who didn't even live in the street. Told me there might be trouble if I didn't move. I wondered if I should tell the police, but Leanne said not to, she said it would all just get worse if we started getting people arrested, so I left it alone. It was upsetting though. These were friends, you know? People I'd known for years, friends and neighbours, turning against me because they wanted to cash in. But...'

He looked down at the letter again, then held it out to Cora, a slight tremor in his hand.

'But nothing like this. This is dreadful. That poor girl...'

Cora took the letter and Arthur leaned back in his chair, closing his eyes.

'Are you alright, Mr Everton?'

Nathan's voice was gentle. The old man twitched slightly, then opened his eyes. He nodded.

'Fine, thank you. It's just a bit of a shock.'

Cora and Nathan exchanged glances, then Cora slid the letter back into her folder and turned back to Arthur.

'Can I ask you just a couple more questions, and then we'll leave you in peace? We've been told that Leanne was on to something... had discovered something, that she believed might help her win the fight with the developer. Did she tell you what that was, by any chance?'

Arthur frowned, shaking his head.

'No, no idea about what that could be. Sorry.'

'That's OK. Just one more thing. You said earlier that when Leanne... when Leanne died, it shocked you. You obviously knew her reasonably well – where there any signs, any indication that she was feeling low or depressed

134

or scared? Scared enough to do something like that?'

Arthur sat forward in his chair, his dark eyes fixed on Cora's.

'None. None at all,' he said vehemently. 'On the Wednesday evening, we'd been celebrating. We'd been told we didn't have to sell up after all, you see. Our homes were ours again, for as long as we wanted to stay in them. Leanne was over the moon. We got together, over at Gladys's, for tea. She's a great baker, Gladys – made a cake, big Victoria sponge it was, to celebrate, and we were all chatting and laughing and then we gave Leanne a round of applause. She'd been the driving force behind it all, you know? It was her campaign that made the developer change his mind, I'm sure it was. And she told me, right there, that it was one of the best days of her life. And then the next day, she jumped off that bridge and killed herself. Greatest shock of my life, that was. Never ever saw it coming. Still makes no sense to me, but then I suppose you never know what's really going on in somebody's head, do you…?'

His voice tailed off and he leaned back in his chair again, passing a shaky hand over his eyes.

Nathan nudged Cora and stood up.

'Mr Everton, we're very sorry to have upset you. We won't take up any more of your time. Thank you so much for talking to us,' he said.

'Yes, thank you very much. Are you OK, Mr Everton?'

Cora reached over and touched the old man on the arm, and he straightened up again and looked up at her, his eyes wet.

'I'm alright, my dear. But you just remember, when you're writing your story. You just remember to say what a great girl Leanne was. Hard working, loyal, community-

135

minded. Not like a lot of the kids nowadays. She was a good girl, one of the best. Like a granddaughter to me, she was. So you remember to say all that, right?'

Cora nodded.

'I will, Mr Everton. I promise you, I'll remember.'

19

Back out on the street, Cora and Nathan waited until they were a few yards away from Arthur Everton's home before they spoke.

'Poor old man. And, a bit like Liam, a man astounded that Leanne would take her own life, when she was in such a good place. You have to admit, it does seem more and more odd, the more we learn about all this, doesn't it?' Cora glanced back at number seven.

Nathan nodded slowly. 'Maybe, yes. But as Arthur said, you never really know what's going on in somebody's head. She might have been putting on a good act, but still been really depressed underneath it all. We can't assume anything, Cora. Where to next?'

'I know, I know. OK, hang on…'

She rooted in her handbag and pulled out her list of names and addresses.

'Right – Mark and Caroline Sinclair. Number three. They wanted to move. They have two children, said their house was getting too small but couldn't afford anything bigger, according to Leanne's notes. The offer from Greythorpe to buy at way over the market value must have been like manna from heaven for them. Very keen to sell up, it says here. Wonder if they'll be in though, in the middle of the afternoon?'

'Only one way to find out.'

They stopped outside number three. Light glowed from the downstairs window, and when Cora looked up she could see that one of the first-floor windows was open a crack, its white curtain billowing in the light breeze.

'Looks like we're in luck,' she said, and they walked up the short pathway. Cora rang the doorbell, and a few moments later the door was opened by a small, lean woman in a black velour tracksuit, with short dark hair in a pixie cut and a small, pointy nose.

'Yes?' she said, looking them both up and down.

'Caroline Sinclair? I'm Cora Baxter, and this is Nathan Nesbit. I wonder if we could have a few minutes of your time?'

Cora repeated the story she'd told Arthur Everton, but instead of inviting them in, Caroline Sinclair shook her head, a frown creasing her smooth brow.

'I have no interest in talking to you, none whatsoever. What that girl did is no concern of mine. She was a little busybody, if you ask me. Riled the whole neighbourhood with her selfish little campaign. Now if you don't mind, I'm busy, the kids will be home from school soon and I'm in the middle of cooking their dinner.'

She started to close the door. Cora held up a hand.

'Mrs Sinclair, please, just one question then? Leanne had received some hate mail, threatening letters, during the campaign. Did you know that? Would you have any idea who might have sent them?'

She flicked her file open and pulled out one of the letters, this time the one that said:

'WHY WON'T YOU LISTEN? WE'VE WARNED YOU MORE THAN ONCE. STOP YOUR CAMPAIGN AND BACK OFF, YOU STUPID LITTLE BITCH. BACK OFF OR PAY THE PRICE.'

She held it out in front of Caroline Sinclair, who stared at it for a moment. Then, very suddenly, her face flushed bright red. She opened her mouth for a couple of seconds, then closed it again. When she spoke, her voice was sharp.

'What? What letters? I've never seen that before. I don't know anything about any letters. Now please go away!'

She slammed the door, and Cora and Nathan could hear rapid footsteps in the hallway inside, then silence. They turned to look at each other.

'Well,' said Nathan. 'What a strange reaction. Is it just me, or does Caroline Sinclair know a little bit more about those nasty letters than she just made out?'

'I think you might be right,' said Cora. 'A slightly over-the-top reaction, to say the least. Did she write them herself, though, or just knows who did? Either way, we can't prove it, can we? There's absolutely nothing in those letters to indicate who wrote them – it could have been any of the neighbours who wanted to sell up. Although Arthur said it was a fifty-fifty split in the beginning, so that's only four possible houses they could have come from.'

'Want to knock on all of them, then? Is there any point?' Nathan sounded sceptical.

Cora shrugged. 'Probably not. I mean, they're horrible letters, but we still have no reason to think they directly influenced Leanne's death, do we? There's a big difference between writing a nasty letter and actually physically hurting someone. And getting letters like that isn't nice for anyone, but are they enough to drive someone to kill themselves? Possibly, I suppose, if the person is in a fragile state, but again we can't prove that. I'm not really sure what we've gained here, Nathan, other than finding out that Arthur Everton is another person who didn't feel that Leanne was suicidal. And that there really were pretty strong feelings around here about what Leanne was doing, from the people who felt she was scuppering their chances of getting a good payout. But we sort of knew all that already. I don't know if it's worth talking to anyone else, what do you think?'

'No, let's go home. I think you're right. Nobody's actually going to admit sending those letters, after all. But I think it was still worth coming today. It gives us a clearer picture. Leanne was a heroine in some quarters here, and an interfering menace in others.'

He shrugged, and Cora slipped her hand into the crook of his arm as they headed back towards the car.

'Thank you, again, Nathan, for doing all this with me,' she said. 'I don't say it often enough, but I really do appreciate it. You're the best.'

'I am, aren't I?' he said with a grin. 'Fancy showing that appreciation by buying me a quick coffee at that café round the corner before we go home?'

She grinned back. 'You'll turn into a coffee one of these days. But OK. Done,' she said.

As Cora and Nathan enjoyed their hot drinks, back at number three Flower Street Caroline Sinclair was sitting at her kitchen table, nursing a glass of red wine just poured for her by her best friend and neighbour Tracy Leonard, who lived across the street at number six. On the cooker top, a pan of chicken curry intended for the children's dinner was slowly boiling dry, but the two women were oblivious, both in a state of mild panic. Tracy, who was as round and curvaceous as Caroline was lean and pointy, picked up her own glass with a slightly shaky hand, took a gulp of Shiraz and wiped her mouth.

'Shit, Caz. Are you sure she said she was a reporter?'

Caroline nodded, eyes wide.

'And she said she was looking into the events that led up to Leanne Brimley's death? Did she say why? I mean, it's been in all the papers, hasn't it? That it was a straightforward suicide? And that she had a history of depression? What is there to look into?'

Caroline shook her head.

'She didn't say. I didn't ask her, Trace. As soon as she mentioned those letters... well, I freaked out, didn't I? Thank God Mark wasn't here. He's been racked with guilt about what happened, Trace. He can't sleep, he's off his food...'

She sank her face into her hands and a huge sob wracked her slender body. Her friend leaned across the table and gripped her upper arms.

'Caz, stop it. You have to pull yourself together, this isn't helping anyone. And the kids will be home in a minute, do you want them to see you like this? No? Then stop it. Here, wipe your eyes and drink that wine down.'

Caroline took the tissue and scrubbed at her face, mascara streaking her cheeks.

'Sorry, Trace. I'll be OK in a minute. Thanks for coming round. I don't know what I'd do without you.'

She smiled weakly, and Tracy smiled back.

'That's a good girl. Caz, I feel for you, I really do. What happened... what Mark did... well, it was bad. Really bad. But we all have to put it behind us, don't we? We have to put it behind us and move on. The girl is dead now, it's too late. Don't worry about that reporter, she can't prove anything, can she? You didn't tell her anything. So just carry on as normal. And Mark will be OK. Give him time.'

Caroline looked at her friend, and her eyes filled with tears again.

'Oh, Trace, I hope so. I really, really hope so.'

20

John Smith smiled as she turned and grinned at him, then returned her gaze to the TV screen. It was cosy in the small lounge, and they were currently the only two in there, the others down the hall in the kitchen making biscuits or cupcakes or something. He hadn't really been listening, not interested in what anyone else was doing. He was content just to sit here, holding her hand, his thumb running repeatedly back and forth across her knuckles in the way she liked. He'd left work early this evening, keen to get here to see her before it got too late. Randall hadn't minded. He was good like that, a good boss, and it *was* Friday after all. It had been a long week. John felt the stresses and strains of the day slowly leaving him as he relaxed against the cushions, feet up on the padded pouf that sat in front of the slightly threadbare but still comfortable sofa. He didn't even care that she was engrossed in some inane cartoon show that he would never have chosen to watch by himself. He took pleasure from the immense enjoyment she seemed to be getting from the silly programme, her eyes shining, little giggles escaping her pink mouth. She turned to him again, checking to see if he was watching, and he grinned at her and squeezed her hand.

'I'm watching, don't worry,' he whispered.

In reply she slipped her hand from his and gently squeezed his biceps, and he tensed his gym-honed arm so the muscles popped and danced under her fingers. She nodded happily, and tipped her head to one side so that it rested on his shoulder, her hair curling softly against his neck. He inhaled, breathing in the clean scent of her, then closed his eyes, the smile still playing on his lips.

'But WHY can't we put my Lego Batman on the top of the tree? He would look WICKED!'

Cora, hands full of baubles, looked down into Harry's enthusiastic green eyes.

'Well, because... because a fairy is more *traditional*, Harry. I just don't think Batman would look quite right. And he wouldn't be very comfortable either. He'd have a branch up his bottom until January. The fairy's used to it, she does it every year. We could use a star instead though, if you really do strongly object to the fairy. Would you prefer a star? I've got one, somewhere in that box...'

Harry, who'd been rolling on the floor giggling since Cora mentioned Batman's bottom, nodded vigorously.

'Hahaha, Cora! Yes alright, a star would be WAY better than the stupid fairy. I won't put my Batman up there. I need him anyway, to play with. Shall I find the star?'

He stood up and scampered over to the big cardboard box Cora had brought from her flat in Cheltenham, and started rooting through it. It was nearly five o'clock, the sky already black outside the windows of Adam's west London apartment, and the seven-foot Nordmann fir he'd installed in the corner of the living area last night was already looking considerably more glamorous than it had half an hour ago. Harry's mum had dropped him off with Cora mid-afternoon as planned, and as soon as he'd dumped his bag in his bedroom and wolfed down a sandwich, the seven-year-old had insisted they start decorating the tree, 'to surprise Daddy when he gets home from work'. Cora, who adored Christmas and all its trappings, had happily agreed. She had checked on Adam's own Christmas decoration stash a few weeks back and declared it woefully inadequate. Now, she placed the final bauble – cream-coloured, silk-covered and decorated with tiny feathers – onto the tree and went to help Harry locate the star. Her box was filled with decorations collected over the years, a few from her childhood, donated by her parents when she'd first moved into her own flat, but mostly purchases of her own. In contrast to her style of dress, which she preferred to keep sleek and classic, Cora adored the ornate, the whimsical and the quirky when it came to festive décor. This would be the first Christmas she and Adam spent entirely together, and she very much hoped he'd approve of her taste, having given her carte blanche to decorate his home as she saw fit.

'Here it is!' said Harry triumphantly.

'That's it, well done.'

Cora plucked the star, a sparkling silver ceramic creation, from his eager fingers, wiping a little dust from one of its points. Perfect, she thought.

'Right – if I lift you up, do you think you can pop this right at the top of the tree? That sticky-up branch at the top goes into this hole on the star, see?'

'I see. Yes, lift me up, lift me up!'

She gave the star back to him and hoisted him onto her shoulders, groaning loudly and only half in jest about his weight, and Harry leaned over and carefully eased the decoration into position.

'Done it!' he said proudly.

'Brilliant! Looks great, doesn't it? Just jump off and I'll switch the lights on.'

She bent double and the child leapt from her shoulders, then hopped up and down with excitement as Cora flicked the power switch.

'Wow wow wow! It's AWESOME! Daddy is going to love it, Cora!'

'Do you think he will? I hope so. I love it too. We're a top team, Harry. High five!'

She held a hand up and they slapped palms, both grinning widely. Then she slipped an arm around his shoulders and he snuggled into her side, falling silent as they both stood and gazed admiringly at the tree. It really did look beautiful, Cora thought. The star had been the perfect finishing touch, atop the soft, glossy foliage into which hundreds of tiny white lights were now entwined, the big feathery baubles nestling amidst silver snowflakes and trails of white velvet ribbon. Bach's celebratory *Christmas Oratoria*, playing softly on the radio, was the perfect musical accompaniment to the festive scene. Less than three weeks until Christmas, Cora thought happily. A Christmas that would be spent with the man she loved more than she'd ever loved anyone before. She still had to pinch herself sometimes, finding it hard to believe her luck. Nobody else, no previous boyfriends, had ever really 'got' her, not like Adam did. She didn't need to explain herself to him, didn't need to justify her life choices. He just *got* it, and he loved her as much as she loved him, even though she knew he found her infuriating at times. And then there was Harry, the child who had stolen her heart. He hadn't changed her attitude to having children of her own – she knew nothing would ever change that. She had always known she didn't want to be a mother, in just the same way as most of her friends always knew they *would* want children some day. But being a stepmother was great. Cora liked to look at children simply as little people – some she liked, some she didn't. And she adored Harry, not just because he was Adam's son but because he was such a lovely little person in his own right, funny and sweet and clever. She looked down at him now, his eyes shining as he continued to stare at the tree, and decided that tonight would be all about the three of them. And no thoughts of bridges, horrible deaths or nasty neighbours were going to spoil it.

'What do you think about one of these robots?'

Adam stopped to read the marketing blurb on the price tag.

'It says it can walk, talk, jump, climb over obstacles, pick things up, take orders – guys, do you think Harry would like this?'

Detective Inspector Glenn Arnold peered over his shoulder and nodded his approval.

'Cheaper and less hassle than a dog, mate!' he said.

'I wouldn't mind it myself, boss,' added Detective Constable Gary Gilbert.

The three police officers, all of whom had worked together for a number of years, had finished work early this afternoon, deciding to sneak off while things at the station were quiet, and get some Christmas shopping done. Adam had a special gift planned for Cora, and was secretly already growing anxious about whether or not she would like it. But Harry was much easier to please, and he was determined to buy his son what he called 'real' toys this year, growing tired of seeing the child and his friends so frequently engrossed in their games consoles. Harry had definitely developed a love for books recently, which was great, but the computer games were still a little too popular with the boy and his schoolmates for Adam's liking. And, as this was probably the calm before the festive storm, he and his colleagues had decided today that they might as well make the most of it. Crime rates were often high over the Christmas period, giving the police more shoplifting, alcohol-fuelled public disorder, drink-driving and domestic violence to deal with. If the criminals were taking it easy today, the police could seize the chance to go shopping.

Glenn, who was clutching a bright red pedal car for his young daughter, moved off down the toy store aisle, and Gary, who had no children but was pretending he did so he could chat up the busty brunette sales assistant, turned back to where she was demonstrating the voice-changing abilities of a frightening-looking alien mask. Adam tucked the robot into his trolley next to the elaborate building set and pogo stick already in there and scanned the shelves, looking for more inspiration. He added a book on dinosaurs to his pile, and then stood back as a weary-looking teenager in a lurid green elf costume staggered past him, hauling a black sack, and disappeared into a ramshackle Santa's grotto at the end of the shop. At the sight of fresh presents arriving, an excited murmur ran down the queue of hassled parents and tetchy children snaking down the aisle.

A remote-controlled helicopter caught Adam's eye and he grabbed it, as Glenn and Gary, who was now wearing the alien mask, re-joined him.

'Are-you-ready? Hurry-up-or-you-will-be-exterminated. We-want-to-go-to-the-pub.'

Gary's voice was a robotic monotone. Adam laughed and turned his trolley in the direction of the check-out.

'OK, give me two minutes – nearly done. But just one quick pint and then I'm off – Harry's here for the weekend and Cora wants to decorate the tree tonight.'

'You're a proper little family now, you three, aren't you?'

Glenn, tall and muscular, with white teeth shining

against his black skin, punched his friend gently on the arm. Adam grinned.

'We are. It's great, Glenn.'

'Well, I'm delighted for you, mate. You deserve it. Come on, let's pay for this lot. Gary's going to collapse from dehydration if we don't get some booze into him in the next ten minutes.'

Twenty minutes later they were ensconced in a booth in the nearby Coachman's Inn, a century-old pub with an open fire blazing at one end and an enticing selection of real ales. Shopping bags piled high under the table, and a family-sized bag of cheese and onion crisps split open for sharing, the three police officers clinked glasses.

'Well, this is a rare treat for a Friday evening,' said Gary.

'It is, but as I said I can't stay long,' said Adam. 'Apparently Cora and Harry have a surprise for me.'

He re-read the text he'd just received and smiled. He'd bet a hundred quid that his son and girlfriend had already decorated the Christmas tree together, but he wouldn't spoil it for them by telling them he'd suspected what they were up to. He'd practice his 'surprised' face on the way home, he decided, and took another mouthful of beer.

'What's Cora up to these days, anyway?' asked Glenn, wiping foam off his top lip with the back of his hand. 'Got anything on the go that we should know about?'

Adam smiled wryly. His colleagues were all too aware that in recent times his girlfriend had got somewhat more involved in one or two police investigations than she probably should have.

'Well, as a matter of fact, she is looking into something,' he said, and on the other side of the table Glenn and Gary both leaned towards him, instantly interested.

148

'She was driving home from work a few weeks ago when a girl came off a bridge and smashed into her car. Actually landed on her bonnet – what are the chances, eh? Pretty horrific. Anyway, the coroner ruled it a suicide – there was a note, and a history of depression and so on. But Cora's found out a few things that make her think – well, not that it *wasn't* suicide, exactly, but that someone might have encouraged the kid to jump, maybe. I'm not sure there's anything in it myself, but you know what she's like when she gets her teeth into something…'

'I remember, yes,' said Glenn with a grin, and Gary nodded.

Adam sighed. 'She's a tough cookie, but I can't help worrying about her sometimes. Remember in the summer, when she was investigating the Marcus Williams murder and went off to New York with that bloke she barely knew? I mean, obviously that all worked out fine, but still. She does tend to put herself in some slightly risky situations without really thinking things through first. One day, she might not be so lucky.'

Glenn and Gary nodded. They both remembered Adam talking about the New York trip, and the case that had resulted in Cora flying out there. The Marcus Williams murder had been a little too close to home for comfort.

'Boss, have you thought about getting a tracker app put on her phone? I mean, she might not be very keen, but at least if she gets herself into any trouble and can't contact you, you can see where she is.'

Gary waved his mobile phone at Adam.

'You could tell her you'd only use it in emergencies? My girlfriend's got one, and honestly it makes me feel better and her feel safer – she's got a fifteen-minute walk back from the tube in the dark, and she says she feels much happier knowing I could find her if some yob

149

dragged her down an alleyway or something. Providing he didn't nick her phone of course.'

Adam frowned.

'Maybe. It's actually a good idea, Gary, although as you said, she might not be too keen. But I'll suggest it tonight. Thanks.'

Adam waited until Harry, still shiny-eyed with excitement about the Christmas tree and Daddy's hugely surprised face when he saw it, was finally tucked into bed before he made the suggestion to Cora, and as he had suspected her initial reaction was one of outrage.

'What? So you can see where I am at any second of the day and night? Not that that I have anything to hide, Adam, but that just sounds a bit too stalkerish for comfort for me!'

But when he'd explained that he'd only ever use the app in emergencies, and that he'd have it on his phone too, she calmed down a little.

'It works both ways, Cora. We'd both only use it if we couldn't get hold of each other and we thought the other might have a problem. I promise, it's just a security thing. What do you think?'

He leaned towards her on the sofa, pushing her soft brown hair back off her face and dropping a kiss on her forehead. She smiled, the slightly cross look in her light green eyes softening, and reached a hand up to stroke his cheek.

'Damn you, Adam Bradberry. I can't deny you anything when you look at me like that. Go on, let's download the stupid app. But you have to fill my wine glass first, *and* order the pizza. Deal?'

Adam kissed her again and smiled.

'You drive a hard bargain, Baxter. Deal.'

Later as they sprawled on the sofa, fingers entwined,

watching a repeat of *The Graham Norton Show*, Cora suddenly sat up straight.

'OK, so if we're really doing this security thing, let's add another layer. I was reading this book – I can't remember what it's called – but the girl in it had a word she'd use to let her boyfriend know if she wanted to leave a party or whatever without making a fuss. She used to say "cigarette", even though she didn't smoke, so he'd know she wanted to go home. Can we have one of those too? Not for leaving parties, but... I don't know, say I get into some sort of awkward situation and I need to let you know I need help, but there isn't time to explain what's happening? I could just say one word and you'd understand there was a problem. And you could do the same if anything bad happens to you. What do you think?'

She looked at Adam eagerly and he laughed.

'You've changed your tune! Well, personally I think the app is enough, but it you want to... what word will we use then?'

'Errrm...' Cora looked around the room, seeking inspiration. Her gaze fell on the pizza box on the coffee table, one slice of Sloppy Giuseppe still remaining.

'Mozzarella!' she said.

'Mozzarella? Are you sure?'

'Yes. Mozzarella is a great word. Mozz-a-rella!'

She giggled and sank back onto the cushions, then laid her head on his shoulder and kissed his neck.

He squinted at her suspiciously. 'Are you a little bit drunk, Cora Baxter?'

'Might be. Only a teeny bit though. I love you. Love mozzarella too. That pizza was yummy.'

Adam laughed.

'I love you too. OK, mozzarella it is. Not that you'll remember that in the morning. Bed?'

She nodded sleepily.

'I will, you know. But yes. Bed.'

21

'Well I reckon he's going to propose soon. Valentine's Day, maybe? I bet you a fiver, Nicole!'

Rosie plonked herself down in one of the chairs at Cora's dining table and wagged a finger at her friend. Opposite her, Nicole was shaking her head as she turned her laptop on.

'Nope, not Valentine's Day, definitely not. That would be cringe-makingly soppy. Adam's not the type. And they've only been together, what, just over a year and a half? It's not that long really, is it?'

Rosie ran her hands though her red hair, which she'd yesterday had cut into a elfin crop and wasn't quite sure about yet.

'No, but they're *so* perfect for each other, Nicole. And think how much fun we'd have at the wedding. We haven't been to one in ages. Honestly, I think he'll…'

Her voice tailed off as Cora entered the room, carrying a tray laden with mugs, a huge teapot and a plate of cupcakes. She looked quizzically at Rosie, who was suddenly tapping urgently on the keyboard of her own laptop, head down.

'You think who will do what, Rosie? Why did you stop talking when I came into the room?' she asked, suspiciously.

'Oh, nothing important. Idle chit-chat. About… about that new BBC drama that started last night, you know, the one with, errrm, thingy in it…'

Rosie flushed and carried on typing. Cora narrowed

her eyes.

'Hmmm. OK, well I'll let you off, for now. Let's get this tea poured and see if we can find anything. How are we going to do this? Shall we split it into sections?'

She finished filling the three mugs, then pushed the plate of cakes into the middle of the table.

'Thanks, Cora. Yes, let's divide it up. What do you suggest?'

Nicole selected a chocolate and raspberry cupcake and bit into it with a happy sigh. It was Sunday afternoon, and she and Rosie had arrived at Cora's as planned half an hour ago, a couple of hours after she'd returned to Cheltenham after her weekend in London with Adam and Harry. Slightly hungover, and having gone for a short run around the park which only succeeded in making her feel rather sick, Cora had declared it a booze-free Sunday, but had softened the blow by producing the box of cakes from Mattino's, one of their favourite local cafés. After a quick gossip, they were now getting down to the real business of the afternoon – a spot of brainstorming about Manchester, its possible connections to Randall Greythorpe, and why Leanne Brimley had written the word, and heavily underlined it, on her map.

'Well, we know Greythorpe went to university there. And yes, that's kind of, well, so what? So, what else could it be? I'm wondering if Randall and his partner are maybe involved in something dodgy up there, and Leanne found out? I'm just pulling ideas out of the air here though. Nicole, can you look at that? See if you can find anything that links Douglas Granley and Randall Greythorpe in Manchester?'

Nicole nodded, mouth still full of cake.

'Shhure,' she mumbled.

'And Rosie, can you see if there's anything online

154

about any new housing developments in Manchester that Greythorpe might be linked to? Maybe Leanne found out he was doing the same up there as he was here, trying to buy up people's homes and upsetting them? Again, just a thought. He did mention when I met him that he was looking at some other developments further north, so you never know.'

'OK, no probs.' Rosie smiled, and delicately wiped a cake crumb from her lip before turning back to her screen.

'I'm going to try to see if he has any other business connections in Manchester, or is involved in any organisations or charities, stuff like that,' said Cora, and switched on her own computer. 'There *must* be something. Everything else Leanne wrote on that map links to Randall Greythorpe in some way – the club and the possibility of under-age girls there. So Manchester must be linked too. We just need to find out why.'

'What are you going to do about checking out that under-age thing properly, seeing as your visit to the club was inconclusive? And can I have another cake, please?' asked Nicole, hand already out-stretched towards the plate.

'Course you can. And I think I'm going to have to go back to Leanne's brother, Liam,' Cora said. 'Discreetly, obviously. He doesn't know about the housing estate drawing and the notes on it, because we found it on Leanne's USB stick. I don't want to lose his trust by telling him we kept something of hers like that – I feel so guilty about it, but it's too late now. But I might just sound him out, see if Leanne ever mentioned Midnight Diamonds to him. I've been wondering if maybe she knew someone who worked there. She'd obviously worked out that Randall was linked to it, but I can't see how she'd know about any under-age staff unless somebody told her. I mean, it's unlikely she visited as a punter, isn't it?'

'It is. I'm having another one too. They're just too damn delicious, Cora.'

Rosie's hand wavered for a moment above a Black Forest cupcake, then she picked up a lemon meringue one instead.

'I know. And good hangover fodder. I may have had a *teensy* bit too much wine last night,' Cora admitted.

'Nothing new there then,' muttered Nicole, then ducked as Cora threw a pen at her. They all laughed, then settled down to work.

In Bristol, DCI Gordon Gregory swallowed the last of his third pint and banged the glass down onto the table.

'BUGGER IT!' he said.

Opposite him, DC James Jordan, who was still nursing his second drink, frowned. He glanced around the pub, taking in the groups of families and young couples still enjoying a late Sunday lunch, the remains of roast beef, pork with crackling and side-dishes of vegetables littering the tables.

'I think you're getting yourself into a state about nothing, boss,' he said. 'Look, let me get you another one and we'll talk about this logically, OK? And – no offence - but maybe less of the loud Scouse swearing? There are kids in here, and in your position... well, you don't want a complaint about drunk and disorderly behaviour in a public place on top of everything else, do you?'

Gregory looked at his younger colleague with a surprised expression on his ruddy face, then nodded.

'Suppose you're right. Go on, get me one more then we can talk it through.'

He grinned as Jordan made his way to the bar. There had been a time when the kid would never have dared to speak to him like that, but he'd grown some balls in recent months. That was good. He had the makings of a fine copper, had young James Jordan. A better copper than Gregory himself, if he was honest. He'd done a lot of thinking over the past few weeks, since he'd been suspended. He knew he'd messed up in the past, more than once, had done things he shouldn't have. Things that broke the law. Bad things. And covering for his dumb-arse brother was the least of them. But it was too late to go back now, too late to fix things. Some things just weren't fixable, were they, even if you realised after you'd done them that you'd done something really, really awful. He couldn't fix them, so now he just needed to get this suspension over with, get back to work, then keep his nose clean enough to get to retirement age and keep his pension. He'd been worrying about that bloody strip club all week. It could ruin things for him, if anything got out. Then he'd never be able to leave this miserable country and all he'd done here, retire to the sun somewhere and start afresh. And he wanted to, desperately. Spain maybe. Spain would be nice…

'Here you go, boss.'

Jordan was back, carefully placing another pint of beer on the table in front of Gregory before putting a half down next to his own only partially-empty drink.

'Cheers. You're a gent.'

Gregory took a slug from the glass and wiped foam from his lips with the back of his hand.

'OK, let's talk about this.'

Jordan leaned towards the senior officer, keeping his voice low.

'So, last weekend you were in Midnight Diamonds?

And you saw Cora Baxter, the TV reporter, sitting outside in a car? And you think she recognised you, going in.'

Gregory nodded.

'Errrm... can I ask why you were there, boss? I mean, I thought you were steering well clear of the place, after... after what happened...'

He paused, reddening, remembering the awful thing that Gregory had finally admitted to him, the dreadful thing he'd done. He had confessed everything when they'd gone to the pub together on the day of Leanne Brimley's funeral. Before that, Jordan hadn't known the full details, had suspected that something had happened but hadn't known exactly what it was or how bad it was. He did now though, and he heartily wished he didn't. Gregory glanced quickly around the bar, checking to see if anyone was close enough to hear the conversation, then shrugged.

'Just for a drink, mate. I thought it would be safe now, you know? I mean, she's dead, isn't she? And Dougie, the boss, well he's become a bit of a mate. You know that. No big deal. It's not so bad – you should come with me sometime. Nice scenery to look at, if you know what I mean. But if that stupid little reporter bitch is on my case again... shit, Jordan. We've got to do something about her.'

James nodded slowly, but his heart sank a little at Gregory's use of the word 'we'. He'd do a lot of things for the boss, but he wasn't going to... well, he wasn't sure what Gregory had in mind right now, but he was fairly sure he wouldn't want to be a part of it. Certainly not if it involved that TV reporter. He thought back to the last time he'd spoken to her, when she'd called to tell him she'd found a memory stick belonging to Leanne Brimley. She'd said there'd only been a map on it, but what if she'd been lying? What if there was something on it about the club, and about Gregory? But no. If there *had* been, she'd have done something about it by now, wouldn't she?

He took a large gulp of his drink. He knew Gregory had met Douglas Granley, the club owner, in a pub when he'd first moved to Bristol to set the place in Rotunda Street up. They'd hit it off, and Gregory had helped the guy sort out the licenses and other stuff you needed to get a place like that off the ground. He'd always had a suspicion that Gregory had received some sort of payment in kind for his help, but when he'd finally told him the details, when Gregory had finally confessed to him what had happened, with the girl... he swallowed hard. He didn't like where this conversation was going now, and he was dearly wishing he'd made up an excuse when Gregory had phoned him earlier to suggest a couple of Sunday afternoon pints.

'Look, Cora Baxter hasn't made contact or anything, has she? Maybe it was a complete coincidence that she was outside the club that night, nothing to do with you at all? Wouldn't she have confronted you or something by now? I mean, it's been a week.'

Gregory rubbed his eyes with meaty, nicotine-stained fingers.

'James, she's a sneaky little bitch. She'll be biding her time, mark my words. You saw what she did to me on live TV. Yes, I made a mistake. I should have let my moron of a brother take his punishment instead of trying to protect him. But she didn't have to do that to me, expose me like that. She's a little bitch trying to make a name for herself. But I'm trying to get back to work now, clean up my act, and she could scupper everything. If she knows what happened...you know, with the girl... and she goes to the brass, I'm done for mate. It'll all be over.'

159

Jordan thought for a minute.

'OK, I get that. But she was just sitting outside in a car. She didn't come in, follow you inside, did she?'

Gregory shook his head. 'Don't think so. Didn't see her if she did.'

'So, as I said, it might have just been a complete coincidence. She could have been waiting for somebody else out there. How would she know you were going to turn up that night, anyway? No way she could have known, is there?'

Gregory nodded. That was true. It had been a spur of the minute decision to go to the club that night. There was no way she could have known. But still…

'I don't know. Seems a pretty big feckin' coincidence to me.'

He sighed heavily, then thumped a fist on the table.

'BITCH,' he hissed.

Jordan looked around nervously.

'Boss, seriously, less of the swearing. Listen, I'll give her a call tomorrow. I'll think of some excuse, try and find out what she was up to there. But stop worrying, OK? I'm sure there was nothing in it.'

Gregory wiped sweaty palms on his trouser legs and nodded.

'OK. Cheers, mate. You're a pal.'

He picked up his glass and drained his pint.

'Just one more?' he asked.

John Smith loved his Sunday afternoons. He always spent them with her, unless Randall needed him to work, but that was rare. They'd decided to go to the beach at Weston-super-Mare this afternoon, take a brisk walk along the sand, despite the chill wind. She loved the beach, would scamper ahead of him like a child, always wanting to paddle no matter how cold it was.

'You're crazy, completely and utterly mad!' he would yell affectionately, as she ran towards the waves, ripping off her shoes and socks, discarding them on the sand and shrieking as the icy water washed over her toes. He always brought a small towel in his backpack for their beach visits, knowing that when her feet were numb she'd come running back to him, teeth chattering, wanting him to warm her up. He'd sit her down on one of the benches that lined the seafront then, wrap her feet in the towel, rub them until the circulation got going again. He'd do anything for her, anything to see her smile, to see the sparkle in those beautiful eyes. And then they'd walk, hand in hand, along the promenade, have some chips maybe, plain for her, dripping with curry sauce for him. And she'd look at him and laugh as the sauce dripped down his chin, and he'd laugh too, completely content just to be with her.

Yes, John thought, Sundays were the *best*.

22

Today's café was small and prettily decorated, windows draped with frilly curtains in a ditsy floral fabric, matching cushions on the seats of the pine chairs at every polished table. In contrast, the waiter taking their Monday morning breakfast order was dressed head to toe in black, with spiky dark hair, a nose stud and thick black eyeliner – applied so perfectly that Cora was slightly jealous – completing the Gothic look.

'I'd love a bacon roll, actually,' Cora said, scanning the menu.

'How hungry are you? I've got a small one or a big one.' The waiter's pencil was poised over his pad.

'I'm starving. How big is your big one?'

There was a snort from Nathan on the other side of the table. Cora glanced at him, then turned back to the waiter.

'It's huge,' he said. ''bout, I dunno, this big? Can you manage that?'

He gestured with hands about nine inches apart. Nathan snorted again, and beside Cora Rodney sniggered.

Frowning – what was wrong with them this morning? – she thought for a moment, then nodded.

'Great, I'll have the big one. I'm sure I can cope. Thanks!'

Nathan and Rodney exploded into laughter as the waiter, who had started to blush, walked off and Scott, who'd just arrived back from the toilets, looked at them with a puzzled expression. Cora shrugged.

'Don't ask me,' she said.

Nathan leaned forward and tapped Cora's menu.

'Cora's asked the waiter for his big one. He showed her how long it is and asked her if she could handle it, and she said she could. And first thing on a Monday morning too. She's a right little goer, our Cora, isn't she?'

'Ah. Nice one, Cora. Start the week as you mean to go on, eh?'

Scott grinned and sat down and, the penny dropping, Cora rolled her eyes.

'Oh, for goodness' sake! How old are you, six? You're such idiots. Shut up. The poor waiter will refuse to serve us if you keep that up, plonkers.'

Rodney was still tittering.

'Sorry, Cora. You know what it's like. Post-live hysteria. We'll be OK in a minute.'

He took a deep breath, snorted again, inhaled once more then pressed his lips tightly together for a moment.

'OK, I'm done,' he said firmly.

Nathan sniggered again then straightened up.

'Me too. Bloody hell, we seem to spend our lives in cafés, don't we? Another day, another town, another café. You've got to laugh or you'd cry. When I finally retire, I never want to see another café ever again, I swear. So… any news?'

'About the Leanne story? No, sadly. Rosie and Nicole came round yesterday and we blitzed the Manchester thing over tea and cake but drew a complete blank. Other than Greythorpe going to uni there, we couldn't find a single other connection. Douglas Granley didn't study there – I mean, Randall did tell us they were old school friends, not uni mates, but we wondered if they might have Manchester in common too for some reason. Couldn't spot anything, though. In fact, other than mentions of him in relation to Midnight Diamonds,

163

Dougie only popped up on an ancient photo of a further education college football team in Newcastle. So we still have no idea why Leanne had written the word Manchester on her housing estate plan, I'm afraid... oh sorry, hang on.'

Her phone was ringing and she grabbed it from the table and answered the call.

'Cora, good morning! It's DC James Jordan here, from Avon Police. Spare me a minute?'

The officer sounded cheerful and a little cocky, surprisingly friendly today compared with the last time Cora had spoken to him, when he'd slammed the phone down after she'd offered to return Leanne's memory stick.

'Errrm... well, I'm just having breakfast with my crew. We're in Dorset on a story. But yes, I can speak for a minute. What can I do for you?'

'Well, it's just an enquiry, really, related to... well, related to an investigation I'm working on.'

He paused, and Cora waited.

'Well, it's about last weekend – Friday the twenty-ninth, to be precise? A, errrm... a patrol car was driving down Rotunda Street in Bristol, and one of the officers said he thought he recognised you, sitting in a car parked up on the street. Quite late at night too. So, well, as we have a... an important investigation going on in this area, we just wondered what you were doing there?'

'What I was doing there? Really?'

Cora hesitated, not sure how to reply. What an odd phone call. Why did DC James Jordan want to know what she was doing sitting in a car over a week ago? And she didn't remember any patrol car passing by. Had there been one, really?

'Yes. Were you... were you working on a story maybe?'

The voice was less bright now, some of the swagger gone, a little more hesitancy in his delivery. He sounded nervous, Cora thought.

'This is a very odd question, but OK. I was just there waiting for someone,' she said at last. 'A couple of friends of mine were having a drink in the club opposite, and myself and another friend were there to give them a lift home. That's all, not working on a story.'

She crossed her fingers. It was only a tiny lie, after all.

'Oh, OK. Great, thank you. Just didn't want to, you know, jeopardise the investigation by letting the press in on it too early.'

Jordan sounded relieved.

'We'll tell you all about it as soon as we can though,' he added hastily.

'OK, well, thanks. Better get on with my breakfast now though,' said Cora. She rolled her eyes at the boys, who'd been listening to the exchange with puzzled expressions.

'You do that. Sorry for the interruption. And if you need anything from us at any point, do get in touch,' said Jordan.

Slightly bemused, Cora ended the call, then filled in the blanks for the others.

'I mean, I didn't see any passing patrol car that night, did you, Scott?'

The engineer shook his bald head. 'Definitely not. Bullshit.'

'So clearly, this question about what we were doing there has come from our suspended police officer friend DCI Gregory, hasn't it? Probably buddies. Is he scared we're following him, waiting for him to mess up again, do you think?'

Cora looked at her colleagues one by one.

'Maybe,' said Rodney. 'Or maybe we're missing some sort of connection here. We have a dodgy cop, visiting a rather sleazy club flagged by Leanne Brimley on her map of the Elmsley Park development. Is he somehow connected to that development too?'

'Doubt it, but...' Cora thought for a moment, then remembered something.

'Hey, remember when I rang up to tell the police I'd found Leanne's USB stick? It was DC Jordan I spoke to then too. When I told him there was just a map on it, he questioned me a bit. Seemed to want to make sure there was nothing else on it. When I said no, he lost interest.'

'Hmmm.' Nathan scratched his chin. 'If Leanne was interested in the club, maybe she was also aware that a senior cop hangs out there. Maybe Jordan was wondering if there was any mention of Gregory on her memory stick? And lost interest when you said it was just a map?'

Cora nodded. 'Maybe, yes. But none of that really helps us, does it? All we have is a dodgy cop hanging out in a strip club, something which Leanne may well have known about if he did it regularly, as we're fairly sure now that she knew a bit about the place because of its links to Randall Greythorpe. But I can't see how DCI Gregory and his nocturnal habits could be connected to the new housing development, or to Leanne's death? Unless... oh gosh. Unless Leanne confronted DCI Gregory at the club for some reason, and he... well, he...'

'What, he pushed her off the bridge? Or threatened her, and made her so scared she jumped?' said Scott. There was a slightly sceptical edge to his tone.

Cora sighed. 'Oh, I know, I know. It sounds ridiculous. He's a police officer, isn't he? Not a very nice one, true. But still a police officer. He's hardly likely to go around doing things like that. It's just so confusing.'

Nathan exhaled heavily. 'It's all a bit odd, admittedly. I don't know what's going on, Cora, or how all these threads tie up together. But Leanne Brimley somehow seems to have links to the Randall Greythorpe development, the strip club, and possibly now to this DCI Gregory as well. Curiouser and curiouser.'

She nodded, then looked up as the still-blushing waiter arrived with the first of their breakfast orders. Curiouser and curiouser indeed, she thought.

'So, nothing to worry about, boss. She was just there waiting for a friend, and I'm fairly sure she was telling the truth. We would have heard something by now if she had any suspicions about you, wouldn't we?'

James Jordan had phoned Gordon Gregory as soon as he'd put the phone down after his conversation with Cora. He smiled as he heard a relieved-sounding 'phewwww' on the other end of the line.

'Great work, mate. That's made me feel a lot better. You're right, she wouldn't hang about, would she? She'd have been on to it like a rat up a drainpipe if she had a sniff of what went on. I owe you a pint.'

'No worries, boss. See you soon.'

Jordan ended the call. As he walked to the coffee machine, he felt a sudden pang of guilt. Yes, it was nice to make the boss happy. But should he really be covering this up? He was a police officer after all, and what had happened... well, it had been bad. The girl was so... so young. He thought for a minute, thought about the implications of telling somebody senior about what he knew, about what Gregory had done. Then he shook his head. Grassing on a colleague? No. He couldn't do it. It would be OK. It was all over now, and nobody would ever know. He poured himself a drink and headed back to

167

his desk.

At five o'clock, back home in Cheltenham and wearily preparing for another 2 a.m. start tomorrow, Cora decided to call Liam Brimley. He'd be home from school now, and after this morning's conversation with James Jordan, Cora was becoming more and more convinced that the "something Leanne was on to" was connected to Midnight Diamonds. She had discovered something important, she must have. But why were the police, and DCI Gregory in particular, so concerned about Cora being seen near the club, she wondered? If there was something illegal going on there, and they knew about it, surely they'd just deal with it and not worry about a reporter who happened to be in the area? It was all very odd. Having decided to be as vague as possible with Liam about her reasons for asking about a strip club – he was only fifteen, after all – she dialled his number and waited. He answered within a few seconds.

'Cora! Good to hear from you! I've been wondering… well, have you come up with anything yet?'

'Oh, Liam, nothing really, no. I'm so sorry. I'm still working on it though. And something's come up that may or may not be related. I don't know if you can help, but did your sister ever mention a… a club, in Bristol, called Midnight Diamonds?'

'Midnight Diamonds? Oh yeah, sure. That's that lap-dance place, right?'

The teenager's tone was matter-of-fact.

'Well, yes. You know of it, then?'

'I've obviously never been there, if that's what you mean.'

Liam laughed.

'But yeah, Leanne talked about it a few times. She had

this mate at school, Fee. Short for Fiona. Anyway, they were best mates for years when they were younger, then not so much at secondary school. Fee got a bit wild, Leanne said. Trouble at home too, I think. I'm not sure exactly what. Anyway, when Leanne went on to sixth form, Fee left school. She was only sixteen but Leanne said she'd heard she'd got a job dancing at that club. She must have used her fake ID, Leanne said. She was worried about her – they weren't exactly best mates anymore, but they still hung out a bit. Not sure how recently she'd seen her though. And what has this got to do with anything, Cora? I don't understand. It's not relevant, is it?'

'Liam, I don't know. Probably not, no. It's just something we're looking into. Do you mind if I don't explain further just yet? I'll update you as soon as there's anything concrete, is that OK?'

At the other end of the line, the teenager sighed.

'Yeah, sure. I appreciate what you're doing, I know you're crazy busy. And Leanne would appreciate it too. Thanks, Cora. Speak soon, yeah?'

'Definitely. Liam, do you know this Fee's surname, by any chance?'

'Fee Taylor,' he said instantly. 'And she's got a second job too, if that helps. Works in Top Shop at Cribbs shopping centre. Saw her there a few weeks ago.'

'That helps a *lot*, Liam. Thanks so much. Talk soon. Take care, OK?'

Cora ended the call and grinned. Perfect. So Midnight Diamonds *was* employing young girls, girls under the age of eighteen. Well, well, well. She still wasn't quite sure what it all meant, but she was sure now about what her next step would be. Miss Fee Taylor would be getting a visit.

Liam slipped his mobile back into his pocket and, the prospect of a couple of hours of maths and geography homework weighing heavily on his mind, opened the living room door. To his surprise, his mother was standing there, so close to the door that he actually bumped into her.

'Mum! What are you doing? Are you alright?'

He sniffed cautiously. She smelled of coffee and perfume. Good, he thought. But Lisa was staring at him, anger in her blue eyes.

'Who was that, Liam? Who were you talking to?'

Liam swallowed. Had she heard everything? If Mum knew he'd asked a reporter to look into Leanne's death…

'Answer me, Liam!' His mother was shouting now, her mouth so close to his face that tiny droplets of spittle spattered his skin.

'No… nobody important,' he stuttered. 'Just… just one of her friends from school. She wants to hold a charity evening for that… for that animal charity Leanne loved, you know the one? She's trying to track down some of the girls who left the school, to ask them to join in too. I told her Leanne would appreciate it. She would, wouldn't she, Mum?'

He reached out tentatively and touched her arm. She flinched slightly but didn't back away, her breathing slowing.

'Oh, well, fine,' she said. 'I'm going out now. I won't be long, just a few hours, OK? But don't speak to anyone else. Nobody we don't know. Not about the night Leanne died, OK? Promise me? Promise me, Liam!'

She gripped both of his hands tightly, tears suddenly springing to her eyes. Liam pulled his fingers free and wrapped his arms around her, resting his head on her shoulder, a feeling close to despair rushing over him.

'It's OK, Mum. I promise. Everything's fine. I love you, Mum.'

Lisa let out a little sob.

'Love you too, son.'

23

The rain was torrential again, hammering so loudly on the roof of Cora's TT that she could barely hear the radio, the exuberant strains of Mozart's *The Marriage of Figaro* virtually drowned out by the noise. Wipers on top speed, she left the M5 and took the Cribbs Causeway turning, heading for The Mall. The big out-of-town shopping centre just north of Bristol was one of her favourite places to indulge in retail therapy, but today she wasn't planning to spend any money. Well, probably not anyway. Today, she was on a mission. This was where Liam had told her Fee Taylor worked, and Cora was very much hoping the girl would be on shift on this wet Thursday afternoon. It had been a madly busy week thus far, she and her crew spending Monday in Cornwall, Tuesday in Norfolk and yesterday in West Wales, and she was exhausted. This morning, on a story in Wiltshire, after first being assigned to a story in Liverpool and then in Shropshire before the news desk finally made up its mind, she and the boys had revisited an analogy they'd once come up with to try to explain to their friends exactly how ridiculous their job could be sometimes.

'Imagine your job was doing piles and piles of paperwork,' Cora would say. 'So you spend all day doing mountains of paperwork in London. And then at seven in the evening you get a phone call from your boss, saying actually, we've decided we don't need any of that paperwork anymore, you can rip it all up – but there's some really important paperwork that needs doing up in

Liverpool, so we need you to go there right now and start again. So, you drive to Liverpool and do more paperwork till midnight, and then get up at 4 a.m. and do yet more paperwork. A few hours later you have breakfast and then, just as you're hoping you can go home, you get a call from your boss telling you there's another, brand new lot of paperwork to be done in Shrewsbury. So you head there, and spend all day doing that new lot of paperwork, and it's really difficult and complicated and you're totally exhausted, but you get through it, and you call your boss to tell her it's done, and she says, oh, actually we don't need that anymore – did nobody let you know? Sorry about that, it's been a bit chaotic here, we forgot to tell you. Or – even worse – you do paperwork all day, and then drive to, say, West Wales ready to get up and do more paperwork at 4 a.m., and at 1 a.m. you are sound asleep when you get a call saying, whoops, sorry, we've changed our minds, we need you to get up NOW and drive to Surrey because there's some even more urgent paperwork there…'

Cora's friends, a few of whom for some reason still thought her job was glamorous, soon realised it wasn't after the paperwork explanation. She worked the longest hours of anyone she knew. Now, she yawned as she spotted a parking space and slid the Audi into it. A few minutes later, umbrella still dripping by her side, she walked into Top Shop, where *Christmas Lights* by Coldplay was playing on the sound system. Spotting an assistant rearranging a rail of sparkly party dresses, she asked if Fee Taylor was in today. The girl, acne-ridden cheeks covered with thick make-up, nodded.

'Yep, over there. In the burgundy top, see?'

'Thanks.'

Cora crossed the shop floor, weaving her way between

tables laden with jeans and stacks of colourful knits, and stopped in front of the young woman, who was folding T-shirts. She looked up with wary eyes when Cora said her name. Fee was wearing polka dot tights under a tight black mini-skirt, the burgundy top a batwing style with beaded embellishment at the neckline. She was slim but curvy, and extremely pretty, long dark hair pulled up into a loose ponytail. She wore just a hint of mascara and deep red lipstick, her skin pale and lightly freckled.

'Yes, I'm Fee. Who are you?' she asked. Her accent was strong Bristolian.

'My name is Cora, Cora Baxter. I'm a reporter, and I wanted to chat to you briefly about Leanne Brimley, if that's possible? I'm... well, I'm looking into the circumstances that led up to her death. And I believe you were friends? You might be able to help me.'

Fee stopped her folding.

'Not sure how I can help – she topped herself, didn't she? And we weren't that close, not so much recently anyway. But...'

She paused. 'Well, OK. She was a nice girl, Leanne. I'm due a break in five minutes, can you wait? There's a bench just outside, meet you there?'

She gestured towards the main doors and Cora nodded. True to her word, five minutes later the teenager slid onto the bench next to Cora, who was flicking through emails on her phone and listening to a nearby busker who was currently murdering *Fairytale of New York*. She hadn't thought buskers were allowed in here, and was now very much wishing they weren't. She slipped her phone back into her pocket, as Fee pulled a cereal bar from her bag, unwrapped it and took a bite.

'Sorry, starving,' she mumbled. 'Go on then, what can I do for you?'

Cora smiled. 'Don't worry, I know what it's like, I have to grab food when I can in my job too. What I really wanted to talk to you about was a club called Midnight Diamonds. I believe you work there as well as here, or certainly that you did recently?'

Fee swallowed and stared at Cora for a moment, then looked around uneasily.

'How... how did you know that?'

Cora hesitated, not sure whether to reveal her source, then decided it couldn't do much harm.

'Liam told me. Leanne's younger brother? He said that you'd managed to get a job there after you left school, even though you were only sixteen? And that Leanne was worried about you.'

Fee was looking down at her hands, fingers twisting the cereal bar wrapper.

'Oh. Please, don't tell anyone? Not many people know I work there,' she whispered. 'I'm too young, even now I'm seventeen. I'm not doing it so much now that I have this job too, but I got kicked out of home a few months back and rent is so expensive... I was a bit desperate, you see. I'd left school and I couldn't find anything, not even a shop job, and I was skint. Then I met one of the girls from there in a bar. We got chatting in the loos, you know how you do, and she said she danced at Midnight Diamonds and how she made hundreds of pounds a night. It sounded so easy, and I love dancing, I'm good at it. And I don't mind my body, taking my clothes off, you know? But she said you had to be eighteen to work there. So I used my fake ID, we all had them at school, and I went in for an audition and got the job. The boss, Dougie... well, I think he knew damn well I was only sixteen. I could tell by the way he looked at me when I showed him my

ID. But he let it go. Some of the men who go there... well, they like younger girls, know what I mean?'

She glanced at Cora then looked back down at her lap. The cereal bar was crumbling now, and she swiped a hand across her black skirt, knocking the pieces to the floor.

'When you say they like younger girls, do you mean... do you mean it goes further than just dancing?' Cora's voice was gentle.

Fee shook her head vehemently.

'No! There's strict rules. They're not allowed to touch us, not in the club. And we only go topless, not the whole way. Not even when we do the private dances, even though a lot of the men ask us to. But sometimes... well, sometimes you meet someone there who's nice, you know? Who buys you presents and stuff. And if you decide to... well, to take things further outside of the club, well that's your business. That's *my* business, OK?'

She sat up straight, a defiant look in her eyes now.

'And what's this got to do with Leanne dying, anyway? What are you here for?'

Cora touched the girl gently on the arm, trying to reassure her. Something had just occurred to her, and she urgently needed to ask another question.

'It might not have anything to do with her death at all, it probably doesn't in fact, it's just an avenue I'm pursuing. But can I just ask you a couple more things? Fee – when you... when you get together with customers outside of the club, does money change hands? And does the club make anything out of that?'

Fee stared straight ahead of her, back stiff. Then she turned to look at Cora again.

'Why? I don't understand these questions. Look, sometimes it's just gifts, sometimes it's cash. It's not like being a prostitute. These are men we meet and get to know at the club, who ask to take us out sometime and like to treat us. It's not like we pick them up on a street corner. I'm not a hooker, OK? But yes, sometimes Dougie asks for a cut, if I get cash. He says I wouldn't have met the men if it wasn't for his club, and he's right, I wouldn't. A lot of clubs fire girls for doing stuff like that, but he said he wouldn't. So I give him a cut. Only fair, right?'

'Sure, yes.' Hoping her feelings weren't showing on her face, Cora smiled. This poor kid, being totally exploited. This was horrible.

'So, you talked to Leanne about this? She knew?'

Fee nodded. 'Yeah. We'd lost touch a bit after I left school, and I think she disapproved when she heard what I was doing for a living too. Then suddenly one day she rang up and asked if we could meet up for a coffee. I was upset that day... I'd had another row with my mum earlier, and Leanne was always a good listener, so I went and met up with her, ended up telling her everything. She was a bit of a goody-goody, but she was nice. I knew I could trust her. She was really interested in the club for some reason, not sure why, never had been before. But she said I shouldn't be doing it, what I was doing. Said I was better than that. It made me think, so I looked for another job after that, found this Top Shop one. I still do the club, but not as much. Just a couple of nights a month, if I'm short. Might not even go back after Christmas, I've been promised more hours here, maybe a place on the management trainee scheme. And I've started seeing somebody, he works up there in Waterstones.'

She gestured with her head.

'He probably wouldn't like it, would he, having a girlfriend who works part time as a stripper? And even

177

though it's fun, and the money's great, Leanne was probably right. It's not good, is it? Not for young girls, working in a place like that.'

'I think she *was* right, yes. Fee…' Cora wasn't sure she even wanted to ask her next question, almost afraid of what the answer would be.

'Fee… you got the job at sixteen. Can I just ask… are there any – any girls there *younger* than that? Under sixteen?'

Fee stared at her hands for a few seconds, then shrugged. 'Maybe. There's one or two, I think. Some of the Eastern European girls, they look really young when they're not all done up. But I can't be sure. Everyone lies about their age, don't they? And with make-up and everything…'

'I know, it's difficult. Fee – did Leanne know about all this? Did you tell her?'

Fee nodded.

'Yep. She was really interested, like I said. Suppose her life was quite boring, compared to mine.'

She laughed, and then stopped herself abruptly.

'Sorry. Seems wrong to say things like that, now that she's dead.'

Cora patted the girl's arm.

'Don't worry, I know what you meant. Fee – I'm really keen to run a story on this club. Do you think any of the girls would speak to me, on camera? Maybe if we hid their faces and disguised their voices or something? Would you talk to me officially, on the record?'

'What? Are you crazy?' Fee looked aghast. 'Of course they bloody won't. Me neither. Never in a million years. They'd lose their jobs for a start, if Dougie got a sniff of it, which he would. No way. Forget it. Not a chance.'

Cora sighed. 'OK, I knew it was a long shot. Sorry to

ask.'

'It's OK. I know it's your job. Not going to happen though, sorry. Hey, how long have I been out here? Hang on.'

Fee dug into her bag and pulled out a mobile phone. She tapped on the screen, checking the time, and then turned to Cora.

'Shit, I need to go in a minute, my break's nearly over. Look, I still don't know why you're so interested, but as I've told you this much there's one more thing you might want to know. Leanne asked me how Dougie got away with it, you know, hiring under-eighteens. I think he's just a very good liar, to be honest. He pretends he doesn't know. But… well, he has a friend who's a cop too. I think the copper helps him cover it up, keeps other cops away. He's in there a lot. Tall Scouse bloke, always red in the face. Dougie calls him Gordon. And he likes the young ones, too. I've seen him with them. Well, with one of them, a girl called Sofia. That's how Dougie gets away with it, I reckon. He's in bed with the pigs.'

24

The water was brown, little patches of slime and pieces of debris sluggishly floating past as Cora made the phone call, her waders submerged to the thighs.

'Sam, the houses are completely cut off by the floodwater. I've spoken to some of the residents on the phone and none of them have waders, and they say they're not prepared to get into the water to walk out to me for an interview without them, they don't feel safe. And there's no point in me wading in to them, because Scott can't get the truck close enough to broadcast. I'm sorry, but I don't think I can make this work.'

At the news desk in London Sam sighed heavily.

'Cora darling, I hate to do this to you, but Betsy is adamant. She wants a family for the eight o'clock news, and nothing less will do. Look, you've got Nathan's little boat, haven't you? Great piece with you floating across the park in it at seven, it looked fantastic. Loved how you pointed out the swings and slides and everything half under water. But now you're going to have to use it to get us a family. Float round to the houses in it, let them jump in, then you hop out in your waders and pull the boat back to the dry ground where the truck's parked for the interview. Problem solved!'

Dumbstruck, Cora stared at the scene in front of her. The lashing rain of yesterday had taken its toll on this flood-prone area of Somerset, bursting riverbanks, trapping residents in the upstairs of their homes and closing roads and railway lines. Cora and the boys had received the call from London in the early hours, and after much time wasted driving in frustrated circles, constantly being cut off by floodwater, they had come across this little hamlet. The homes at one end of the small cul-de-sac were surrounded by five feet of water, the small park across the road underwater too, but Scott had managed to find a patch of higher ground nearby to park the truck on, and enable their earlier broadcasts. As Cora gazed around her, a swan sailed regally past her on what was normally a main road and, at the bottom of the small hill, an old red telephone box sat forlornly, dirty water filling its interior to the halfway mark.

'So – have I got this clear? Sam, you want me to haul a heavy boatful of people out of the cul-de-sac and all the way along the street until we reach dry land? Like…like a *donkey*? Come on, seriously?' Cora said into her phone.

Sam laughed. 'Well, not like a *donkey* as such. Like the intrepid reporter you are, Cora. Will you do it? Please? For me?'

'Oh, BLOODY HELL. Yes, alright, I'll do it. But if I do my back in I'm sending my chiropractor bills to Betsy. Speak later.'

'You're a star. Bye, Cora.'

'You really were an angel to do that this morning. Great interview. Loved how the little girl was sobbing over her "drowned" teddy, really tugged at the heartstrings. Well done, you. Did your back survive? Here, have a flapjack.'

Sam held out a paper plate.

'Oh, go on then. And yes, my back survived. But honestly, Sam, I do worry about you sometimes. I think the spirit of Jeanette lives on in this newsroom, and every now and again a hint of it sneaks its way into you. That poor little girl! She was heartbroken.'

181

'Och, don't say that! I'm not that bad. Just know what makes good telly. Shut up and eat your flapjack.'

Cora accepted the plate and took a large, satisfying bite of her cake, then frowned as she noticed something a little odd on an adjoining desk.

'Errm… Sam, why is there a half-eaten chicken sitting there? And are those…are those *candles* sticking out of it?'

Sam glanced across at the desk and nodded.

'Yeah, that's Kelly's birthday cake. Kelly, the new trainee producer? She's on some sort of detox diet and can't eat cake. So the guys got her a spit-roast chicken instead, and stuck a few birthday candles in it. She was thrilled. Chicken cake. Great idea, eh?'

Cora stared at the mangled carcass in bemusement.

'Well… yes, I suppose so. Gosh, Sam, this place just gets weirder. Anyway, where were we?'

'I was saying what great telly it was this morning,' Sam said. 'But enough of boosting your ego. Come on, are you going to fill me in on the Leanne Brimley investigation, then? Let's use Betsy's office, she's out for the rest of the afternoon. I'll carry the teas.'

'OK. *Loads* to tell you. Not sure what any of it means though.'

Cora spoke through her mouthful of flapjack, delicately spraying crumbs onto Sam's desk. Luckily her friend was already marching off towards the editor's glass-walled corner office.

'You go, I'll wipe it!' hissed Wendy, who'd been discussing graphics with one of the other reporters at a nearby desk. She winked at Cora, who winked back and headed off after Sam.

She still felt a little damp in one leg after this morning's broadcasts, her left wader having sprung a small leak as she'd dragged the boat and its live cargo to their broadcast position. Pulling uncomfortably at her trousers, she closed the office door and sank down onto the sofa. Being called to London this afternoon was a bonus, she thought – a chance to talk through what she and the boys had discovered so far about the Leanne case, and an unexpected Friday evening with Adam, whom she hadn't planned on seeing tonight as he was working over the weekend. He'd be wanting an early night, which was completely fine by her, she thought lasciviously.

Between sips and nibbles, she brought the senior producer up to date. Sam listened quietly, then stood up and walked to the flipchart which sat on a stand in the corner of the office. Turning the pages until she found a blank one, she picked up a black marker pen and started to make notes.

'Right, let's do this bullet-point style, so we're clear about what we've got,' she said. 'First, a girl, a bridge, a suicide note and a coroner who rules she killed herself. Fairly clear cut.'

She drew a line down the centre of the page.

'But, opposite that, we have a mysterious car on the bridge at the time she came off it, plus a brother who says she would never have voluntarily jumped.'

'And now a neighbour who backs that up,' said Cora. 'Old Arthur Everton seemed pretty shocked by it too.'

'True. So *more* than one person who believes she wouldn't have done it.'

Sam made another note.

'So, the question is, did Leanne kill herself, as the officials in this case – the police and coroner – seem to think? Or was she coerced into it somehow - or, worst case scenario, but unlikely due to the suicide note, was she pushed? That sum the basics of this up?'

'It does, yes,' Cora said.

'OK. So Leanne's brother said she was "on to something" as he put it, but we don't know what, although you now think it's probably something to do with Midnight Diamonds, right?'

Cora nodded, her mouth full of flapjack again.

'OK, so let's list people of interest. We have the property developer Leanne was at loggerheads with, who's also part-owner of the club along with his sleazy mate, and who seemed to suddenly cave in and let Leanne win her fight against his building plans.'

She wrote Randall Greythorpe's name on the page.

'Then we have some neighbours who were furious with her for scuppering their chances of making a fat profit on their houses, one of whom probably sent her those threatening letters. And finally, we have a dodgy copper who seems to be somehow involved too – certainly Leanne believed that he was helping to cover up what was going on at the club, because that's what her friend Fee told her. And then there's the thing about him liking the younger girls…'

She shuddered, made a final note and stood back from the chart.

'They seem to be the main players, right?'

Cora nodded again, staring at the board.

'Blimey. Quite a lot going on here, then. How on earth does it all link to Leanne's death? Or does it?'

Cora sighed.

'I really don't know, Sam. I keep swinging backwards and forwards on this. One day I think her death was definitely a bit suspicious, the next I don't. It's the suicide note that bothers me – it was typed on her own laptop and then printed out. It seems totally genuine. But then, there was the car on the bridge too, remember. And Liam being so sure she wouldn't have killed herself, especially as she was so happy that day. And, on the flip side, she did have all these people who weren't too fond of her at the time she died. I keep coming up with crazy theories. Maybe Randall Greythorpe suddenly dropped his plans for the bigger estate because she was blackmailing him about what was happening at the club? And then maybe she threatened to report him anyway, so he got really mad? Or maybe one of those neighbours was so furious about losing out on a property windfall that they decided she had to be punished? I don't know if she ever confronted DCI Gregory about hanging out in the club, and what he was up to, but if she did, he wouldn't be too happy with her either, would he? So, lots of potential suspects. But at the same time, I can't really see any of those people actually forcing her off a bridge. I'm starting to think this is all a waste of time, especially now that I've seen it all laid out in front of me like that. There may have been lots of people around Leanne who had a grievance against her, but would any of them really resort to trying to kill her? I can't see it, honestly.'

Sam sat back down on the sofa and patted her friend's hand.

'Well, maybe it's all been a waste of time when it comes to Leanne's death, yes. But you did sort of know that from the start really. You were just being nice and trying to help her little brother out, because of how Leanne died right in front of you. It probably *was* suicide, Cora, and for reasons we'll never really understand. But this whole thing has definitely *not* been a total waste of time. You've discovered that a famous architect and property developer is involved with a club which is employing under-age girls. We know that because Fee has confirmed it. And we also have the possibility that some of those girls are so young they are under the age of sexual consent, and yet they may be having sex with customers outside the club. That's huge, Cora – huge! But we'd need to be pretty damn sure of our facts, before we did anything with it…'

'And of course, our senior police officer, currently suspended from duty, who also hangs out in said club,' Cora said slowly. 'Fee mentioned the name Sofia, in particular, as a girl he liked. But again, I only have her word for it, and she won't speak to me on the record. I'd need to be able to prove that somehow, and have solid proof too. We can't go and accuse a police officer of something like that otherwise, especially this particular police officer. He's got it in for me enough already. Wonder if I can find this Sofia girl, or one of the other younger ones?'

'You could try, yes,' said Sam. 'And what about visiting your friend Randall one more time? Confront him about the club again. I know you've asked him about it before, but you know a lot more now. Tell him you have it on good authority that things are not as they should be there, see how he reacts. To be fair, he may not even know. He told you he's pretty much a silent partner, didn't he? Maybe he doesn't get involved with the day to day goings on there at all. But still, worth a try.'

'It is. Good idea, Sam. I'll ring his PA right now and make an appointment.'

She thought for a moment, then pulled her mobile phone from her pocket and dialled the number. John Smith answered within three rings, his voice bright and efficient.

'John, would it be OK to pop in briefly at some point over the next week? I, errrm, want to show you Randall's interview footage. Just to make sure you're both happy with it before we broadcast?'

Beside her, Sam raised her eyebrows. No news organisation *ever* showed an interviewee footage "to make sure they were happy".

'Tomorrow? Well, I'll just have to check that my cameraman is free, seeing as it's Saturday, but hopefully we could both be in Bristol by late morning, if that would work for you? Thanks, John. See you then.'

Cora ended the call.

'Yes, Sam, before you say anything, I know we don't show people edited footage. How else was I going to get back in there? And that interview's not actually for broadcast, remember?'

'Fair enough.' Sam looked at her watch. 'Got to go in a minute. And Cora, obviously if and when we have something solid, we need to report the shenanigans at the club to the police. We can run a report, yes, it's a great story. If it's all true, these men are horribly exploiting young women, children practically. But this needs investigating on a criminal level, not just by us. OK?'

'Of course. But just give me a bit more time to gather evidence, please?'

'Sure. Look, I have a meeting, my love. Got to run. Enjoy your weekend, and keep me posted, OK?'

'I will. Catch you next week.'

The two women hugged, and went their separate ways.

'John, I told you under no circumstances to let that woman back into this office! What the hell are you doing?'

Randall Greythorpe was standing next to his assistant's desk, eyes flashing with anger.

'Randall, I... I just thought it would be a good idea, to see the interview footage. You know, to make sure they haven't edited it to show you in a bad light or anything. I mean, after the questions Cora asked you about Midnight Diamonds and everything? It was nice of her to offer it, they don't usually... I mean, that's all she's coming for, it's not another interview or anything. She'll be in and out. I'm so sorry... do you want me to call her back and cancel it?'

John sounded close to tears. Randall glared at him, running his hands through his dark quiff, then turned and marched back to his own desk.

'It's too late now. Let her come, but she'd better not be here for long. And make that the last bloody time, John. I mean it,' he said over his shoulder, his tone exasperated. He sat down and pushed a pile of papers aside so roughly that they slid off the desk and fell to the floor. What was that reporter really coming here for – or was he just being paranoid? Dougie had been on the phone a few days back, telling him about a copper friend who'd spotted a breakfast TV reporter hanging around outside the club one night – was it the same one? His gut told him it was. Why was she so interested in the club? And in Leanne Brimley? He pressed his fingers to his temples, feeling a stress headache bubbling. Things were going so well, he had so many big plans for the future. Could this interfering TV news reporter spoil things for him? Randall lifted his head and stared out of the window opposite his desk. It was already almost dark, and his own reflection looked back at him. She needed to be kept away from him, he thought. Cora Baxter needed to *back off*.

At his own desk, John Smith sniffed and took a deep breath. He hated it when Randall shouted at him. He'd go and see her again after work tonight, he thought. Sit with her a while, maybe have dinner together. She'd make him feel better. Just looking at her had the power to do that, to change his mood, to lift him up and remind him why he worked so hard. All she had to do was smile at him and his heart would soar, and the troubles of the day begin to melt away. He smiled. Yes, he'd go and see her this evening. He looked at his scribbled list of things to do, squinting as he tried to read his own writing. He could get through this in a couple of hours, and then go. He might screw up now and again, but he was damn good at his job, he knew he was. He tapped his mouse to wake up his laptop screen and got back to work.

25

'We really need to start meeting in museums. Or art galleries. Or *pubs*. Seriously, how many cafés have we talked about this story in recently? Must be a world record.'

Nathan rolled his eyes despairingly. It was eleven o'clock on Saturday morning, and he and Cora were sitting in the coffee shop on Bristol's Thornton Street, just round the corner from Flower Street and the new housing development. Outside the steamed-up window the winter sun was shining brightly on a group of boys playing with what looked like a remote-controlled helicopter, which buzzed overhead as they ran up and down the quiet road, laughing and pointing skywards. Otherwise, all was peaceful, the café empty apart from two elderly women gossiping over coffee and toasted muffins while Cora and Nathan nursed their large mugs of tea.

'I know. It's getting quite comical. It's just easy, though, isn't it? And we do need to talk about this, before we do it. I'd rather do it over a leisurely breakfast than just sit in the car or something, wouldn't you?' said Cora.

'Suppose so. So, you're just going to come straight out with it, while we're showing them the interview footage?' asked Nathan.

He licked his finger, which he'd just wiped across his plate, collecting the last smears of ketchup from his sausage and egg sandwich.

'Animal,' said Cora. 'And yes, I suppose so. Don't really know how else to do it. Wonder how he'll react?'

'No idea. It'll be interesting though. And what next, after we've given him a chance to comment? Which I bet he won't do, will he? If we're going to run a report before Sam makes us hand all this over to the police, we need someone to talk on camera…'

Cora sighed. 'We do, and I can't see anyone doing that. None of the girls will do it, will they? Fee Taylor made that pretty clear. Unless we can find someone who's left Midnight Diamonds maybe, a former employee, who might be willing to talk to us? Won't be easy though. I'm not sure we're going to get a report out of this at all, Nath. We're fairly sure of what's going on there, but proving it's going to be impossible. I mean, Fee said she thought there might be some very young girls working there, but even *she* wasn't sure. She said everyone lies about their age, and that it's hard to tell with all the make-up and everything. So maybe there are, maybe there aren't. And if not, then all the club could be done for is employing some under-eighteen dancers.'

'But there's the other stuff too,' said Nathan. 'You know, the little matter of the girls having sex with punters, and Dougie Granley taking a cut? I guess that's also going to be impossible to prove though.'

Cora took a sip of tea and nodded.

'Really difficult. I've been reading up on it, and the law's so complicated. For example, it's not actually illegal for a girl over the age of eighteen to go off and have sex with a customer outside the club. And it's not illegal for him to pay her for it either, again as long as she's over eighteen. It's stuff like soliciting on the street and kerb crawling that's illegal. But it *is* against the law for an *under-eighteen* to be paid for sex, even though she's technically over the age of consent. And of course, if she's under sixteen, it's all illegal. And if Dougie *is* taking

191

a cut, hence sort of acting as a pimp, well that's illegal too, but... oh, it's hopeless. We have no solid evidence for any of it. It's all just so sleazy, Nathan.'

Nathan nodded slowly, picked up his napkin and wiped his mouth.

'It is, yes. And I suppose what it also is, Cora, is a totally separate issue from the story we started with. This was supposed to be us checking out Liam's theory that his sister's death might not have been as straightforward as it seemed. It's kind of bizarre that we're currently on such a different track. I know we've got pretty much nowhere in looking into Leanne's death, but I don't think we should forget it entirely, and get totally distracted by all these tangents. Let's try to remember the Leanne connection in all this, eh? Ask Randall Greythorpe if he knows what's going on at the club, yes. But also tell him that you believe Leanne knew there were underage girls at his club, some having sex with clients, and ask him if that's why he let her win her campaign. Was she blackmailing him? Although he's hardly going to admit it though. Oh, bloody hell, here we go again. We're never going to get anyone to admit anything, not to us, are we?'

Cora stared out of the window, a sudden wave of despondency washing over her. Nathan was right, she thought. Why was she even bothering with all of this? It wasn't going to bring Leanne back, was it? Nobody they'd met so far could really have had anything to do with the girl's death, it was ludicrous to think so. And did she really care enough about a sleazy nightclub story to carry on pursuing it? It was pointless. But they were here now...

'Oh, come on, let's just go and do it,' she said, pushing her chair back from the table and standing up. 'And then maybe we can just leave it, and concentrate on nice things like Christmas.'

'Alright. I'll go and pay. Meet you outside in a minute. Go and get some sunshine, top up your vitamin D levels while you can.'

Cora nodded her thanks, and as her cameraman headed to the till she slipped her coat on, wrapped her woollen scarf tightly round her neck and stepped out into the street. It was a perfect cold, crisp morning, and she found herself smiling as she watched the excited boys who were still tearing up and down the road, whooping as their helicopter did loop the loops. Shading her eyes with her hand, she squinted as she tried to focus on the little blue machine humming overhead.

'Oh, I thought it was a helicopter. It's not, it's a drone,' she said, as Nathan appeared at her side, hoisting his camera onto his shoulder.

'Cool. Kids nowadays, eh? When you think about the sort of toys *we* had…'

He paused as one of the boys, the one clutching the remote-control unit, skidded to a halt in front of them.

'Oi, Billy! Take this for a minute!' he said, passing the controller to one of his friends, who yelled 'Yay!' and ran off with it. The first boy grinned up at Nathan and pointed to the camera.

'Are you a telly cameraman? That's what I want to be, when I grow up. Hi, I'm Josh.'

He held out a hand, and Nathan shook it with a grin.

'Hello, Josh. I'm Nathan, and this is Cora. And yes, I'm a telly cameraman. She's a reporter.'

'Wicked.'

He looked about twelve or thirteen, with intelligent dark eyes and tousled blond hair.

'That your drone?'

Nathan gestured skywards and Josh nodded.

'Yes! Got it as a birthday present from my uncle. It's awesome. Got a twelve megapixel camera and shoots 4K video at thirty frames per second.'

'Wow, that's impressive. Isn't it, Cora?'

Nathan glanced sideways at Cora, grinning mischievously.

'Ermm, yes. Very impressive,' she replied, hoping the boy would not realise what Nathan clearly knew – that she did not have the slightest clue what he was talking about.

'So, what sort of footage are you getting?' Nathan asked.

'Stuff of the new housing development mostly. I started as soon as I got it. I'm going to shoot the whole thing from start to finish, and then edit it together all speeded up, you know? So you can see it go from a big empty space to a whole new estate in a couple of minutes.'

'Good idea. A sort of time lapse thing? That'll look great.' Nathan smiled at the eagerness in the boy's face.

Josh nodded. 'And then I'm going to try to sell it to the boss of the development. He might want it for his website or something, I thought.'

'Very enterprising. Well, very nice to meet you, Josh. We need to get off now, but good luck with your project. You'll go far with ideas like that. Aerial photography is big business.'

'Thanks! OK, better get my drone back. Billy! Billy!'

Josh turned and ran off up the road in pursuit of his friend, and Nathan turned to Cora.

'Smart kid. Right – let's do this. Gareth is making lasagne for lunch, and I said I wouldn't be late. Fifteen minutes in and out, OK?'

'No probs.'

Three minutes later they were inside the site office,

John Smith fussing around them offering tea and biscuits while Randall sat silently in one of the tub chairs in the reception area, sipping coffee from a tall glass mug. He didn't look entirely pleased to see them, Cora thought, as Nathan set up his camera, hooking it up to a monitor so he could play the edited interview footage for the two men.

As they watched though, Randall seemed to relax, nodding approval and even smiling once or twice, John's twitchiness also visibly quietening as his boss's mood improved. When the tape ended, both men grinned.

'Great interview, Randall! Really great. Thank you so much, guys. Do you know when it will be broadcast yet?'

John was rubbing his hands together, on his feet now.

Cora shook her head, mentally crossing her fingers.

'Sorry, I don't. Should be soon though. Think they're waiting for a day when property prices are in the news, something like that, so it all ties in, you know?'

Randall nodded.

'Makes sense. And thank you for showing it to us. We're very pleased. Now if you don't mind, I need to get on. Various calls to make. It might be the weekend, but work never stops in this business. Much like your own, clearly.'

He smiled, showing his even white teeth, and Cora took a deep breath and glanced at Nathan. It was now or never.

'Yes indeed, news doesn't stop at weekends, sadly! Errrm, just before we go though... I have one quick question, which has emerged from some... well, some additional research I was doing when I was putting the interview together. It's in relation to Midnight Diamonds.'

'Midnight Diamonds?'

John, who'd been gathering up the tea and coffee mugs, stopped what he was doing and stared at Cora, a worried look on his face. Randall's smile faded.

'I told you last time. I'm a silent partner in that club, more or less. Just an investor. If you have any questions about the day-to-day running, you'll need to speak to Dougie Granley.'

His tone was pleasant, but there was a slight edge to it, Cora thought.

'Well, yes, I remember. But I just wanted to run this past you, if you don't mind?'

She spoke quickly, not giving either of the men time to object.

'I've been talking to a girl who's an occasional dancer there. She's only seventeen, Randall. And she was actually only sixteen when she got the job. Which as you must know, isn't legal, not for that sort of work. And, even more worryingly, she's told me that there are girls there who are even younger – maybe even *under* sixteen. And that some of these young women are... well, providing additional services to some of the customers, outside the club. Are you aware of any of this?'

'WHAT?' Randall's expression was one of revulsion. 'What are you talking about? That's absolute rubbish. Whoever told you that is clearly lying. Dougie would *never*...'

'No, no he wouldn't!'

There was panic on John's face as, still clutching the biscuit plate, he rushed across the room to stand at his boss's side.

'And another thing.' Cora spoke quickly, aware that they had now very much outstayed their welcome.

'We know that Leanne Brimley, the girl who was protesting against this development, was also aware of what was going on at the club. Did she confront you about it? Is that why you decided to...'

'What the hell are you implying? How dare you come in here and throw accusations like this around?'

Randall's tone was icy cold. John's mouth was wide open, his eyes wide. He looked horrified.

'Guys, this is all a big mistake. You can't… I mean, you'd have to have proof, wouldn't you, to make this public? You have no proof, do you? Do you?'

His voice was shaky, and Randall put a calming hand on his assistant's arm.

'John, they don't have proof, because it's simply not true,' he said. 'And now they're going to leave.'

Cora and Nathan watched in silence as he turned and walked towards his partitioned off desk area. When he reached it, he looked back over his shoulder.

'I don't expect to see you here again,' he said coolly. 'I appreciate the interview you did with me, but I think that concludes our business. Goodbye.'

He disappeared behind the partition. John was standing stock still, looking distraught.

'I think… I think you do need to go. I'm… I'm sorry,' he stammered.

Cora and Nathan exchanged looks.

'Of course. Thanks for your hospitality as always, John. We'll see ourselves out,' Cora said.

A minute later they were outside, walking briskly towards the site gate. When they reached it, they stopped simultaneously. Nathan exhaled loudly.

'Well,' he said. 'What do you make of *that*?'

As Cora and Nathan made their way back to their cars, they were being watched from a distance by Caroline Sinclair and Tracy Leonard. The friends and neighbours were standing on the doorstep of Gladys Parker's house, number four Flower Street, after an enjoyable morning coffee and gossip session. They'd just been finishing off with a final, extra little gossip before returning to their families and their Saturday chores, when Tracy gasped.

'Shit, Caz. That's that bloody reporter again, isn't it?'

Caroline peered down the street, wrinkling her small pointed nose.

'Oh my God. It is, isn't it? What's she doing back here, Trace? Did she come out of Elmsley Park?'

She ran her hands frantically through her short dark hair as her friend nodded.

'Think so, yes. Look, calm down, Caz. She's not been back to see you, has she?'

Caroline shook her head.

'Or she hasn't tried to talk to Mark?'

'No! No, I didn't even tell him about her. He's in a bad enough way without the extra worry of that. I can't tell him, Trace!'

There was a note of panic in Caroline's voice. Tracy grabbed both of her upper arms and shook her, very gently.

'So there's nothing to worry about, is there? She's probably just interviewing what's 'is name or something. You've got to stop worrying about this. Put it behind you. We all have to, OK? What's done is done. Right?'

Caroline took a deep breath.

'Sorry, Trace. I know you're right. It's just that…you know, when I think about it…'

Tears suddenly filled her eyes, and Tracy sighed.

'Well, you can't go home in this state. Come on, come to mine. The kids are out. We'll have another cuppa and get you sorted, alright?'

Caroline nodded gratefully and slipped her arm through her friend's.

'You're an angel, Tracy Leonard. Don't know what I'd

198

do without you, I really don't.'

Tracy sighed again.

'Get yourself in even *more* trouble, that's what. Come on. Let's get that kettle on.'

26

Inside the site office, Randall was on the phone to Douglas Granley.

'I mean, WHAT THE F...'

He paused, suddenly aware that John was dealing with a walk-in on the other side of the room, a passer-by who'd just come in to enquire about how soon the show home would be ready for viewing. He lowered his voice, but there was still menace in his tone.

'Dougie, it's totally unacceptable for me to have TV reporters barging into my office and asking me questions like that, do you understand?'

On the other end of the line, Dougie was apologising profusely. He had a strong Geordie accent, which became even stronger when he was upset or angry.

'Mate, I'm so sorry. Gordon Gregory, my copper mate, he reckons she's out to make a name for herself – she did him over on TV recently, right little cow by all accounts. Everything's fine here, mate. Nothing to worry about. Deny everything, and I'll do the same if she comes near me. It'll blow over.'

'It better had. Keep your nose clean, Dougie, or else. Get it?'

'I get it, I get it. Chill, Randall. It'll all be fine.'

Randall grunted and slammed down the phone. Cora Baxter had 'done over' a police officer on television? Really? And now she was after him. The thought chilled him. He stood up and walked around the partition which separated his desk from the main office, moving slowly, thinking. John was at the door now, waving his customer off. He turned to Randall with a cheery smile.

'That's another one really interested. Got a deposit ready and everything. As soon as that show home's up and running we're going to sell out super fast, mark my words, boss!'

Randall fixed him with a steely glare.

'Right now, I couldn't care less, John. I wish I'd never started this frigging development. We get rid of one trouble-making woman and another one lands on our doorstep. So you listen to me. If you ever let Cora Baxter near me again, you're fired. And I mean that, John. I know how much you need this job, but I will not hesitate to get rid of you, OK? Understand?'

The colour was draining from John's face, his hands suddenly shaking.

'I understand. I'm so sorry, Randall. You won't see her again. Please don't fire me. You know how much I love…'

'Well do your job, then,' Randall snapped.

John nodded.

'I will. I will. I promise.'

27

Cora and Nathan were leaning against his car, discussing what had just happened in Randall's office.

'I mean, he certainly reacted as if he didn't know anything about what was going on at the club. John looked horrified too. Do you think they really don't know, Nath? Or are they just bloody good actors?'

Cora shivered. The sun had gone in now, grey clouds scudding across the sky. Nathan shrugged, plunging his hands deep into his coat pockets.

'I'm not sure. It actually seemed like a genuine reaction to me. But who knows? They certainly didn't like it when we brought Leanne into it though. But how far does that get us? As John kindly pointed out, we have no proof, do we? Just the word of Fee Taylor, a teenage girl, and a hunch that Leanne might have confronted Randall with what she knew. We can't prove that, we can't prove any of it. And even if we could, how do we link any of it to Leanne's death? We don't have enough, Cora.'

She sighed. 'I know. Oh Nathan, what the hell are we doing? Is it time just to knock all this on the head? I mean, there's the note, for goodness sake. We can't get away from that simple fact. It's extremely likely that this was just a straightforward, tragic suicide, despite Liam's doubts, and despite all the nasty people around Leanne and all the odd goings on.'

She reached into her bag and pulled out her file, then flicked through it until she found the suicide note.

To my family and friends. I'm so sorry. It's been a long

few months and I can't take it anymore. It's too hard. I apolojise for what I'm about to do. I know this is going to come as a terrible shock, but I want you to know that I know what I'm doing. This is my decission and it's the right one for me. I love you. I will always love you. But I can't stay with you any longer. Please try to understand. Leanne xx

They both read it silently, Nathan leaning over Cora's shoulder. She closed the file again and turned to look at him.

'Look, what if I try one more thing? Just one? I'll call Fee Taylor, see if she can give me a number or any contact details for that Sofia girl she mentioned, the one she said was friendly with DCI Gregory. It's worth talking to just one more girl from the club, even if Fee does think none of them will talk on camera. Maybe *she'll* talk to me. Maybe she had some dealings with Leanne. And if not, well…'

'If not, we put this to bed. Nobody could have done more, Cora, to try to get to the bottom of it all. But maybe there's nothing to get to the bottom *of*. Not in relation to Leanne's death, anyway. There's definitely some sort of sleazy news story here, even if we can't prove any of it. But as far as somebody else being somehow involved in that poor kid jumping off a bridge… well, I just don't think so. Never really did, to be honest. Come here, you.'

Nathan pulled her into a hug and she hugged him back gratefully, then released him.

'Thanks, Nath. Don't know what I'd do without you. Now, go! Don't want Gareth's food spoiling. Have a good weekend and I'll see you on Monday.'

'OK. But keep me posted, right?'

'I will. Bye.'

She waited until he'd driven off, then got into her own car, turned the engine on to generate some heat and reached for her mobile to call Fee Taylor.

'Sofia? Sofia Dobrescu?'

The young waitress in the baggy black dress and oversized pink trainers turned, a startled look on her face, as Cora called her name. The coffee shop in a side street off Bristol's Broadmead shopping area was packed with couples, groups of teenage girls and families with small children, all jostling for space at the closely packed tables and along the stand-up bar areas around the wall, shopping bags piled at their feet and winter coats slung over chairs. It was warm in here, the windows steamed up, beads of sweat on the brow of the harassed-looking young man in an ill-fitting suit who stood behind the counter. He must be the manager, Cora thought, noting that all of the other staff wore casual black uniforms, the girls in dresses, the boys T-shirts and dark jeans. Fee had been reluctant to help at first when Cora had called her, saying she hadn't seen Sofia for weeks, but she had finally relented. She had told Cora she didn't have a phone number for the girl but knew she sometimes did shifts at the Cosy Café. Not feeling very hopeful, Cora had battled her way through the hellish traffic of this almost-Christmas Saturday, queued for twenty minutes to get a parking space in the nearest multi-storey, and located the coffee shop. Asking the first member of staff she could grab if he knew a waitress called Sofia, he'd grinned and gestured over his shoulder.

'Romanian bird? Aye, over there, wiping tables.'

Now, Cora smiled reassuringly as Sofia approached her, a wary look on her thin face. She was tiny, with a delicate, bird-like bone structure and shoulder-length straight blonde hair, eyes so dark they were almost black.

'Sofia, I'm sorry to bother you, I can see you're very busy. My name is Cora Baxter, and I'm a journalist, working on a story. Fee Taylor told me where I could find you. Fee? She's a dancer at Midnight Diamonds, the club you also work at?'

Sofia, who had frowned when Cora mentioned Fee, nodded and smiled. One of her front teeth was slightly chipped.

'Oh, Fee, yes. She nice.'

Her accent was strong, the words clipped.

'But why you want me? I do nothing wrong. And is so busy, today, you see...'

She gestured behind her, waving the blue dishcloth clutched in her hand.

'Yes, I can see that. Have you got just a minute though, to talk? Don't worry, you're not in any trouble. Or could I meet you later, after work?'

Sofia shook her head. 'No, I busy later. Meet someone, boyfriend.'

She glanced at the counter at the back of the room and turned back to Cora.

'Come, outside. Boss not looking. But must be quick, OK?'

'Of course.'

Cora followed as Sofia weaved her way between the tables and pushed the front door open, slipping through it and out into the street, then turned right and stepped into a narrow alleyway where wheelie bins were lined up next to a towering stack of empty cardboard boxes. It smelled deeply unpleasant, a pungent mix of rotting vegetables and a hint of stale urine.

'OK, what you want? I have done nothing wrong. I just work, go home, work again. I good girl, you know?'

Sofia's dark eyes flashed defiantly. She looked so young, Cora thought – her skin was make-up free, a dusting of acne on her cheeks, her lean frame swamped by the thin woollen dress. Fourteen, fifteen? How old was she really?

'Look, Sofia, this is a bit complicated, but again let me

promise you you're not in any trouble. I've been doing some research into Midnight Diamonds for a story I'm working on, and I thought you may be able to help me out with a couple of things. First of all, did you ever meet a girl called Leanne Brimley? She was seventeen, long reddish-brown hair?'

Sofia frowned and shook her head.

'Leanne? No, I not know her.'

'OK, don't worry. So, Midnight Diamonds. As I said, I've been doing a bit of research, and it's come to my attention that some of the girls working there are under eighteen, which is illegal for a start. But also, something else – that some of the girls, even the younger ones, are... well, are having sex with customers, for money. Somebody mentioned a police officer, called Gordon Gregory, who goes to the club, and who you might be... well, who you might be friends with. Is that true?'

Sofia had been listening intently, the wary expression back, but when Cora mentioned Gregory's name her eyes widened, a frightened look crossing her face. She gasped and stepped backwards, pressing her body against the concrete wall behind her.

'Gordon... no, he not my friend. I know him but... no, he *not* my friend.'

She wrapped her thin, pale arms around her body, the blue cloth still in her fingers, and Cora reached out a hand and gently touched the teenager's shoulder.

'Sofia, I'm sorry, I didn't mean to upset you. You do know Gordon Gregory, then? How old are you, Sofia? Do you mind telling me?'

'Eighteen,' the girl said quickly. She shivered and stared at the ground. The cloth had begun to drip, dirty brown water making a little pool at her feet, and she started to wring it out, twisting it between chapped fingers.

'You don't look eighteen. Are you, really?' Cora's voice was gentle.

Sofia's hands dropped to her sides. She looked Cora in the eye then glanced anxiously towards the street.

'I need to go back. I'm sixteen, OK? A few weeks ago, my sixteenth birthday. But please, tell nobody. Is hard to get good work, pay is bad when you are young. Please?'

'I won't tell anyone, I promise.' Cora felt a lurch of sympathy for this small, frail girl. Where were her parents? What were the circumstances that had brought her here, that had caused her to have to make a living like this, when she was so young? Cora was desperate to know more, to help her somehow, but now was not the time.

'Sofia, can I ask you something else? Did you ever sleep with Gordon Gregory, or any other customer, for money?'

She flinched as Sofia flung her head back, face suddenly flushing deep red.

'I not a whore! I do what I have to do to live, OK? But I not a whore! No more questions. I go. I not want to talk any more.'

She was shivering violently now, and Cora knew she would get no more information, not now.

'I'm so sorry, I didn't mean… you go, Sofia. Get back into the warm. But if you ever *do* want to talk, or if you need any help… please, call me.'

She pulled a card from her bag and pushed it gently into the girl's free hand. Sofia glanced at it, then at Cora, and a tear ran down her cheek. She nodded.

'I go. Goodbye.'

She stepped out of the alleyway and headed back into the cafe. Cora watched her go, the fragile teenager in the too-big clothes, and felt a wave of anger. This wasn't right – how could a strip club take on a girl like that, who looked little more than a child? What was wrong with people? What the hell was Dougie Granley playing at? And if Randall Greythorpe knew, what the hell was wrong with him too? Why did he let it go on? Surely he knew the damage it would do to his reputation, to his business, if it was made public? And then there was DCI Gregory. Sofia clearly knew him better than she had admitted – she had looked terrified when Cora had mentioned his name. But he was a *police officer*, for goodness sake. Why would she be so frightened of him? Did he frighten Leanne too, like that? Is that why she jumped off Clarton Bridge? This stank, every single bit of it. And whatever was going on at that club had to stop. But if nobody would talk to her on the record, and everyone was denying everything, how on earth could she make that happen? With a feeling close to despair, and unable to get Sofia's tiny, haunted face out of her mind, Cora made her way back to her car.

'It might be time to give up now, Cora, seriously. It's taking over your life. Work on the news story for a bit longer if you must, I know that's your job, but stop obsessing about it so much. And forget the Leanne Brimley angle. I know that poor girl is constantly on your mind, but I really think you need to move on. It was a tragedy, yes. But she's not your responsibility, and nor is her brother. You need to leave it, honestly. It's not good for you.'

Nicole squeezed Cora's waist as she passed, on her way to the fridge for wine. They were in the big kitchen at the back of Rosie's house, the delicious aroma of red mullet being baked with spicy potatoes wafting from the oven.

Cora turned from the counter where she'd been pouring crisps into a bowl and looked at Nicole.

'You're probably right. I don't really know what to do next, certainly as far as Leanne's death is concerned anyway. We can't prove a single thing. Can't prove a single thing about any of it. I'm going to tell Sam she might as well report the club to the police on Monday though. If they can at least look into what we believe is going on there, then *something* good will have come out of all this. I think I'm going to give Liam a call in the morning too, see if I can pop in and see him, explain that I think we need to just leave things be now. I feel like I'm letting him down, but what can I do? I've tried. I've *really* tried, we all have.'

'We have. You have. You're right Cora, time to leave it now. Chill. Take some time out. Have a baby…'

Rosie, who had just come into the room, arms full of cuddly toys, ducked as Cora aimed a crisp at her head.

'I was joking! JOKE! Now move out of the way, I need to get these toys in the washer before they notice they're gone.'

'Hmmm. Not funny,' said Cora, then grinned, and both Nicole and Rosie laughed. Her friends had pretty much given up on trying to persuade her to change her mind about motherhood by now, after years of gentle, well-meaning jibing, but the occasional little comment still crept in, now and again, although now thankfully it was generally in jest. In the past, Cora had entered into discussions with people who questioned her choice, wanting to try to justify it, but she no longer felt the need to explain it to anyone. It hadn't always been so easy to put an end to a 'baby' conversation though, and as she carried the crisps into the sitting room, she remembered the time the three of them had almost had a major row about it. It had been one summer afternoon a couple of years ago after far too many glasses of wine in Nicole's sunny garden, when Rosie had tentatively suggested that Cora 'didn't know what she was missing'.

'I'm not missing anything!' Cora had yelled,

209

infuriated, slamming her glass down so hard on the wooden patio table that the stem had cracked. 'That bloke in the pub the other day who'd just climbed Everest, he said *that* was the most amazing experience in the world and the rest of us didn't know what we were missing, but I don't want to rush off and climb a mountain, either! We all don't have to experience *every* amazing thing, do we? Yes, I'm sure it's amazing for you, but *your* amazing is not *my* amazing, OK? I don't want to climb Everest and I don't want to have a bloody baby, and I am *not* missing out. Why do you only do this about babies? Why don't you - I don't know – why don't you go out and harass lesbians and tell them how great sex with men is, and they'll regret it if they don't try it?'

She had looked wildly round the garden. 'Why don't you go and grab that blackbird over there and tell it swimming is the best thing in the world and it doesn't know what it's missing out on, eh? And make it get in the pond? Because it would drown, that's why! And that's what will happen to me if I have a baby – I'll drown in misery. So SHUT UP!'

The poor blackbird, which had been quietly rooting for worms in the flowerbed at the far side of the garden, had abruptly taken flight, as if it had understood every word Cora had said. At its panicked flapping, she had laughed suddenly, her slightly drunken tirade over. Rosie and Nicole, who had been staring at her with horrified faces, had collapsed into relieved giggles. It had only been a few months after that that Cora's then-boyfriend, Justin, had ended their relationship, blaming her feelings about having children, despite previously having declared he had no interest in becoming a dad. Cora had been devastated. Another woman, she could compete with, but a sudden longing for a baby – well, she could do nothing about that. He'd been so nice to Rosie and Nicole's kids while they were together, and she'd been so delighted by that at the time, so happy that he was making such an effort to fit in with her friends, knowing how important they were to her. After he left, she'd seen it all differently – while he was apparently loving the childfree life he shared with her, was he secretly increasingly wanting the family life her friends lived, instead? Had spending time with them made him realise something was missing from his own life? Apparently so.

When she'd started dating Adam, it was one of the things she'd made sure he was aware of almost from day one, but fortunately he'd completely accepted her as she was. She knew that he would never put any pressure on her to change, and she loved him even more for that. She was so lucky, she thought now, sinking down onto the sofa and taking in the sheer loveliness of Rosie's Christmas décor. Her friend did Christmas so well. Cora gazed around her, taking in the eight-foot tree, festooned this year with the same red, beaded baubles and tiny, sparkling glass butterflies she remembered from a previous festive season, but with the addition of draped, red silk ribbons and little feathered birds dotted among the branches. A twisted holly and ivy garland trailed across the mantelpiece, and candles in glittering holders flickered on the window ledge. The beauty and serenity of the scene calmed her, and she took a deep breath, determined to relax this evening. No more talking or even thinking about Leanne Brimley, Randall Greythorpe, DCI bloody Gregory or Midnight Diamonds, not tonight. It could all wait, just until tomorrow.

28

Cora was at the Brimleys' home by two o'clock the next day. Liam, having willingly agreed to see her when she'd rung him earlier in the day, opened the door with a shy smile and ushered her inside to the lounge. The room felt cold, no fire burning in the grate this time, but *Elf* was playing on the television and a few Christmas cards were lined up along the mantelpiece. Otherwise, the house seemed to be free of decorations. Understandable, Cora thought, considering how recent their family tragedy had been.

'Would you like some tea? Or coffee? Actually, I don't think there is any coffee. Mum... Mum didn't get the chance to go shopping this week yet. So, tea?'

Liam looked even paler than he did when she'd last seen him, his freckles vivid against the milky skin.

'Oh no, I'm fine, honestly. Had one before I came out. Thanks, though. How are you, Liam? How have things been?'

Cora sat down on the sofa and he sat too, perching on the edge of the chair opposite her. He looked uncomfortable, she thought. On edge. Probably nervous about what she was about to tell him. She suddenly felt a wave of guilt. Had she tried hard enough, really?

'Things are... well, OK. You know. Good days, bad days. Mum... she... well, she's struggled a bit, but she's alright. She'll be OK, I know she will.'

He paused for a moment, a stricken look crossing his face, then added, 'She's out now. Errrm...at a friend's.

That's why I said it would be OK for you to come round. I still never told her, you know. That I was worried Leanne's death wasn't as straightforward as it seemed. Didn't want to worry her even more. So, what have you found out?'

Cora, struck again by the intelligence and maturity of this fifteen-year-old, took a breath.

'Liam, I wanted to come and see you today because, well, I haven't really got anywhere, to be honest. We've looked at lots of different possible angles – talked to some of the neighbours, people involved in the housing development, others too who we found might have possible links to Leanne for various reasons. And we've found out some... well, some fairly unsavoury stuff.'

She hesitated, decided not to enter into a more detailed discussion about the strip club with this young boy, and continued.

'But it's nothing that we can directly link to Leanne and that night on the bridge. We do get the feeling that some people aren't telling us everything, and some have pretty much refused to speak to us at all. But unless they do, well, we have nothing, Liam. Maybe the police could get further, make people talk, if you really wanted...?'

He was shaking his head violently.

'No! I can't go to the police. I told you before, that's why I didn't say anything at the time, or at the inquest. I'm a kid, they won't listen to me, will they? And I can't upset Mum any more. That's why I asked you, Cora. I thought a reporter...'

His voice tailed off and Cora could see that his eyes were suddenly wet. He wiped them viciously with the backs of his hands.

'Oh Liam, I'm so sorry. I just don't know what else...'

'It's OK. Sorry, I'm being a baby. I really appreciate

213

you trying. It's just…'

His voice cracked. He took a gulp of air and tried again.

'It's just that whatever you say, or the coroner, or the police, or anyone, I know my sister wouldn't have gone to that bridge that night and jumped off it. I don't understand the suicide note. But she wouldn't have done that, not on her own. She wouldn't have left me here, not like that. She just wouldn't. Somebody made her do it, they must have done. So what do I do now, Cora? What do I do now?'

After Cora had left, still apologising and promising to keep in touch, Liam sank back onto his chair and let the tears run freely down his cheeks. The thought of the TV reporter possibly solving the mystery surrounding Leanne's death had been the only thing keeping him going over the past few weeks, and now that hope was gone. What now? He had nobody now, nobody to help him and nobody to rely on. He sat up, fists clenching as a sudden rush of anger replaced the grief. Where was his mother? He was only fifteen, he needed her. He needed food in the fridge, and a warm room to do his homework in, and he needed *his mother*. He shivered as the rage subsided as quickly as it had arrived. He knew she'd recover, one day. She was just still reeling, wasn't she? They both were. She'd be home tonight, of course she would be. He didn't know what time. It would be late, he was fairly sure of that. But she'd come home. She'd never left him alone at night, not all night anyway. And when she did eventually appear, he'd look after her, like he always did. Protect her. His mind flashed back to the night Leanne died, but immediately he shook his head violently, rubbing his

214

eyes hard as if to break up the images. No. NO. Don't think about it. It was just the two of them now. There was no point in thinking about it. Life just had to go on.

'I miss you, Leanne,' he whispered.

29

'Helen Leeson is one of the single mothers affected by the nursery's sudden closure, and she's been kind enough to invite us into her home this morning to discuss what it will mean for her, and others in her position…'

Still talking, Cora edged her way from the narrow hallway of the flat and in through the kitchen door, Nathan just feet away from her, camera on his shoulder. Behind him, Rodney was awkwardly manoeuvring his boom pole through the doorway. It was twenty past seven on Monday morning, and they were broadcasting live from Peterborough, where on Friday a large children's day-care centre had suddenly announced its immediate closure, plunging the parents who relied on it into chaos as they realised they'd have nowhere to leave their offspring when they went to work on Monday.

The story had tied in beautifully with a piece Morning Live was running that day about lone parents and the various problems they faced, hence Sam's joy when single mum Helen had contacted the news desk to ask if the show could cover her plight. A mum of a three-year-old son and a two-year-old daughter, and with every other nursery in town full, she was now panicking about having to give up her job in a local hair salon unless she could find alternative childcare almost immediately.

Live on air, Cora was now chatting to Helen at the kitchen table, the woman giving succinct, intelligent answers to all her questions, the children playing quietly on the floor at their feet with a pile of toy cars. It was going rather well, Cora thought happily, as she heard the 'one minute' count in her earpiece from the director in London. The morning hadn't started quite so calmly – *both* of Rodney's personal radio microphones, the ones Cora and Helen were supposed to be wearing, had failed during their rehearsal earlier and, with no time for him to work out what had gone wrong, he'd decided to use the boom pole for the live broadcast instead. Normally used for big groups of people or in more spacious locations, it wasn't ideal in such cramped surroundings – angling the long pole, which had the microphone mounted on its end, so that both women could be clearly heard was tricky in the small kitchen, but Rodney was a pro, despite the distraction of the two small children who now seemed to be edging closer and closer to him as their car game spread across the floor. Cora had just launched into her final question when she became aware that Rodney's boom pole had started to swing somewhat erratically over her head. Glancing back at him as Helen began her reply, Cora noted with some amusement that the oldest child was now sitting right in between the soundman's legs, zooming a small red tractor up and down his right calf and making 'Brum! Brum!' noises. The second child, clearly very taken with her brother's antics, grabbed Rodney's left trouser leg – he was wearing a fetching pair of what could only be described as baggy tan slacks today - and pulled herself up, then began to drive the blue sports car she was clutching up and down his thigh. Clearly trying to steady his pole without treading on either child, Rodney leaned forwards, but as he did so the little boy looked up and, aping his sister, grabbed hold of the soundman's other trouser leg and hauled himself up from the floor, giggling. Thrown off balance, Rodney swayed on his feet. The boom pole swung violently to the left and there was a

217

sudden loud CRACK, followed by what sounded like a pile of plates being dropped onto the floor. Mid-answer, Helen's head whipped round, and her eyes widened.

'I, errrm, gosh, sorry. Could you repeat that?' she stammered, eyes flicking again to where the noise had come from.

What on earth…? Cora quickly repeated the question, listened to Helen's answer and wrapped up the interview. Once the director had given them the all-clear, she turned to see Nathan doubled up in silent laughter, tears rolling down his cheeks. Rodney, the two children still driving their vehicles up and down his legs, was ashen-faced. On the floor next to the kitchen counter were at least three ceramic wall tiles, smashed to pieces, the gap where they had been on the wall moments earlier clearly visible. From the satellite truck parked outside, Scott's voice suddenly boomed in Cora's earpiece.

'OK, what the HELL was that noise?'

'Tell you in a minute,' she hissed. Then she turned to Helen, who was staring open-mouthed at the damage to her wall. Before she could speak, Rodney did.

'Helen, I'm *so* sorry. The children… I lost my balance, and the pole…'

Nathan snorted, and Rodney glared at him. Sighing, Cora stood up and took charge.

'Nathan, shut up. Rodney, it was an accident, it wasn't your fault. Helen, massive apologies. This hardly ever happens, but we're insured for damage like this, OK? The tiles will be fixed. Is that alright? We're really, really sorry.'

Helen, who seemed to have regained her composure, nodded and smiled.

'Sure. I never really liked those tiles, to be honest. And the kids shouldn't have been doing that anyway. Kyle,

Annabel! Leave that poor man alone!'

She spoke sharply, and the children looked at each other and sank back onto the floor again, casting sideways glances at their mother as they quietly resumed their game.

'Right, I'll clear up in here. You three go and sit down next door and I'll bring you some tea. We're on again in an hour, right? And tell your friend outside to come in too.'

'We're on again at 8.20, yes. And thank you, Helen, for being so understanding. Tea would be great. Come on, guys.'

Gratefully, the three of them made their way to the small lounge at the front of the flat, and closed the door. Nathan, still grinning widely, punched Rodney on the shoulder.

'Excellent boom work, mate. Smashing, in fact.'

'Oh, shut up. My heart's still in my mouth,' said Rodney, and sank down on the sofa. 'How awful. Lucky she was so nice about it.'

'Well, to be fair it *was* her two little brats' fault,' said Nathan. 'Forget it, Rodders. Sorry for laughing so much. It was bloody funny to watch.'

'Yeah, yeah.' Rodney exhaled, as the door opened and Scott marched in.

'Well? What happened?'

They explained and the engineer guffawed with laughter.

'Bit of a bum in a china shop moment, eh Rodders? Good start to the week.'

He sniggered again, then looked from one to the other. They were all grinning.

'What?'

'*Bull* in a china shop, Scott. Bull. You know, as in

219

male cow,' said Nathan.

'Huh? Don't be stupid. What would a bull be doing in a shop?'

'Well, what would a bum be doing there? On its own? Detached from its body? Which makes more sense, Scott, bum or bull?'

Scott rolled his eyes. 'Not that sort of bum. Not an *arse*. A *bum*. As in, you know, a down and out, a tramp. Goes into the china shop, knocks plates and stuff off shelves...'

Nathan groaned theatrically, then sighed. 'OK. I give up. Bum in a china shop. Fine.'

Scott smiled, a satisfied expression on his face. Cora and Rodney, who'd been listening to the exchange with great amusement, began to laugh, just as Helen pushed the door open, carrying a tray of mugs.

'Here you go,' she said. 'Tiles all swept up and bacon under the grill. Sandwiches to follow. I'll sit in the kitchen with the two little monsters, keep them out of your hair. Help yourselves to milk and sugar, it's already on the table, look.'

'Helen, you're a wonder. Thanks so much,' said Cora. The woman smiled and left the room, and they all helped themselves. Rodney took a sip from his mug and leaned back in his chair with a sigh.

'Two little monsters is right. Haven't had that much hassle with a kid since Aberdeen and the baby simulator, remember, Cora?'

'How could I forget?' Cora laughed, and the others all grinned. That little incident had been about three years ago, when she, Nathan and Rodney had been sent to Scotland to cover a story about an infant simulator – an extremely realistic, 'robot' baby doll which responded just like a real child and had been credited with dramatically reducing teenage pregnancies in one deprived area where it had been used in schools to teach students about the harsh realities of parenthood. The school they were filming at was about to lend the doll to a London school for a term, and asked Cora and the boys if they would mind carrying it back to the capital with them, to save on courier charges. They had happily agreed, and it wasn't until they arrived at Aberdeen airport to fly back to Heathrow that things had started to go a little awry.

Having travelled up on a day return ticket and with hand luggage only, Cora had simply dumped the baby doll onto the conveyor belt at security along with her handbag, chatting to Nathan and Rodney as she did so. Suddenly, she jumped in fright as somebody nearby bellowed 'NOOOOOOO!', and then, to her bemusement, a burly security guard pushed past her, dived towards the slowly moving belt and grabbed the doll, just before it passed under the X-ray machine.

'Madam! Your baby… why would you put your *baby* on the conveyor belt? No, no, no!' the man gasped, horror on his face. Astounded, Cora simply pointed at the doll he was now cradling protectively in his arms.

'Ermmm… it's not real,' she said, apologetically. 'It's… well, it's a sort of robot. A pretend baby…?'

The man's face had been a picture, as had the air stewards' faces shortly afterwards, when Cora had casually tossed the 'baby' into the overhead locker on the aeroplane, precipitating a similarly shocked response. Once everyone had recovered from their fright, the doll had ended up being given its own seat and treated like a VIP passenger by the amused cabin crew, and Cora and the boys had yet another excellent story to add to their growing list of weird and wonderful tales of life at *Morning Live*.

'Sandwiches! Anyone need more tea?'

Helen was back, this time with a plate full of warm bacon sandwiches, which they fell on hungrily. As they ate, Cora's mind drifted back to yesterday. This morning had been a welcome distraction, but she was still feeling pretty dreadful about the encounter with Liam. He'd looked so devastated, and even though she knew that realistically there was nothing more she could do to help him, she couldn't shake off this feeling of sadness and guilt. Had she given up too easily? *Was* there something fishy about Leanne's death, something they'd missed? Or was it all just in the imagination of a grieving teenager, who didn't want to admit that his sister had taken her own life?

She suddenly remembered a thought that had struck her last night, when she'd been lying in bed, unable to sleep and going over and over everything in her mind for the hundredth time. She didn't know if it would be of any use whatsoever, but she'd thought about it again as she'd driven to Peterborough in the early hours, her mind wandering as it always did on her long drives, and she'd convinced herself it was worth a try.

'I know we'd pretty much decided to leave all this alone now, but I want to look at just one more thing. I just feel so... so low about it,' she said, as she filled the boys in on what had happened with Liam. 'Like we – well, like *I*, really – have given up too easily. That poor boy...'

Nathan leaned forwards in his seat.

'Look, we've talked about this. You, and all of us – we've done more than enough. We've investigated what always seemed like a cut and dried case of suicide, and come up with zero evidence it was anything else. Yes, we've encountered some fairly strange and unpleasant people, and yes, there's definitely a news story in all this,

222

or there would be if we could get anyone to actually talk to us on the record. But have we come across anything that makes Leanne's death seem suspicious? I don't think so, Cora. We've tried, and you more than anyone. Let it go now. It was a horrible experience for you, and an absolute tragedy for the poor girl and her family. But it's time to move on. Harsh though this may sound, you owe Leanne nothing, Cora. You'd never even met her. It wasn't your fault she died where she did, right in front of you. It was just a terrible, tragic coincidence.'

Cora looked at him for a moment, then down at her tea cup, biting her bottom lip.

He sighed. 'Go on then. Let's hear it. What's this last thing you want to try?'

She lifted her head and looked back at her cameraman.

'OK. Look, it's probably pointless, but it's just an idea, so hear me out. Remember that boy, Josh? The one with the drone?'

Nathan nodded. 'Yep. Nice kid.'

'Well, he told us he was using it to shoot footage of the housing development, didn't he? To make his time lapse video and then try to sell it to Greythorpe when it's all done. I was just wondering – would it be worth trying to have a look at his footage? To see if Leanne is in any of it?'

Rodney frowned. 'Why would Leanne be in any of it?'

'Well, we know she visited the site office, and that things got a bit heated and she was pretty much turfed out, don't we? I mean, I know the footage will only be of the exteriors, but what if it shows her being forcibly ejected from the office? Or maybe there was an altercation outside, possibly? If there was any violence shown towards her, maybe we could show the footage to the police, and…'

Her voice tailed off. Now that she was saying it out loud, it sounded ridiculous. She looked around the room, at the three faces wearing expressions ranging from doubtful to downright sceptical. Nathan was the first to speak.

'Seriously? I mean, first, even if Leanne did have a serious argument with someone at the site, even if it was more than just "heated", as Liam put it, that doesn't mean they had anything to do with her death, does it? She was leading a protest against the developers, things were bound to get a bit intense if she visited them. And second, what are the chances of Josh sending his drone up at the exact time when Leanne was visiting? He's at school all day, isn't he? There are hours and hours when he's not capturing any footage. It's a ridiculously long shot, Cora.'

She groaned, put her cup down on the coffee table and covered her face with her hands.

'I know, I know,' she said, through her fingers. 'But can we just try? Just a quick look? And then I'll stop, I promise. We can forget about the whole thing. Please?'

She looked up, gazing imploringly at Nathan. He sighed and shook his head.

'Oh, bloody hell, you know I can't resist when you do the puppy dog eyes thing. Fine. I'll come with you and we'll take a look, *if* we can find Josh and *if* he'll let us. We don't even know where he lives, for goodness' sake. And then that's it, OK?'

She smiled. 'Thank you! I'll ask Sam if we can hold off on reporting Randall and the club and all that stuff to the police until we've done it. Love you, Nath.'

She blew him a kiss and he raised his eyebrows.

'Yeah, yeah.'

'Well, I think you're both mad,' said Scott. 'Bloody waste of time. Accept it, Cora. The story about that poor girl's death being suspicious is dead in the water. Might as well try to bring a pig back from the dead by giving the kiss of life to a sausage.'

They all laughed, and the little knot of tension that had been twisting Cora's stomach since she'd spoken to Liam suddenly loosened, just a little. Scott was probably, she feared, absolutely right, but they had done their best. They would do this one final little check, and then forget about it. It was only a week until Christmas, after all. She was determined that this Christmas, her first to be spent with Adam and Harry, would be the best ever. It was time to put this awful tragedy behind her, and move on.

30

'Aaaa-CHOO! Aaaaa-CHOOO!'

Cora took an exaggeratedly large step backwards as Nathan had what must have been at least his tenth sneezing fit of the day.

'Urgh, sorry Cora. I'm definitely coming down with something. I'm going straight home to bed after this. Come on, he *must* be out in the street – look, there's the drone again!'

'Well, walk ahead of me then. I don't want your germs, not with Christmas almost here.' Cora followed as Nathan led the way down Thornton Street where they'd parked their cars near the café, and round the corner into Flower Street. As luck would have it, they'd been assigned to a story in Cardiff this morning, so Cora and Nathan had seized the chance to head to Bristol this afternoon, seeing as it was pretty much on their way home. And luck had continued to favour them, their concerns about having no idea where the boy with the drone lived abating when Nathan spotted the little machine buzzing overhead as soon as they'd reached the neighbourhood. As they rounded the corner, Nathan stopped walking abruptly and pointed up the road.

'There he is. Got your story straight?'

'Yep. Come on, let's do this.'

Josh was alone this time, his face screwed up in concentration as he manoeuvred his drone back down the street towards him from where it had been flying over the new housing development. When Cora and Nathan approached he glanced at them, returned his attention to his toy and landed it neatly at his feet, then turned back and grinned.

'Hello!'

'Hi, Josh, remember us? How's the drone, any good footage?'

'Course I do! Yeah, not bad. I've started editing the early stuff, it looks OK!'

'Great!' Nathan paused. 'Josh, we were wondering if you might be able to do us a favour? Cora, can you explain?'

Josh looked expectantly at her. 'I'll help if I can. Is it to do with my drone?'

'It is, actually,' Cora said. 'Well, more to do with the pictures you're shooting. Did you know Leanne Brimley? She lived at number one, but she... she sadly died recently.'

Josh ran his hands through his messy blond hair and nodded. 'Yeah, I knew her a bit. I know her brother a bit better, Liam? He's older though, so we don't really hang out. She killed herself, Leanne, didn't she? Jumped off that Clarton Bridge?'

Cora cleared her throat. 'Well, yes. You see, we're trying to put together a piece about her final days – you know she was active in the community, protesting about the housing development and so on?'

Josh shrugged, a 'so what' expression on his face.

'Well, we suddenly thought you might have some footage, with her in it. Maybe visiting the development? We might be able to use it in our report. We'd pay you, of course, if it was broadcast. Is there any chance we could take a look?'

Josh looked doubtful.

'Well, I s'pose so. I don't know if there are many

227

people in it really, I don't look closely at it until I start editing. Haven't seen her in any so far, I don't think. There's an awful lot of footage too. I shoot some nearly every day after school, and more at weekends. But yeah, if you have time to look, I don't mind. Want to come now? My mum and dad won't be home from work yet but they won't care.'

'That would be wonderful, thank you so much, Josh. Do you live nearby?'

Cora smiled gratefully at the boy, who grinned back, then ducked down to scoop up the drone from the pavement.

'Just down there, number twelve,' he said. 'Come on.'

Five minutes later they were all settled in front of Josh's laptop at the dining room table. Number twelve turned out to be an immaculately clean, tastefully decorated family home, the two main downstairs rooms having at some point been knocked into one large sitting/dining room. French windows opened onto a small, paved rear courtyard, dotted with architectural plants in tall, graceful pots. Fairy lights twinkled on a white, glittery fake Christmas tree which sat in the front window, and various festive candles and figurines adorned the mantelpiece and side tables.

'Just give me a minute... OK, I've saved everything in this folder as I've gone along. It's all in date order, a separate file for every day, so I don't get mixed up. So, where do you want to start? My birthday was the first of November and I started shooting the next day, the second. The first few days are just practice stuff though, mainly of the empty building site, because they didn't start building until the seventh.'

Josh waved a hand at his screen.

'Very, very organised. I'm impressed,' said Nathan,

and the boy beamed.

'Very organised indeed. But what that means is you didn't start filming until just a few days before Leanne died, so that narrows it down a lot. Probably not much hope of her being in your footage after all,' Cora said. She sighed.

'Oh well, let's have a look anyway. Leanne died on the seventh, didn't she? I didn't realise that was the same day building started. So I suppose it makes sense to start there, and work backwards. Can we do that?'

'Course.'

Josh clicked on the file marked *7th November* and the footage started to play, a little wobbly at first, the drone clearly taking off and doing some slightly erratic loops before steadying. Suddenly there was a perfectly clear aerial image of Flower Street, the light a little dim but cars and houses clearly visible.

'Wow. I didn't expect such good pictures,' Cora said. 'Is this legal, by the way? Do you know, Nathan?'

He nodded. 'I'm thinking of getting one for work. Would be really handy in floods and such like, when we struggle to get access. You just have to keep it in sight, and under four hundred feet in altitude if I remember correctly. Supposed to keep it a certain distance away from people and vehicles too, but it looks like you've followed all those rules, Josh.'

The boy nodded.

'There's a Drone Code. It's like the Highway Code, but for drones?' he said. 'My uncle went through it all with me when he gave it to me. Didn't want me getting in trouble with it. You can't fly near airports, and it's fifty metres from people and stuff. You get used to it pretty quick.'

Cora was watching the screen closely, fascinated by

the view as the little drone flew down the street and over the fence surrounding the housing development.

'This is brilliant, Josh,' she said. 'And you're right, Nath. This would be fantastic for work. Do you think Betsy would fork out for one?'

'Hope so. Really is good quality, isn't it?'

Josh was beaming again, clearly delighted.

'It'll be better in the summer, when it's brighter. I've been shooting after school but there's not much light left this time of year. It's still not bad though. There's a time code too, and the date, see?'

He pointed to the bottom left of the screen, as the pictures wobbled again, the drone taking a sharp left and dropping a little lower in the sky.

'Oh, I might be breaking the Drone Code a bit there. Wanted to get a closer shot of some of the diggers and stuff. They look wicked, all lined up like that, don't they? You can see the workers too, they stand out quite well in their yellow coats, even though it was starting to get dark around then.'

'And there's the site office,' said Cora. Now that the drone was flying closer to the ground, the pictures were even clearer, despite the increasingly low light levels. She peered at the screen, watching the builders in their luminous vests crossing the yard in front of the office, then another person entered the shot, walking quickly towards the building. Cora frowned, then gasped.

'Josh! Can you slow this down, or zoom in or anything?'

He nodded. 'Both. What bit?'

Cora pointed at the screen. 'There. That person. Can you get me a better image?'

'Cora? What is it?' Nathan frowned and pulled his chair closer to the table, then sneezed violently.

'I'm not sure... hang on. And use a tissue Nathan, *please*. Josh and I do *not* want your cold, do we, Josh?' said Cora, sounding exasperated.

'Not really, thanks!'

Josh laughed, and reached for his keyboard, and Cora stared at the screen as he hit some keys. The image on the screen grew larger and slowed, and she watched, her heart suddenly pounding, as the figure became clearer, walking towards the site office, a flash of red hair and a dark coat. The woman – and Cora was sure now that it *was* a woman – paused for a second as if knocking on the door, then vanished inside.

'Wow. Wow.' Cora's breath was ragged. 'Can we zoom on, see her coming out again?' she asked.

Josh nodded, but seconds later groaned. 'Oh, sorry. It ends a minute later, look. I was running out of battery and I was scared I wouldn't get it back over the fence, if I remember right. The charge only lasts about twenty minutes, you see...'

'Don't worry, don't worry. Just rewind, let me see that bit again.'

Cora was chewing anxiously on a nail, eyes glued to the screen as the footage was replayed. When the figure reached the door of the office she yelled 'STOP!' Both Josh and Nathan jumped.

'Cora, for God's sake. What is it? Is that her? Is that Leanne?' It was Nathan's turn to sound exasperated.

'Sorry.' She leaned forwards, scrutinising the picture. The long reddish-brown hair, the dark coat ...it was. It *was* her, she knew it was. The image of the dead girl slumped on the road flashed into her mind. This might mean absolutely nothing. But then again, it might mean everything.

'That's Leanne Brimley,' she said. 'I'd bet any money

231

on it. That's her. And the time is, what? Four sixteen in the afternoon. Four sixteen on Thursday the seventh of November, and she's alive and well and at the site office of Randall Greythorpe Developments.'

'And? So?' Nathan was frowning again. Cora took a deep breath.

'And almost exactly two hours later, she was dead.'

31

Adam poked his cheese and pickle sandwich with the end of his pen, then pushed the plate aside. He wasn't particularly hungry after the large bowl of porridge he'd devoured for breakfast just a few hours ago; he'd only wandered down to the canteen for the sandwich to ease the boredom of wading through the enormous stack of paperwork on his desk. He would probably have eaten the sandwich anyway though, but the phone call he'd just had from Cora had dampened what little appetite he had. He loved his girlfriend with all his heart, and he tried to support her in everything she did, but this slightly annoying habit of... well, of getting *involved* with things, could be a tad frustrating at times. He'd thought she was about to abandon her latest quest, having told him just the other day that she'd now come to the conclusion that there was nothing in it, and now suddenly she was all fired up again.

The first call had come last night, when she'd phoned him in a state of some excitement, buzzing about something she'd seen on some kid's drone camera footage which had made her suspicious about Leanne Brimley's death all over again.

'I'm not jumping to any wild conclusions, honestly Adam. I'm trying to keep a very open mind about this. But don't you think it's a little bit weird that Leanne visited Randall Greythorpe's office the very next day after she'd heard he'd given up trying to make her sell her home, looking perfectly normal, and that a couple of hours later she was dead?' she had said.

Adam had replied wearily. 'Not particularly. It was suicide, Cora. Lots of people who commit suicide have seemingly completely normal days before they do it, and seem totally fine to everyone around them. That's why it often comes as such a terrible shock to their friends and families. You don't know what goes on in people's heads, Cora. What awful, private battles they're facing.'

'I know. I know that. And I know there was a suicide note. But why kill herself then, that day? And what was she doing at the site office just a couple of hours beforehand? She was really happy for the twenty-four hours before that, by all accounts, so something must have happened in that office, something bad. It *must* have. Something that resulted in her death. Come on Adam, don't you think it's odd? Or am I reading too much into it?'

'I think you might be, yes. Come on, darling. Put it to bed now. Please, for me?'

There'd been a pause, Cora silent on the other end of the line, then she'd sighed.

'Oh, OK. I suppose I'm going to have to leave it there, aren't I? But... well, I'd really love to go and see Greythorpe just one more time, Adam. He probably won't even see me, after our last visit. But I really, *really* want to ask him what she was doing there. I mean, what happened? Did he threaten her or something? Could he have frightened her into doing something as awful as leaping from the bridge?'

'Cora, he's hardly likely to tell you, even if something did happen, is he? Think about it. He's already told you not to come back. You'd be putting yourself in a potentially very confrontational situation, and what are you going to get out of it? Absolutely nothing, that's what. Please, don't do it. It's pointless.'

Phone in one hand, Adam ran his other across his blond crop of hair in mild frustration.

'Oh, and you really should have talked to Avon Police by now about what you think's going on at that club, too. Why the hold-up?' he asked.

'We are going to, I promise. I just need to talk to Sam about this footage of Leanne at the site office and get her take on it first. I'll do that as soon as I can, first thing tomorrow. I'll let you know what she says, OK? I love you. Can't wait to see you on Friday.'

He'd told her he loved her too and they'd ended the call. But this morning, she'd phoned again to tell him she'd chatted to Sam and the senior producer had agreed that she should attempt to tie up this final loose end, and go back and ask Greythorpe about the footage.

'She agrees with *you* really, Adam. She's warned me to be very careful, given how angry he was last time we met. And she also thinks he won't tell me anything, even if there's something to tell. But she thinks we should do it anyway. And then we'll stop. None of this is going to bring Leanne back, and as I keep saying, at least I've tried, haven't I? I just don't think there's anything else I can do after this. Oh, and don't worry, Nathan's coming with me. We're going to go after work on Friday afternoon. Sam said she'll do her best not to send us too far away for the show that day.'

Relieved that at least she wasn't going alone, Adam had grudgingly told his girlfriend to 'go ahead then, but be careful – don't antagonise him!' Now, he glared at the sandwich, the edges of which were already starting to curl, then cast his eyes around the room. It was fairly quiet today, just a few officers dotted around, heads down at their desks or on the phone. In the corner next to the

235

photocopier, the sad little artificial Christmas tree that had been dragged out of storage annually for at least the past decade drooped dejectedly, its spindly branches bending under the weight of a couple of ancient cracked baubles, a Christmas cracker somebody had saved from their festive drinks do a few days ago and, incongruously, a couple of packets of Maltesers, balancing precariously in the faded foliage. He stared at it for a moment, then shrugged and turned his thoughts back to Cora. Sometimes, he wished he had a partner who was a little bit less… actually, no, that wasn't true, was it? He adored Cora Baxter. He'd never met anyone quite like her – funny, clever, beautiful, headstrong, determined and unswervingly loyal. He knew that this mission she was on was simply the result of her incredibly kind-hearted and caring nature, and he felt bad for berating her so much about it. The fact that the girl had died through absolutely no fault of Cora's was irrelevant to her. She *felt* responsible in some way, and he knew he simply had to let her get on with it until, in her mind, that responsibility had been absolved. He hoped that would happen by Friday, he suddenly thought with a wry smile – it would certainly make for a much more relaxed weekend. He'd been looking forward to it for ages, fervently hoping that there wouldn't be an urgent case suddenly needing his attention and keeping him in London. Friday would be the twentieth of December, the last weekend before Christmas, and he and Cora were due to spend it in Cheltenham, celebrating a "mini Christmas" with Rosie, Nicole and their families. He'd then return to London, picking up Harry from his mum's in Swindon on the way, and wait for Cora to join them on Tuesday, after *Morning Live*'s Christmas Eve show. Their first Christmas together, just the three of them. A warm glow crept over Adam as he envisaged waking up on Christmas morning, Harry's shrieks of excitement, a champagne breakfast and then Cora's face when he gave her the very special gift he'd picked out for her. Would she like it? The warm glow was suddenly replaced by a little flutter of nerves. Bloody hell, he hoped so.

32

It was snowing lightly on Friday morning, Cora shivering despite her full set of thermal underwear, two jumpers and thick down jacket as she clambered out of her car in the lay-by just down the road from the M5 motorway bridge. It was shortly after 5 a.m. and they were in Somerset - Sam being true to her word and assigning them to a story as close as possible to Bristol this morning – to cover that annual story beloved of news desks everywhere: the great Christmas getaway. With just days until the festive season proper, today would be one of the busiest of the year on the UK's roads, and the motorway bridge should give them a bird's eye view as traffic started to build through the morning.

'Morning! Cold enough for you?'

Climbing out of his own car a little further down the lay-by Rodney, face barely visible inside the huge, fur-trimmed hood of his floral parka, waved a gloved hand. Cora headed towards him, grinning. Nothing about Rodney's attire particularly fazed her any more, although she did frequently marvel at the way the soundman seemed to be able to hunt down garments she couldn't even imagine existed. A *floral* parka? Really? Although it was actually rather pretty, she thought as she got closer. She wouldn't mind it herself.

'Nice coat, Rodders,' she said.

'NICE COAT? Are you drunk, Cora? It looks like he's gone mental in a flower bed. Have fun rolling around, did you, Rodders? Lots of crap stuck to you though. Want me to brush it off?'

Nathan appeared out of the darkness and launched himself at Rodney, who yelled and attempted to get the cameraman in a headlock.

'Get off me, Nathan! It's five a.m. and I haven't even had my coffee yet. I can't fight you without coffee… urgh, stop it…'

Cora rolled her eyes, shivered again and wandered across the snowy road, looking for the best live position. Behind her, the boys were still jostling each other like puppies let out to play. She squinted into the early morning gloom, blinking as snowflakes settled on her eyelashes. There, that would do. Right at the far end of the bridge the road rose slightly, with a flat grassy verge which would be a perfect spot to set up the camera. She turned and walked back to the lay-by.

'You two finished yet? We'll do it there, OK? Look, Nathan.'

Nathan, who had stopped attacking Rodney, was now nudging him on the arm instead, and grinning.

'What?' said Cora.

'Nothing really – it's just that you'd better not go wandering off this morning – against the rules here, apparently. Make sure one of us comes with you, OK?'

Nathan grinned widely. Rodney, who seemed to be peering at something just past where Cora was standing, suddenly snorted with laughter.

'What are you going on about now?' Cora, puzzled, turned to look. In the blackness she could just make out two signs. The first said NO PICNICS, and the second…

'Oh, very funny. Hilarious. "BICYCLES MUST NOT BE LEFT UNATTENDED". Me? I'm a one-man woman now, as well you know. Honestly, what is wrong with you two this morning?'

But she couldn't help laughing. No matter how much they all might moan about their horribly early call-out times, the cold, the long hours, the unceasing weariness, this was what kept them doing this job year after long year. The banter, the comradeship, the fun. She loved her job, and she loved her crew. Still smiling, she headed for the truck to see Scott, hoping he'd have the kettle on.

It wasn't until they were sipping their third cup of the morning, in their down time between the seven and eight o'clock bulletins, that Cora remembered the last time she'd covered a story on a motorway bridge. It had been a couple of years ago, when a teenage boy had survived, but suffered serious injuries, after a fall from a bridge over the M40.

'Can't believe I didn't remember that until now,' she said, cupping her hands around her mug to warm them. The snow had stopped falling now, the world outside the truck covered in a delicate white blanket.

'Yeah, I'd forgotten that too. Near Junction Four, wasn't it? He was lucky to be alive. AAA-CHOO!'

Nathan sneezed violently, sniffed loudly and reached into his coat pocket for yet another tissue. Despite his energetic start to the day, he didn't look very well, Cora thought, looking at his red-rimmed eyes and pale face.

'You OK, Nath? Think that cold's getting a grip.'

He sniffed again and nodded morosely.

'Think it is. I feel pretty shitty, actually. Another biccie might help though.'

He reached for another chocolate digestive from the packet on the shelf that ran along the back wall under Scott's racks of monitors and control panels.

'Anyone else?' he asked.

'No, thanks,' said Cora, and the others shook their heads, Scott engrossed in his crossword, Rodney scanning

Twitter for the latest news. Nathan took a small bite of the biscuit and then put it down on the shelf.

'Actually, I'm not really hungry,' he said.

'Bloody hell, mate. You *must* be ill,' said Scott, looking up from his crossword.

Cora made up her mind. 'Nathan, you need to go straight home to bed when we're cleared from here, OK? I know you said you'd come back to Bristol with me to see Greythorpe but you really don't need to, I can easily do it on my own. I've got the copy of the drone footage anyway, and you're going to ruin your Christmas if you keep pushing yourself like this. Go home, rest. OK?'

Nathan hesitated for a moment, then coughed and nodded.

'OK. If you're sure. They probably won't even let you into the office after what happened last time, so I don't think you can get yourself into *too* much trouble. And I do feel pretty ropey. An afternoon on the sofa is quite appealing, if I'm honest. Thanks, Cora.'

Cora was half-wishing she'd opted for an afternoon on the sofa herself by the time she finally parked her car outside Randall Greythorpe Developments later that day. After breakfast with the boys, she'd decided to do some quick last-minute Christmas shopping at Cribbs Causeway on the way back to Bristol, a decision she was now deeply regretting. Arriving at the shopping centre before midday, she'd spent a stressful couple of hours battling crowds and queues before returning to her car laden with shopping bags. Aiming to be at the housing development office well before three, she'd headed for the M5 only to suddenly be faced with stationary traffic, backed up on the approach to and on the motorway itself, following a three-vehicle accident. With no obvious sensible detour, the journey ended up taking her an hour and a half, and it was now almost 4 p.m., the sky already nearly dark. Cursing under her breath, and now just wanting to get this over with as quickly as possible so she could get home in time to greet Adam and get ready for her weekend with the gang, Cora marched through the gate on Flower Street and headed for the site office.

She had deliberately not made an appointment this time, thinking it might be more prudent to just turn up and hope she could charm her way in. Reaching the door, she took a deep breath and tapped on it with her knuckles, paused for a moment and then pushed it open. Inside, John Smith was sitting behind his desk, brow furrowed in concentration as he tapped on his computer keyboard. As she walked in, he looked up, and his eyes widened.

'Cora! What… what are you doing here?'

Cora crossed the room and stood in front of his desk, smiling in what she hoped was a reassuring manner.

'John, I'm so sorry to barge in unannounced like this, but I was just passing and, well, I have one more question for Randall…'

John half-rose from his seat, mouth opening as if he was about to speak, but Cora kept talking, raising a conciliatory hand.

'I know, I know, he probably isn't going to be too keen to talk to me. But this is absolutely the last time, I promise you. There's just something I want to show him, to get his view on… is he here?'

John was on his feet now, and shaking his head.

'Cora, I'm sorry, he's not. He left at lunchtime. He's headed to friends in London for Christmas and he wanted to miss the worst of the traffic. And to be honest, I don't think he *would* see you, even if he was here. Is it anything I could help with, do you think?'

Cora thought for a moment. John would probably have

been here, wouldn't he, when Leanne came to see Randall? And, no doubt, heard or even witnessed any altercation that might have taken place. It was worth a try. She nodded.

'It might be, yes. Thanks, John. Let me explain.'

33

'Is this about Midnight Diamonds again? Because honestly, Randall really is just an investor. He has nothing to do with the daily running…'

'No, no it's not. It's about Leanne Brimley.'

John, who had been shuffling papers on his desk, looked up sharply.

'Lea… Leanne Brimley? What about her?'

Cora, now sitting in a swivel chair on the other side of the desk, paused for a moment, wondering how much to say. Oh, to hell with it, she thought.

'Look, I didn't mention this before, but we've been actively looking into her death. There've been some concerns, from her family and friends, that it might not have been as straightforward as the police and coroner seem to think. Not a simple suicide, I mean. There's a possibility that someone may have coerced her, or bullied her into jumping off that bridge…'

She stopped talking, aware that John was now looking at her with a horrified expression, his face flushing a violent red.

'Are you OK?' she said tentatively. He ran a hand across his short dark hair and cleared his throat.

'Fine, yes. I'm fine. But why? Why do you think it wasn't… wasn't suicide? And what has that got to do with us?'

Cora reached into her bag and pulled out the memory stick onto which she'd copied the drone footage of Leanne at the site office.

'Well, for a few reasons really. I can't really go into it all, but I just wanted to ask you – well, ask Randall really – about this.'

She waved the stick at him.

'It's footage captured by a local kid, playing with a drone. It shows Leanne visiting this office late on the afternoon of the day she died. That was the seventh of November. It was the day after Randall told her that her fight was over, that he'd be going ahead with the smaller development and that he wouldn't be trying to buy her house anymore. Is there a diary you could check for me or something? It looks like Randall had a meeting with her that day, the seventh, for some reason. The thing is, a couple of hours later she was dead, so I was wondering...'

'No. No.' John stood up abruptly. 'Randall keeps his own diary. I don't... I don't remember if she was here or not. There are so many meetings, you know? Do you... do you want some tea?'

'Errrm... well, OK then. Thanks. Black is fine.'

'OK. Stay there, back in a minute.'

John rushed from the room, and Cora stared after him, her mind racing. Why was he so nervous? Something was definitely not right here. Something *must* have happened that day, and John clearly knew about it. But could she persuade him to tell her about it? He seemed to be incredibly loyal to his boss. Would he cover up something so serious though, if indeed Randall *was* somehow involved in what had happened to Leanne on the bridge? She desperately needed to find out what had happened between Leanne and Randall that afternoon. But how on earth was she going to get it out of John? Beg? Threaten to go to the police? She just wasn't sure what would work. She sighed, wishing Nathan had been able to come with her. From the kitchen area on the other side of the door

John had vanished through, she heard the clatter of cups. He'd be back in a minute, and she had no idea how to go about this. Thinking hard, she leaned forward and idly flipped through a few of the papers on the desk. Messages for Randall, mostly, it seemed.

Mr Carter called, wants to arr. meeting ASAP after Xmas...

Bricks order – need conf. quantity...

Bill Levens apolojises for cancelling conf. call, will rearr...

She sat back in her chair, deciding she'd simply have to ask John if Randall and Leanne had argued that day, and watch his reaction. But then what? Even if he admitted it, how could she prove...

Hang on. She grabbed the last note from the pile and read it again.

Bill Levens apolojises for cancelling conf. call, will rearr...

Apolojises? That was weird. That was the same misspelling as in Leanne's suicide note, wasn't it? She stared at the piece of paper, just as the door opened and John reappeared.

'Tea,' he said breezily. Cora turned to look at him, still clutching the note, and he frowned.

'What are you doing?' he asked.

34

'Errrm… sorry, I wasn't being nosy. I just spotted this note, and the spelling mistake…'

She paused, embarrassed to have been caught red-handed. John crossed the room and put her tea down on the desk.

'Oh, spelling! I'm rubbish at it,' he said. 'My handwriting is shocking and my spelling is even worse. What have I spelled wrongly? Randall's always pointing it out. I try, but I'm slightly dyslexic, you see. Show me?'

Cora held out the note.

'It's the word "apologise". It should be with a "g", not a "j"', she said.

He nodded, his lower lip jutting out.

'Ah, right. Always get that wrong. It sounds like it should be a "j" though, shouldn't it? Anyway, this Leanne Brimley thing. I don't remember if she was here or not that day, as I said. But even if she was, I don't see why it's important.'

He was cheerful again, his tone brisk and businesslike.

'Well, it may not be, of course. But I really just wanted to speak to Randall, maybe ask him how she was that day – her mood, you know? Or whether there was any sort of row, argument, anything like that?'

John laughed, settling himself back into his chair on the opposite side of the desk.

'Argument? Course not. Randall doesn't do arguments. Not with people like her, anyway. And what would they be arguing about? Her fight against the larger development was over, wasn't it? She was probably here saying thank you or something! But, as I said, I really can't remember, and as Randall's away now for Christmas…'

He shrugged, a 'what can I do?' expression on his face. Cora looked down at the note, which was still in her hand.

'OK. But John, this note. There's something a bit odd.' She hesitated. 'It's just that Leanne's suicide note had exactly the same mis-spelling of the word "apologise"…'

She paused again, unsure what it meant, if anything. John stared at her, then at the note. Had the colour suddenly drained from his face, or was she imagining it? He looked back at her again.

'Well, it's a common mistake to make, isn't it? I'm sure lots of people spell that word wrong. What are you suggesting, Cora? Why are you here?'

His voice sounded dry, croaky. He cleared his throat.

'What do you want, really?' he said and then, keeping his eyes fixed on her, he slowly opened his desk drawer, reaching a hand inside it.

She stood up, feeling uneasy. The mood in the room had changed, and she suddenly felt the urge to get out of there. Maybe this had been a mistake. He was definitely acting oddly.

'I'm just trying to get to the bottom of things,' she said. 'But as you say, Randall isn't here. Maybe I'll come back when he is? I'm sorry to have bothered you…'

John, his hand still inside the drawer, nodded slowly.

'The problem is, you have bothered me, Cora. You've bothered me a lot.'

His voice was calm now, measured.

'OK, well, I'm sorry. I'll… I'll go now, get out of your way.'

She bent down and grabbed her bag, then turned towards the door.

'Too late. Far too late now. You're not going anywhere, Cora.'

She turned back towards him, puzzled, then gasped in horror. John was standing up now, and in his hand was a gun. A gun, which was pointing straight at her.

35

Cora's entire body was trembling, her brain unable to process what was going on. As she'd frozen in shock at the sight of the gun, John had grabbed her arm, marched her to the corner of the room and pushed her roughly to the ground, ripping her handbag from her grasp and flinging it across the office, its contents scattering. Keeping the gun trained on her, he'd locked the front door and flicked the main lights off. Now, he sat at his desk, chair turned to face her, the gun pointing steadily at her. He was breathing heavily, and even though he was now just an outline in the semi-darkness, the room illuminated only by the lights in the yard outside and by one small desk lamp, Cora knew he was sweating. She could smell it, the sharp, acrid smell of perspiration and fear. She sat in silence, trying to calm herself enough to gather her thoughts. What the hell was going on here? *Did* Randall have something to do with Leanne's death, then? Was John covering for his boss? But it was John who had the spelling problem. Did *he* write the note, then? But it had been written on Leanne's own laptop, so how could he have…? Her brain was whirling, none of this making sense. Why was he holding her at gunpoint now though, if Leanne's death was a simple suicide? Why did he even *have* a gun? Nobody had guns in their desk drawer, did they? Not in real life. This was ridiculous. What on earth was she going to do? How was she going to get out of…?

'I never wanted to hurt anyone, you know.'

She jumped. His voice was quiet, sad. Talk to him, she

suddenly thought. Talk to him, and keep talking, while she figured out how she was going to get out of this mess.

'Who, John? Who didn't you want to hurt? Who are you talking about?' she asked gently.

'I always wanted to be an architect, you see.'

He carried on as if he hadn't heard her.

'I was always drawing, as a kid. Houses, tower blocks, huge extravagant mansions, all with big turrets and underground tunnels and secret rooms and... well, I was always sketching something, and it was always a building of some sort. I was so passionate about it. The only thing I was passionate about really, other than my sister. I really loved my sister. Still do. She's amazing.'

He stopped, shifting in his seat, but Cora could still see the outline of the gun, and it was still pointed in her direction.

'Your sister? Tell me about her.' She tried to keep her voice calm and soothing, but even she could hear the tremor as she spoke.

'Maisie. My little sister. She's a few years younger than me. I'm thirty-five and she's nearly thirty-one now. I'm dyslexic, but she had severe learning difficulties. *Has* severe learning difficulties. She's like a three-year-old, you know? But like the happiest three-year-old you could ever imagine. Still in nappies, even now. But never stops smiling and laughing, loves flowers and birds and being out in the garden, running on the beach, watching silly cartoons on the telly... she's amazing. Just being with her makes me happy...'

His voice tailed off.

'That's lovely. She sounds... she sounds great, John. So...what happened to your architecture? Did you try to pursue it?'

Cora had no idea where this conversation was going,

only that she had to keep him talking, keep him distracted. Surely a security guard or somebody would come by, eventually? There must be security guards around the clock, mustn't there, on a development like this?

'Oh, I got a place, amazingly. A place to study architecture. A really good one too, one of the best architecture schools there is. It was at Manchester Uni,' he said.

Manchester? Cora's heart started beating even faster. Leanne had written the name of the city on her map. So John had studied there too, as well as Randall? This must be the Manchester connection then. How had they missed it? But they hadn't been looking at John, had they? He hadn't seemed important...

'I was over the moon. I'd worked so hard to get there. But once the course started, well...' He sighed, a deep, trembling sigh.

'Well, I just couldn't keep up. I tried, so hard, but university was a whole different ball game from school, a whole new level. Worked myself into the ground, spent hours and hours in the library every night trying to get the work done, but my dyslexia... well, in the end, I had to quit. I failed my end of first year exams, and retook them, and failed again. And just when I was trying to decide whether it was worth repeating the year, my parents...'

He paused, and Cora heard a sniff. Was he crying?

'My parents died. Can you believe that? Not just one of them, and then the other a few months or years later. That's what normally happens, doesn't it, to most people? But not to me. Mine died at the same time, on the same day. Together, in a car crash. And of course Maisie lived at home, with them, so suddenly there was just us. Me and Maisie...'

His voice cracked.

'Oh, John, I'm so sorry. That's just *awful*.'

Despite the situation, Cora couldn't help but feel a pang of genuine sympathy for the man. What a dreadful thing to happen. He sniffed again, and the gun dipped as he took one hand from it to wipe his eyes, then steadied again.

'It was, yes,' he said. He took a deep breath.

'So, I had to quit uni then of course. No choice. I probably wasn't going to make it as an architect anyway, and suddenly I needed to get a job, needed to support us. Mum and Dad left us the house, and a bit of cash, but not enough to pay for full-time care for Maisie. And if I'd stayed home and looked after her myself, the money would soon have run out. So I found a home for her. That sounds horrible, but it's not. It's a really nice place, and she's really content there. It's in the countryside, but near Weston so she's got the seaside nearby too. Maisie loves the seaside. Always wants to go on donkey rides though, and doesn't really understand why she can't, why it wouldn't be fair on those little donkeys. She's an adult who thinks like a small child, as I said. But she's happy, where she is. I visit all the time, whenever I want, a few times a week sometimes, and I know she's really well cared for. But it costs, you know? So I did anything really... couple of jobs at a time, for years. Waiter, cleaner, receptionist, telephone sales... but I always kept up with what was going on in the property business, and in the architecture world. Randall had started to make a name for himself, and I started following his career closely. He went to Manchester too, you see, a few years ahead of me, and I often thought, if I wasn't dyslexic, maybe that could have been me. I could have had a career like his.'

There was a touch of bitterness in his voice now, along

with the sadness. Cora said nothing, listening carefully, watching him in the gloom. *Put the gun down*, she urged silently. *Put it down*.

John cleared his throat, his tone more cheerful all of a sudden.

'Anyway, I kept an eye on the job ads in the professional magazines. I thought, OK, maybe I'm not an architect, but maybe I can still work alongside them in some way. And then I saw the ad for this job. Randall Greythorpe was advertising for an assistant, a PA. I knew straight away that it was the perfect job for me, so when I got an interview I pulled out all the stops. I knew I could learn so much, I knew this was the closest I could ever get to the job of my dreams. And I bloody wowed him in the interview – I knew everything about everything and everyone in the business. He offered me the job on the spot, and I took it. Only problem was, I hadn't been a hundred per cent honest on my CV...'

He paused, adjusting his seating position again.

'Well, I'm sure you're not the only one. Lots of people do it, don't they? Almost everyone has a little white lie on their CV.' Cora kept her voice light, reassuring.

'Maybe. But you see, the job ad said you had to be a graduate. And I wasn't, was I? I'd left at the end of year one. But I wanted it so much, and I figured, who ever checks? New employers take up references from previous employers, don't they? But do they ever call your university to check you've really got a degree? Course they don't. So I put that I had a degree in architecture from Manchester, and of course I knew the place and lots of the same lecturers he knew and all that stuff, so he totally believed me. We had a bit of a laugh in the interview, chatting about one particular lecturer who had a really strange walk. It was the icing on the cake, I'm sure that's what swung it for me. That was the only lie I told though, the one about having a degree. I was honest about my dyslexia – told him that was why I'd eventually decided not to pursue a career in architecture myself, that my condition made it too difficult, that the degree had been struggle enough, but that working with him would be the perfect compromise. I got the job the same day. And we became... well, friends I suppose. Of a kind, anyway. He's a funny one, Randall. High-maintenance. But under it all, there's a good heart. And over the past few years I never lied to him about anything else, ever. He knows about Maisie, about my parents, everything. And he hates lies, hates dishonesty. I learned that about him pretty quickly. So I knew I'd have to keep that one secret, that lie I told him. It's even on our website, in the *"Meet the team"* section – there's a little bio of all the staff here, and mine says I have a degree from Manchester. That makes me feel bad sometimes, but... well, it's too late now, isn't it? And Randall would never have found out, because who would have told him? Until... until Leanne Brimley came along.'

He paused, and Cora's breath quickened. Leanne? Surely it wasn't *John* who...

'Ohhh, she was a clever one,' he continued. He was speaking more quickly now, a slightly frantic edge to his voice.

'She was determined to stop us building the bigger housing estate, and she was prepared to do anything to win. She was facing a lot of opposition and pressure from her neighbours, the ones who *did* want to sell up. Things were getting heavy, and she was getting tired of getting hassled, so she decided to play dirty. So one day I get a phone call, and she tells me she's been checking us out, both of us, me and Randall. She knows about the club, and Randall's connections with it. She says things aren't right there, and that she's going to go to the papers about it if he doesn't drop his plans for the bigger estate. I didn't know whether to believe her or not – I have no idea what goes on at Midnight Diamonds. But the worst thing was, she also said that she knew my CV was fake. She was really smug about it on the phone, said she bet Randall didn't know that, and she threatened to tell him if I didn't somehow make him give up his plans for the larger development. I felt sick, but I had no choice. I went to Randall and suggested he think again, that it would be terrible PR if we tried to bully this girl out of the home where her dad's ashes were scattered. I told him to imagine it in the papers, how it would tarnish his reputation. And, thank God, he'd been wavering anyway, and so he just agreed. He just agreed to drop his plans and go with the smaller estate. I couldn't believe it – I'd come so close to disaster and, just like that, I was safe again!'

He laughed, a high-pitched, manic giggle that made Cora shiver. I'm an idiot, she thought. We were all idiots. Why didn't *we* check out John's background? We didn't even think of doing that, we were so fixated on Randall. Leanne did a better job than us, a team of journalists. How could we have been so stupid?

John was speaking again, rocking slowly backwards and forwards in his chair now, still clutching his weapon.

'But then that night I started to think, maybe I'm not safe after all. She still knows, doesn't she? She could tell anyone, at any time. How did I know she'd keep her word? And if Randall found out, I'd be finished. I got the job under false pretences, didn't I? I knew he'd fire me on the spot. And this is the best job I've ever had, and the best-paid too. It means I can look after Maisie and still have a decent life myself. I just knew I'd never get such a good job again... Randall wouldn't even give me a reference...'

His voice cracked with emotion again, and the rocking motion intensified. He was getting more and more agitated, Cora thought. And that probably meant he was becoming more and more dangerous too. She had to calm him down, make him put down the gun, she *had* to.

'But you do the job so well, John. Anyone can see that Randall thinks highly of you, and relies on you. He wouldn't have fired you, not really. He'd have forgiven you. Everyone's allowed one mistake, aren't they?'

Her voice was low, soothing, but her nails were digging into her palms, sweat beading on her brow even though her body was getting colder and colder. The central heating must have gone off, she thought, and she shuddered, glad she still had her coat on.

'Are they?' His voice still had a frantic edge.

'Of course they are. And that's why it would be silly to do anything foolish now, wouldn't it? Don't make any more mistakes, John. Can I stand up for a minute, come and sit next to you? It's really uncomfortable down here on the floor, and it's getting really cold...'

'NO! STAY WHERE YOU ARE!'

He leapt from his chair and took a step towards her, swinging the gun wildly. She gasped and shrank back against the wall, drawing her knees to her chest.

'OK, OK, I'm sorry! It's OK, John, I won't move...'

Cora's mouth was suddenly so dry she could barely speak. He was just a few feet away now, towering over her, breathing heavily. Then he suddenly began to back away again, one hand groping behind him, gun held steadily out in front. When he reached his desk he leaned on the edge of it, and laughed again.

'Well, you know pretty much everything now, don't

you?' he said. 'I might as well finish the story. It makes no difference now anyway, does it?'

Unsure what he meant, Cora remained silent, the cold wall chilling her back as she pressed her body against it.

'It was the day after Randall had decided to go ahead with the smaller development, and work had literally started on the site that morning. We'd already got planning permission for that, you see, so as soon as we'd decided to go ahead with it, it was all systems go. So that morning, I called her, asked her to come in for a cup of tea and some cake, to celebrate, and so that we could all clear the air and make friends after all the aggro about the development. She said she'd love to, and that she only had a couple of classes that day so she could come in sometime in the afternoon. Maybe not so smart after all, eh? So I pick a time when Randall's already left for the day, gone off to London for a meeting, and in she comes, all happy and delighted with herself. And I make her tea, and serve her madeira cake, and we're chatting away and laughing and then I say, how about a drink, and she says no, I don't drink. And I tease her a bit, tell her it's a special occasion, and she should make an exception, and in the end she says why not, maybe just the one, seeing as it's a special occasion and all, so I open some wine…'

He giggled again, and Cora shivered. She didn't want to hear the rest of this story, desperately didn't want to hear what she now feared was coming next. This was sick, horrible…

'…and she knocks it back, and then another glass, and another one. What she doesn't know is that I'd put some sleeping tablets in there too, all crushed up. I struggle to sleep sometimes, so I was prescribed them, and they're pretty strong, so what with those and the booze… well, you're not supposed to drink alcohol with them, you see?

So she's soon getting woozy, starts to nod off in her chair. And after that, it was easy. So, so easy…'

'What was easy, John? What did you do?' Cora whispered, her stomach rolling. She thought she might be sick.

'She had her laptop in her handbag. I turned it on – no password, luckily – and typed a suicide note, and then printed it off. Wiped off the keyboard and everything so I wouldn't leave any prints, then stuffed the note into her coat pocket and put the laptop back in her bag. And then I bundled her out into my car and drove her to Clarton Bridge.'

Cora had guessed what was coming, but now that he'd actually said it, she could feel the trembling starting again. It had been *John's* car then, up there on the bridge. And that meant…that meant…

'And then I dragged her out of the car, and threw her over the edge. And she died.'

He said the terrible words so simply, so matter-of-factly, that Cora suddenly felt chilled to the bone. She hugged her knees tighter to her chest, shaking even more violently. This man is mad, she thought. He *killed* Leanne. It wasn't suicide, and nobody coerced her into jumping either. He killed her. He got her drunk, and drugged her, and physically threw her off that bridge. It was *murder*. I'm being held at gun-point by a crazy murderer. What am I going to do? What…

'And you couldn't keep your nose out, could you?' John said.

'So now, you have to die too.'

36

Adam groaned as the traffic slowed to a halt yet again. The roads were always busy when he drove from London to Cora's at this time on a Friday evening, but on the last Friday before Christmas "busy" was a gross understatement. The journey had already taken an hour longer than usual, and he was now deeply regretting his decision to forgo his usual route – leaving the M4 motorway at Swindon and taking the A roads to Cheltenham – and instead divert to Bristol to pick up a few final gifts at the Mall before taking the M5 north. Shopping, on the Friday night before Christmas? What on earth was he thinking? He rolled his head from side to side, trying to stretch out his tense neck muscles. He was very much looking forward to this weekend though, and he smiled as the car in front moved a few feet forward and he followed suit.

The plans were all in place, a whole weekend of celebrations before he and Cora decamped to London for Christmas. They had both taken the entire weekend off work, and the party would start tonight, when they would be treating Rosie and Nicole and their husbands to champagne and curry at Cora's flat – the curry being delivered, naturally, as Cora didn't cook and she'd insisted he didn't either, not tonight. Tomorrow would be a grand "pretend Christmas" lunch at Rosie's with everyone, children included, and then on Sunday morning the party would move on to Nicole's. She and Will were planning to host a smoked salmon and scrambled eggs breakfast, at which they would all open their gifts to each other. He knew it was going to be a fabulously fun couple of days, if he ever got off this *bloody motorway*. The car in front moved another few inches, then stopped. Adam sighed and wondered if he should ring Cora. There was still plenty of time before he was due to be at hers, but if this congestion didn't ease soon…

'Yes!' He whooped as the vehicles in front suddenly started to move again, and kept moving. It was finally clearing. He'd call her once he'd nipped to the shopping centre and was back on the road, he decided, then grinned, turned the radio on, and started singing loudly, happily and tunelessly along to Mariah Carey.

A few miles away in the site office, John was pacing the room now, muttering under his breath, but turning every few seconds to check that Cora hadn't moved, still holding the gun aloft. She sat rigid in her corner on the floor, heart pounding, mind racing, almost unable to believe that this was actually real. It was like a scene from a scary film, the sort of film she didn't normally allow herself to watch. When you got up regularly in the early hours of the morning, and had to go outside alone to find your car on a dark driveway or in a big, empty hotel car park, it was easy to let your imagination run away with you, to see danger in every shadow and to jump half out of your skin at the slightest rustle of a leaf or snap of a twig. On the rare occasion that Cora *had* been persuaded to watch a frightening film, she'd found herself petrified the next morning, rushing to her car and locking herself into it in blind terror, heart beating at double speed and hands shaking, vehemently vowing to stick to rom-coms in future. But this, what was happening to her right now, was worse than any scene in any of the films she'd ever

261

reluctantly watched. This was a horror film become reality. Could this really be happening? Was it some dreadful nightmare, one she couldn't wake up from? Was she really locked in a room with a madman waving a gun, a man who'd just confessed to killing a teenager and who'd just told her she was about to die too? This couldn't be real, could it? She took a long, shaky gulp of air and tried to order her thoughts, tried to quell the terror, breathe away the panic she could feel starting to creep over her. Think. She needed to *think*, and think quickly. For a second, she considered simply leaping to her feet and rushing at him, trying to knock the weapon from his hand, but she instantly dismissed the idea. He was strong, muscular, and clearly deranged – there was no way she could overpower him. If only she had her bag, her phone… but hang on, her phone wasn't in her bag, was it? It was… it was… or was it?

Trembling so much that her teeth were chattering, she slowly reached her right hand into her coat pocket. *It was*. Her phone was in her pocket, not on the floor on the other side of the office with the rest of the contents of her bag, as she'd thought. Her fingers gripped it tightly, as across the room John slumped onto a chair, still muttering. She heard the words 'bridge' and 'again' and a wave of nausea swept over her. Is that what he was planning then? Not to shoot her, but to throw her off Clarton Bridge, just like he did with Leanne? But how would he get her there? Would he try to drug her too? Could she somehow avoid swallowing the drugs if he did, and just pretend to fall asleep, then try to escape later? Or would he shoot her first, to incapacitate her maybe, and then drive her to the bridge and throw her off? Or maybe he'd shoot her dead, right here, and then it would be her dead body falling off the bridge… Oh shit shit SHIT. She *had* to get out of here, she had to. Could she just hit 999 on her phone? Would the police be able to trace the call? But how long would that take? Would it be too late? They might even dismiss it as a crank call, if she couldn't speak to the operator, mightn't they? Oh shit, oh shit, oh shit. She was panicking again. Adam. She needed Adam, so much...

Adam. *Adam*. Why hadn't she thought of that before? Could she somehow dial his number? He was on speed dial on her phone, she might be able to manage to hit the right key even if the phone was still in her pocket. But what if he thought she'd just dialled his number accidentally, and ignored the call? Despair swept over her again, and then suddenly, it came to her. *The word*. They had arranged that word, hadn't they? The word that they could use if either of them was in trouble, the word they'd agreed on that night when she'd been a little drunk, the night she'd also agreed to let him put a tracker app on her phone. If she could somehow call Adam, and say that one word, he'd know she needed him. Her heart leapt. He wouldn't just know she needed him. He'd know where she was. *He'd be able to see her location*, on the tracker. He could send help. He could call the local police, and send them round. He could save her. But how, how could she do it, without John hearing? Could she text the word maybe, with one hand, inside her pocket? She tentatively ran her fingers across the phone, but it was hopeless. She had no idea what keys to press, couldn't think what order they were in, the fear dulling her senses. She needed to call his number, and somehow...a little gasp escaped her, as she suddenly realised John had crossed the room and was standing just feet away from her, looking down at her.

'John, please.' Her voice was shaky. 'Please, don't do this. Just let me go. I won't tell anyone about any of this.

Just let me…'

'Oh shut up. Of course you'll tell people. You'll be on the phone to the police the minute you leave this room if I let you go, don't talk bollocks. Shut up, and let me think. I need to plan the best way to do this, so that nobody sees…'

He was so close to her now that Cora could feel the heat from his body, smell the sweat. Then suddenly, he backed away, still talking to himself, and slumped back down into his chair. Time was running out, she thought. He wasn't going to think about it much longer, he was going to do it. He was going to kill her. She couldn't wait any longer. She had to do it *now*, right now, or she was going to die, right here in this room. Desperately, she gripped the phone again and touched the key that would speed dial Adam's number. Or was it? Was it the right key? Oh God, she wasn't sure, she couldn't remember…

'Anything you want to say, before you die? Any messages you want me to pass on, anything like that?'

John was leaning forward in his chair, waving the gun at her. From her pocket, Cora heard a tiny "beep" as the call connected. Oh shit, oh please, don't let John have heard that. And now she was going to have to just say the word. It was now or never, but what was John going to think? How could she explain what she was about to do? This was going to sound completely and utterly ridiculous…

'Well, take a few minutes to think about it. No hurry, we've got all night…' he continued.

Cora took a deep breath. 'Mozzarella!' she shouted. 'MOZZARELLA!'

John stared at her. 'What?'

Her heart pounding so hard she thought she might faint, Cora pressed the button to end the call and slid her hand out of her pocket.

'No... nothing. Sorry. I just say stupid things, when I'm nervous. I just...'

'What, you just fancied some cheese? A last meal or something?' His tone was sneering.

She shook her head, suddenly unable to speak, her head swimming as if she was going to faint.

'No last meal, sorry,' he continued. 'You can have a drink though, if you want. There's some whiskey in the drawer here. Might calm you down a bit, make it easier for me. In fact, let's both have a drink, shall we? And then...'

Mumbling again, he reached down with one hand and fumbled in his desk drawer. *Please*, thought Cora. *Please let that have been Adam's number. Please let him have heard me. Please let him remember. Please let him come and find me. Please.*

37

Driving at a steady forty miles an hour now, Adam's heart had started pounding. When Cora's number had flashed up on his phone he had grinned, assuming that she was waiting impatiently for him to arrive and wondering where he was. But all he had heard through his car speakers was one word, repeated twice. Mozzarella. Mozzarella. The call had cut off before he'd had a chance to say anything. *Mozzarella*? That was the word, wasn't it? The word that they'd half-jokingly agreed would be their emergency word, to be used if one of them ever needed the other. If one of them was ever in serious trouble. But why would Cora use it now? Was it some sort of silly joke? In the darkness of his car, he shook his head. He'd heard the anguish in her voice, the panic. This was no joke.

'She wouldn't do that,' he said out loud. 'She just wouldn't. Holy shit. That means she's in trouble. Proper trouble. But where the hell is she?'

He thought for a moment, then started to feel a little shaky as he remembered. She was going to the site office today, wasn't she? But she'd been going with Nathan, and surely she'd have done that hours ago? Could she be still there? Adam flicked on his left indicator and hazard lights and moved swiftly onto the hard shoulder. With hands that were trembling slightly, he grabbed the phone and swiped across the screen until he found the tracking app, zooming in on the map that instantly appeared, a flashing red dot indicating the location of Cora's phone. He frowned, trying to think. Flower Street. That was it, wasn't it? That was the street where the entrance to the new housing development was, where the site office was located. He'd heard her mention it enough times. So why, he thought again, was she still there, at this time of the evening? And what the hell was going on there? What was happening, to make her use that word, and then to cut the call? This wasn't good. This wasn't good at all. Quickly, he tapped the location into his satnav, then reached into the rear footwell for his magnetic blue flashing police light. He turned it on, opened the window, stuck the light on his roof, then moved quickly off the hard shoulder and put his foot down. He had no idea what she'd got herself into now, but he needed to get to her, and fast.

38

Cora was on the verge of panic. She was shivering violently now, the room seeming to have turned from chilly to icy cold, her limbs numb despite the whiskey John had forced her to drink, the harsh liquid burning her throat. He, in contrast, was sweating even more profusely than before, pacing the room again, breathing heavily, rarely taking his eyes or the gun off Cora, her slightest movement seeming to unnerve him. In her corner on the floor, she wrapped her arms around her knees again and tried to keep still, but she was no longer able to hide the tears that were now streaming down her cheeks. She found herself idly wondering where he'd managed to get a gun, and what kind of gun it was. Some sort of pistol, she thought, although she knew that since the Dunblane school massacre back in the nineties handguns had been banned in the UK, other than in Northern Ireland. Was he really going to use it? Was this really how it was going to end? Was she going to die tonight, in this room? Was she never going to see Adam again, never see her friends, her colleagues? Could this be happening? Did that call get through to Adam? And if it did, did he hear what she'd said, and would he remember the significance of the word? A sob escaped her, eliciting a sharp 'Shut up!' from her captor.

Adam. Please, Adam, she thought. I need you. I need you to save my life.

'I'm on my way there too, but you may get there before I do. Thank you so much.'

Weaving his way through the rush hour traffic as he spoke, Adam cut the call to Avon Police and swore as a motorbike sped past him, doing at least sixty in this forty miles an hour zone. Any other day he would have given chase, but not today. All he could think about was Cora. What the hell had happened to make her call him like that, to use that word? He remembered the fear in her voice, and a shudder ran through him. He glanced at his satnav. He was only three minutes away, but he'd suddenly decided to call reinforcements anyway, just in case any of the local police cars happened to be in the vicinity. He'd found it a little difficult to explain exactly what the problem was, deciding that telling them that his girlfriend had shouted the name of a soft cheese down the phone to him, thus indicating that she was in some sort of serious trouble, but that he currently had no idea what that trouble might be, could be tricky to explain. Instead, he'd briskly informed the operator that he was a senior officer with the Metropolitan Police heading for the scene of a potentially violent altercation and requesting back-up. Deeply grateful that a patrol car was indeed just minutes away and was now also headed for Flower Street, Adam overtook a row of cars which had pulled in to the left as they'd seen the blue light behind them. Two minutes away now. What the buggering hell was he going to find when he got there?

'Right. It's time.'

Cora, who had sunk her head onto her knees and was sobbing quietly, jumped violently. John was looming over her, his voice oddly calm now.

'Time… time for what?'

Her voice was barely a whisper, the terror clutching at her throat.

'Don't make me spell it out. You know what. I could do what I did with Leanne... make you drink a bottle of wine, give you some pills and chuck you off the bridge. But somehow I don't think you'd co-operate. So I'm afraid it's going to have to be this way.'

He waved the gun at her jauntily, a half-smile on his face. He's mad, Cora thought. He's really, truly, completely insane. Her throat was so tight she could barely breathe, but suddenly she knew she had to give this one more try. He could shoot her at any second, and he would, she knew that. She needed to talk to him again, buy herself some time. But what? What would make him stop? It would have to be something he cared about. His sister maybe? What was her name again? Maisie? *Maisie,* she thought.

'But, that's so messy,' she said desperately, her voice cracking. She coughed, and carried on. 'I mean, you shoot me here, and there's blood all over the floor, the walls... how are you going to clean it up? And how are you going to get rid of my body? It'll be a struggle, getting me out of here on your own and into your car. What if somebody's walking past, on the street? They might spot you through the gate, John. It's all far, far too messy. You'll be caught, without a doubt. And what will Maisie do then, when her big brother is in prison? She'll be on her own then, won't she? She won't have you coming to visit her any more, will she? And she won't understand why, will she John? She'll just think you don't love her anymore, that you don't want to see her anymore. Maisie, who loves you so much. Who you love so much, John. It will break her heart. Think about that. If you kill me, what happens to Maisie? Who will pay for her care? There'll be nobody to pay the fees, not for that lovely home she lives in. Where will she end up? She needs you.

Think about that, John. Think about Maisie.'

A little gasp escaped John's lips. His eyes had grown wider and wider as he'd listened, and now he stood stock still, his gaze fixed on Cora's face.

'But... but... no, no! You're trying to trick me, aren't you? Stop it! STOP IT!'

He turned away, then whirled back, the gun just inches from her forehead. She shrank backwards, her body pressing hard against the wall. The tears sprang to her eyes again, the sick dread rising in her chest. He was going to kill her, he was going to kill her... talk, keep talking...

'Trick you? No, of course not. Why do you think...?' she gasped.

'Because if I listen to you, if I don't kill you, and let you go, then you'll tell the police, won't you? You're trying to trick me by telling me all those horrible things about Maisie.'

John moved away from her again, backing towards the desk, the gun held straight out in front of him, still aimed at her head. As Cora watched him, she thought she saw out of the corner of her eye a shadow move past the glass window in the door of the office. Was that... was there somebody out there? She flicked her eyes to the door again but there was nothing there, the window just a blank, dark square. Nothing. Nobody. Nobody was coming to save her, not now, she thought dully. This was it.

John was still talking, the manic edge back in his voice.

'If I let you go, you'll tell them about this, and about Leanne. And then I'll go to prison anyway, won't I? But if I kill you, and get away with it like I did with Leanne, well, everything will be OK. Because I *did* get away with

271

it, didn't I? Nobody had a clue it was me. They all thought she killed herself. The police, Randall, everybody. So I can get away with killing you too, and nobody will ever know, and Maisie will be OK. So shut up. Stop trying to trick me. You're a liar. Stop talking. It's over, Cora. It's time.'

He'd been leaning against his desk but now he stood up, his back ramrod straight, and took a long, deep breath. Slowly, painfully slowly, he gripped the gun with both hands, aiming carefully. Whimpering, Cora flattened herself against the wall, panic numbing her brain, as John's finger coiled slowly around the trigger. And then, suddenly, there was an explosion of light and noise, a cacophony of yelling and sirens outside, an enormous bang as the office door slammed open, John spinning around, the sound of a gun going off and then a scream, long and loud and terrified, a scream Cora realised was coming from her own mouth. And then it seemed that the room was suddenly filled with people, running and shouting, and John was on the ground, and he was screaming now too, a bloodcurdling, howling scream of pure anguish. And already on the ground, just inside the door, was Adam. Adam, slumped in a crumpled heap, a bright, damp, red stain creeping across the front of his blue shirt, and his eyes wide open.

39

It was warm in the hospital corridor, the radiators almost too hot to touch, staff rushing up and down in light cotton scrubs and short sleeves, members of the public ambling past slowly, winter coats slung over their arms. It was warm, very warm. So why was she so cold? Not just cold, frozen. Frozen to the bone, so deep-down cold she doubted she would ever get warm again. A cold that hadn't just enveloped her body, but her heart and her mind too, a numbing, icy cold that was rendering her incapable of thought, incapable of emotion, incapable of movement. Motionless, she sat huddled in the rough green blanket that someone had wrapped around her earlier, eyes fixed on the floor in front of her, staring at nothing, thinking of nothing, feeling nothing.

'Cora! Oh God, Cora! I couldn't find you… Cora, are you alright? Talk to me!'

Suddenly, Nicole was kneeling on the floor in front of her, face tight with concern, eyes red-rimmed. She reached inside the blanket, fumbling for Cora's hands, clutching them tightly.

'Cora, please talk to me! Tell me what happened? Are you OK? Are you hurt? And Adam… oh shit, Cora…'

Cora swallowed hard, the cold still gripping her throat, her voice trapped within its icy grasp.

'It was John,' she whispered. 'John Smith. He killed Leanne. He drugged her, and wrote the suicide note on her laptop, and then threw her off the bridge. It was him. He did it. He…'

273

Nicole was shaking her head, her eyes wide and frantic.

'Cora, please. That can wait. Adam…where is Adam? Is he… is he…?'

Cora lifted her eyes to her friend's, and without warning the hot tears spilled out, burning her frozen cheeks, and a fiery pain began to rise in her chest. She gulped, trying to swallow it down, but the pain intensified, and she suddenly wondered if it was true that hearts really could break, and if this was what was happening to her now.

'I've lost him, Nicole. I think I've lost him,' she said.

40

'He's admitted it all, finally. Took them all weekend to break him though. Little shit. Lock him up and throw away the friggin' key, I say.'

DCI Gordon Gregory slammed a pile of files down on his desk so hard that James Jordan, sitting at the desk opposite, jumped and nearly spilled his coffee.

'That John Smith bloke? The one who it turns out murdered Leanne Brimley? Agreed, boss. And good to have you back,' he said.

Gregory had returned to duties earlier on this Monday morning, albeit with a stern warning that if he messed up again, he'd be shown no mercy. He winked at the younger man.

'Good to be back, Jordan. Good to be back. Now, go and get me one of those, will you? I've got some catching up to do.'

'A coffee? Sure. Be two ticks.'

'Cheers.'

Gregory turned his computer on and waited for it to boot up. For all his bluster, he knew he was lucky to still have this job, and he was deeply grateful that the powers that be had decided to give him one final chance. No, he shouldn't have covered up for his brother, and he'd deserved the suspension, he knew that. Alan was a pain in the arse, a violent little shit, and he should have let him get what he deserved from the off, when he did what he did to that old shopkeeper. He was wrong to try to protect him, and he wouldn't do it again. But it was the other thing… well, if his bosses knew about the other thing, he'd be out on his ear, and on his way to prison too, most likely. Now that he'd been given his job back, he'd made up his mind to stay away from Midnight Diamonds in future. He needed to keep his nose clean, that was for sure. He'd started to think that he might not like Dougie Granley, the manager, quite as much as he used to anyway. There was something extremely sleazy about the man, even by Gregory's standards, which were pretty low. He'd started hanging out there now and again a while back, finding it a good place to kick back and forget the stresses of police work – the music was good, the girls were hot, and Dougie was a bit of a laugh. They'd got on alright for a while, Dougie proffering free drinks because Gregory had been so helpful when he was getting the place up and running - and of course because of what Gregory did for a living - and Gregory turning a blind eye to some of the… well, to some of the *choices* Dougie made as an employer. It was easier that way, and more fun, and nobody was getting hurt, as far as he could see. Working conditions were good, the girls were paid a fair wage, even if some of them were clearly too young to be working there legally, but hey, if they needed the money, they needed the money. Who was he to get in the way of commerce?

And then, of course, that little busybody Leanne Brimley had showed up. What a right royal pain in the arse she had been.

She'd accosted him one night as he was going in to the club, told him she was 'investigating' the place for some reason or other, and that during the course of her so-called investigations she'd discovered he was a cop. She had a friend who worked there from time to time, she said, and this friend had told her about 'Dougie's copper friend'

276

who turned a blind eye to what was going on there, and that there were rumours that this copper had slept with one of the girls, and that the girl was young, very young. And although he denied it, denied it outright, and told her she had no proof, and that to make accusations like that about an officer of the law could get her into big, big trouble, the problem was that she was right. Well, almost right. He *had* taken one of the girls home, and she *had* been underage. But he hadn't known that, not at first. She'd been all dolled up in high heels and skimpy clothes and heavy make-up, but he'd honestly thought she was eighteen, or maybe seventeen at a push, definitely not any younger. He might be bad sometimes, but he wasn't that bad. He wasn't a *paedophile,* for feck's sake. The girl's name was Sofia, and she was from eastern Europe somewhere... Poland, Romania, he wasn't sure. They'd gone back to his place after the club closed, and he'd told her there was a hundred quid in it for her if she stayed the night. They'd had a kiss and a fumble, and then she'd slipped off to the bathroom, and while she was gone he'd taken a look in her handbag, just out of interest. And there it was, her passport. She was fifteen years old. *Fifteen.* Almost sixteen, but still. He'd been horrified. She'd looked so much older. How was he supposed to know? How was any man supposed to know, nowadays? It was a friggin' minefield. And he'd already kissed her, touched her. A fifteen-year-old. A *child.*

So he'd done the only thing he could think of to protect himself – told her he was a police officer, and that if she told anyone, breathed a single word to a soul about what had happened, he'd arrange to get her deported immediately. He would never have done it – *could* never have done it, he didn't have the power – but the poor kid didn't know that, and she was so terrified, she'd agreed.

He'd sent her straight home after that, never laid another finger on her. But there must have been rumours or something, because the next thing he knew that little cow Leanne Brimley was on his case. When he denied having anything to do with anyone underage, threatened her, she backed off a bit, said OK, she wouldn't report him because she couldn't prove it, but she still warned him to stay away from the girls, and from her friend in particular – Fee, her name was, if he remembered rightly. He'd stopped going to the club then for a while, decided it was too much trouble. He'd told his colleague James Jordan about it, at first just telling him that a girl called Leanne Brimley had been getting at him for being a cop in a strip club, and Jordan had agreed that Gregory should just lay low for a while, keep away from Rotunda Street. Then of course there'd been the big hoo-ha about his brother, and while he was suspended he'd heard she'd died - that Leanne had topped herself, jumping off a bridge.

He'd finally confessed the full story to Jordan after that, on the day of Leanne's funeral. He'd needed to tell someone, and Jordan was the only colleague he really trusted. The younger man had been a little shocked about the Sofia thing, but he'd seemed to understand, seemed to believe that Gregory hadn't known how young she was. Gregory didn't mind admitting he'd been glad at the time, really glad, about Leanne being dead. He felt a bit bad about that now, she was only a kid after all, but it had meant that the threat had lifted, and that he could finally start going back to the club now and again, having a bit of fun. Not with the young ones though. Never again. He'd made sure, after that, that they were over eighteen, made them prove it. He wasn't going to make that mistake again. And now - well, probably better to stay away from the place altogether, for now. Now that he was back at work. It was probably safer. When he'd seen Cora Baxter, that interfering little bitch of a TV reporter, sitting outside the club, he'd thought the game was up. It seemed that she didn't know what had gone on after all, though, which was a relief. She'd definitely have reported him by now if she knew. He'd dodged a bullet there.

And now it had turned out that Leanne Brimley didn't kill herself after all. She'd been murdered. Murdered by a cowardly little shit who'd done it to save his pathetic little job. And now, the same cowardly little shit had…

At the thought of what John Smith had done to that DCI from the Met, to a copper, to one of their own, Gregory's fists clenched. Give me two minutes in that cell with him, he thought, his face contorting into a scowl. Just two minutes…

'Here's your coffee, boss. You OK?'

James Jordan was standing by his desk, holding out a steaming mug and looking at him with a concerned expression. Gregory relaxed his face and uncurled his fingers, then nodded.

'Fine. Just thinking about something. Something and nothing. Cheers for that.'

He took the coffee. Drink your drink, catch up on your paperwork, he told himself. Keep your nose clean. Not too many years until retirement now. Early retirement, hopefully. You can do it. Think of that apartment in sunny Spain. Or Portugal. Portugal was nice. He could take up golf. Nah, golf was boring. Maybe the south of France. Somewhere warm, with cheap wine. He smiled, took a slug of the hot, strong coffee, and started work.

Back at his own desk, James Jordan was thinking hard as he waited for his computer to boot up. The system was ancient, and painfully slow, and it drove him mad on a daily basis, but today he wasn't feeling very motivated to get started. He'd told Gregory it was good to have him back, and it was, in a way. They were friends of a sort, after all. But the vague feelings of guilt he'd had recently about covering for his boss had been growing stronger. He'd been one of those who'd accepted Gregory's fake alibi for his brother, even though he'd known it was a lie, deep down. But at least Gregory had been punished for that, with his six-week suspension. The girl was different though. Gregory had been delighted when Leanne Brimley had died, awful though that seemed, because she was the only one to have confronted him about what had gone on in the club, the only one who knew, or at least suspected, and the only one who might have the balls to report him. And what had gone on was that Gregory had touched, kissed, a fifteen-year-old. That wasn't right. It was wrong, and disgusting, and it made James feel sick to his stomach. He'd told Gregory he believed him when he said he hadn't known how young she was, but now he wasn't so sure. Should he report him? Could he? But there was no way of proving it, was there? It would be his word against Gregory's, and the girl certainly wouldn't speak up, even if he could track her down. She'd be too scared, Gregory had seen to that. No, there was nothing he could do. He'd just have to forget about it and move on, just like the DCI was doing.

His computer finally awake, he reached for the keyboard and logged in.

41

At the Brimley home in Flower Street, Lisa Brimley was baking Christmas gingerbread men biscuits. Her face was still pale, but her dark red hair was freshly washed and styled, and she even had a little make-up on. It made her blue eyes even more vibrant than usual, matching the soft, duck egg coloured sweater she was wearing with her jeans and fluffy, boot-style slippers.

Liam sat at the kitchen table, half playing a game on his phone and half watching his mother with wonderment. It had been so long, so very, very long since he'd seen her like this. He couldn't remember the last time she'd made biscuits, cooked anything at all, in fact. They'd been living on microwave meals and takeaways since Leanne had died, that's if there was food in the house at all, and nine times out of ten it had been Liam who'd had to prepare it. But ever since Saturday, when the police had called to say they had someone in custody who was being questioned about his involvement in Leanne's death, his mother had started to change, to come out of herself, out of the shell she'd hidden in since her daughter died. And this morning, when the detective had arrived on the doorstep to let them know the man had confessed and was being charged with murder, the transformation had been complete. It was like watching a caterpillar turn into a butterfly, he thought now, smiling as Lisa flitted happily around the kitchen, humming to herself, a smear of flour on her nose. She hadn't had a drink all weekend, had she? She'd actually poured all the wine down the sink last night, four bottles of it. Ever since Dad died, drink had been her comfort. Liam had hated it, and Leanne had hated it even more, but they'd managed, the two of them. They'd looked after each other, and looked after Mum too, when she was really out of it. They'd covered up for her, afraid that if anybody outside the family knew just how bad it was, Social Services might get involved, and they weren't sure what would happen then.

And then Leanne died, and Liam had been left to handle it on his own. That was another reason why he'd been so sure Leanne hadn't taken her own life. She would never, ever have left him like that, left him to deal with it on his own, he was totally convinced of that. And of course, after Leanne, his mother had got worse, much, much worse, and he'd actually got to the point where he wasn't sure if he could cope much longer and that maybe he'd actually be better off in a foster home or somewhere. And he knew why it had got worse too. It wasn't just the grief, it was guilt. His mum had been drunk the night Leanne died, out-of-her-head drunk, the drunkest he'd seen her in months. She was at a friend's house, and eventually the friend had phoned, saying she really couldn't handle Lisa in this state and asking Liam to come and get her. And when Lisa realised, when she was sober enough to understand that while she'd been drinking, her daughter had been dying, she had been ashamed. More than ashamed – mortified, horrified, that she'd been off her nut on booze, that she hadn't been at home, torturing herself that maybe it wouldn't have happened if she'd been there. She couldn't forgive herself, made Liam promise not to tell anyone where she was, what she'd been doing. He'd agreed, but it had been so hard, covering for her all the time, especially on his own. He'd had to cover for her so many times. That last time Cora Baxter was here, his mum had been pissed then too, down the pub on her own. He'd told Cora that his mum was out at a friend's, but he was sure she'd noticed how cold the house was. Mum had been so bad for the few days before that that she hadn't been shopping for food or firewood or anything.

He'd almost wanted to confide in Cora, once or twice, but he'd changed his mind. Too risky. At the thought of her now, he suddenly felt sad. The police officer who'd come this morning had told them what had happened to her, and what had happened to her boyfriend, who was a policeman in London. It was just terrible, he thought, and decided to go out later, buy her a card and maybe a little present, to let her know that he and his mum were thinking about her. It was her, after all, who'd finally got to the bottom of it, who had found out what had really happened to Leanne, even though she'd told him she didn't think there was any more she could do. She'd done it, and she was responsible for this too, this wonderful change in his mother. He'd never told Lisa that he'd asked Cora to look into things for him, and he didn't see the point in telling her now. The realisation that Leanne hadn't killed herself after all had somehow brought Lisa back from her dark place. It sounded kind of weird, even to him, but he thought he understood it. It was as if the knowledge that this wasn't a repeat of what had happened with Dad, that Leanne hadn't *wanted* to die but had been murdered, had made the difference. It was still terrible and shocking and awful, and it would take them a very long time to get over it, if they ever would. But somehow, finding out the truth had healed something in his mother's heart, and brought her back to him. He caught her eye, and smiled.

'OK, Mum?' he said.

She smiled back and nodded. 'I'm OK. Are you OK, Liam? I'm sorry, you know. So, so sorry, about how it's been recently. Things are different now. Nobody can bring Leanne back, but there's closure now, somehow. We've still got the court case to get through, see that bastard go down. But we can do it, can't we? We can do it together. We're going to be alright, you and me, aren't we?'

She crossed the kitchen and wrapped her arms around him where he sat, pulling his head into her chest and ruffling his hair. Liam hugged her back for a moment, his heart suddenly bursting with happiness.

'Yes, Mum,' he said, his face still pressed against her soft sweater, his voice muffled. 'We're going to be alright.'

Down the street at number three, Mark and Caroline Sinclair were getting ready to host a lunchtime drinks party. Most of their friends had stopped work for Christmas by now, and it had been a tough few months. But Mark had just been given a promotion at work, a promotion which meant a lot more money. It was going to make a huge difference, save their bacon really. It was time to celebrate, to put the past behind them and look ahead to the new year which, hopefully, would be a lot better than this past one. As Caroline opened the wine and arranged sandwiches on plates, she thought about Leanne Brimley, and about the news that had spread along the street like wildfire earlier that day, after a police officer had been seen calling at number one. Apparently Liam had called one of his mates shortly afterwards, and he had told his mother, and she had told... well, the news had got out, and quickly. Always did on a street like this.

It had been Mark's idea, to write those letters. He'd

been desperate to sell the house, money troubles beginning to give him sleepless nights and the beginnings of a stomach ulcer. He'd kept it to himself at first, but he'd finally cracked and admitted to his wife just how bad a shape their finances were in, and what he'd done to get them into such a mess. It had turned out that a mate at his work had a mate who ran some sort of investment scheme, and he'd shown him figures, amazing figures that showed huge returns in just a few months. He'd thought it was a safe bet, he told her, an easy way to double their money in a short space of time, so he'd put the lot into it. All of it, all of their savings, and a bit more besides. But of course, it had all gone wrong. The mate of a mate turned out to be a conman, the impressive figures all fabricated, and suddenly the guy was gone and so was all the money. They'd gone to the police, but so far they'd heard nothing – the bastard had been using a false name, and had seemingly vanished into thin air. The cops said they'd carry on working on it, but not to hold their breath. These things could take years, they said. So eventually Caroline had agreed with Mark that yes, selling the house was the way forward, especially for the inflated price Randall Greythorpe was offering. They could pay off all their debts and even have a nice little nest egg left over. But it was an all or nothing offer – Greythorpe wanted all the houses on his list, or none of them. So when Leanne started her campaign to persuade everyone to stay put, and to encourage locals to object to planning permission for the bigger estate too, she needed to be stopped before she got too many of the neighbours on her side, that's what Mark had decided.

'She's just a kid,' he had said to Caroline. 'A few scary letters through her door, she'll soon stop. I'll write them. Nobody will ever know.'

She'd agreed, a tad reluctantly. It seemed a bit of a mean thing to do, especially to a young girl, but hey, if it worked... Caroline had stopped worrying about it, and started daydreaming about the designer handbag Mark had said she could have as a treat with some of what was left over, once the house was sold. Burberry or Marc Jacobs, she'd mused?

The letters hadn't worked though. And then, one night, Mark came in all red in the face and panting, as if he'd been running, and he wouldn't tell her what was wrong. And then, just a couple of days later, Leanne Brimley came off Clarton Bridge. And that's when Mark broke down, and told Caroline what had happened that night he'd come in looking all funny – he'd taken a knife from the kitchen, and waited for Leanne to come home in the dark, dragged her down a side alley, held the knife to her throat and threatened her, told her that if she didn't drop her stupid little campaign he'd kill her. He didn't mean it, not really, of course. Mark wouldn't hurt a fly, literally – he'd spend ages trying to carefully persuade them out through a window if any were buzzing round the living room. But he was just so desperate, so scared of losing the house and everything...

Caroline shuddered at the memory and stuffed a pile of neatly folded napkins into a pint glass on the buffet table. When Leanne had died, Mark had been convinced she'd killed herself because of what he had done that night. He said it must have been because he frightened her so much. It had been such a terrible time, his guilt and anguish eating him up, the strain on their marriage and family almost unbearable. Caroline had told Tracy and she'd been amazing, promised to keep it all quiet, but it had still been incredibly hard to deal with. But now... well, now the truth was out. Leanne Brimley hadn't taken her own

286

life at all. She'd been murdered, by one of Randall Greythorpe's staff. Why on earth would he do that? Caroline shook her head. They'd find out the ins and outs of it eventually, she supposed. For now though, she was just glad that some of the load had finally lifted from her husband's shoulders. She looked at him now, laughing with the kids as they blew up the last of the balloons before their guests arrived. There was still guilt, always would be, about how they'd treated Leanne. That would take a long time to forgive themselves for. Maybe they'd never find peace about that, but that was their punishment, wasn't it? But at least now they knew they weren't responsible for her death. And that would have to do, for now.

Down the road at the site office, Randall Greythorpe was standing quite still in the middle of the main room, still slightly shell-shocked. He'd temporarily returned from his Christmas trip to London last night after hearing the news, and now, as he gazed around his office, the police having finally finished with it, he was still finding it difficult to come to terms with what had happened here on Friday night. He'd left his PA, John, to finish off a few bits and pieces before he began his own festive break. How in the name of sanity did the calm, industrious scene Randall had left behind turn within hours to one in which a terrified TV reporter was being held at gunpoint? And her boyfriend, a police officer, who'd tried to save her...

His gaze fell on the carpet near the door, the wide, dark stain a sickening reminder of how that night had ended, and his stomach heaved. He had no idea where John had acquired the gun, but ever since he'd heard what had happened he'd wondered if Dougie had got it for him. There'd been a spate of break-ins a while back, when

287

they'd first opened up the office, one when John was alone in the building. He'd been punched to the ground and roughed up a little, and after that he'd been scared of being there on his own. Dougie had contacts, and he liked John… yes, I'd bet my life Dougie got it for him, Randall thought bitterly. Stupid, stupid man…

He'd cut all links with his former business partner as of this morning, first calling him to tell him it was all over, and that he was withdrawing all money and support from the club immediately, and then calling the police. Although Dougie had vehemently denied the accusations of employing underage girls when Randall had first asked him about it, he had known immediately, deep down, that Cora Baxter had probably been right. It had been playing on his mind ever since, and then when this happened… well, he couldn't live with it any longer. If Dougie did have anything to do with this, had provided the weapon, then Randall could no longer have anything to do with him. And if the police were looking into that, they might as well know about the underage girl allegations too, and investigate those as well. So the police were on to it now, and he hoped that Dougie would get what was coming to him. He'd taken Randall for a ride along with everyone else, and Randall Greythorpe didn't like being taken for a ride, or being lied to.

He was still in shock too about the news that John had murdered Leanne Brimley, and deeply saddened by the reason. Was he such a terrible boss, that his PA thought he would be sacked for lying on his CV? Randall would have been a bit cross, yes. But John was an excellent PA, and they'd grown into a great team. He wouldn't have sacked him, even though he'd threatened him with that now and again, when he was frustrated. He felt bad about that now. He was astounded though, that the man had gone to such horrifying lengths to stop him finding out his secret. Leanne Brimley had been a minor annoyance, it was true – she'd been a determined young woman, and adamant that her house, and those of her neighbours, would not be demolished to make way for Randall's dream development. In a way, he'd come to admire her for that, admire her grit and tenacity. He'd been irritated by her at first, especially that day she'd come into the office, shouting her mouth off at him when there were potential buyers within earshot. He'd felt quite irate, insisted she left, told her not to come back. But as time had gone on he'd softened, understanding her reasons for wanting to stay in her home and secretly being rather impressed by her perseverance. He'd actually been about to let her have her way anyway, the day John had come to him and persuaded him that letting her win would be the right thing to do.

'Imagine if the papers got hold of it, Randall. Think of the headlines. "*Hard-hearted developer in attempt to destroy girl's memories of dead father*", stuff like that. Imagine the bad publicity!' John had said.

And so Randall had done what he was probably going to do anyway, and they had let Leanne win her campaign, backed down and decided to just go with the smaller development. But it wasn't enough to save her life, was it? Initially, when he had heard that Leanne had died, thrown herself from a bridge, he'd been horrified, instantly thinking that the pressure of her campaign against Elmsley Park had been too much for her, that he had somehow been partly responsible for her death. And now, he thought, he really had been, in a way, because he had employed John. John, who had lied on his CV. John, who was just too scared, too frightened of being exposed. And so he did that dreadful thing, and he nearly got away with it. Nearly, but not quite. He hadn't reckoned on Miss Cora Baxter, had he? Randall smiled a small, sad smile as he thought about Cora. She'd become a thorn in his side too, with all her questions about Leanne and the club... he'd grown heartily sick of her, nervous that she'd do a negative report, make him sound like a sleazy nightclub owner who bullied young women out of their homes, trash his name on national television, damage his reputation and his business. But this... he wouldn't have wished this on her. Wouldn't have wished it on anyone. Randall looked at the bloodstain on the floor again and shivered, then walked to his desk and woke up his laptop. First, he was going to contact the home that John's sister Maisie was in, and tell them that for the foreseeable future *he* would be settling all of her bills. He owed John that, at least. And then, he needed to order a new office carpet, and then call round the employment agencies and find a new PA who could start immediately after Christmas. Murderous employees or not, business came first. Randall found the care home number and picked up the phone.

At Avon Police HQ, DCI Gordon Gregory had just finished telling DI James Jordan a particularly filthy joke, which had left the younger man sniggering into his cheese and pickle sandwich. Pleased with himself, Gregory stood up and stretched, intending to pop out for a quick fag break before tackling his next mound of paperwork, when he felt a heavy hand on his shoulder. Surprised, he turned round to see two burly detectives, their faces serious.

'Alright, lads? Come to welcome me back? Good to see you!'

Gregory held out a hand, but the taller of the two shook his head.

'Got a fella in the cells, think you might know him?

Name of Douglas Granley. Runs a sleazy strip joint down in Rotunda Street. Midnight Diamonds. Name mean anything to you? Because yours certainly means something to him. He's had quite a lot to say about you, in fact. So we think we need to have a little chat with you, DCI Gregory. Can you come with us please?'

Gregory closed his eyes for a moment, and the image of the Spanish apartment with its sunny terrace and fridge eternally full of cold beer, the image that had been getting him through this rather tedious first day back at work, flickered, faded, and then vanished.

'Oh, SHIT,' he said.

At his desk nearby, James Jordan had been listening wide-eyed. As Gregory was led past him, still swearing, Jordan smiled in wonderment. Bloody hell, he thought. Isn't karma a wonderful thing?

42

'Adam. Oh, my darling, darling, Adam.'

The tears streamed down Cora's cheeks as she stroked his hand, so cold and still on the white sheet, her whole body aching with love for him. This man, this wonderful man, who had been at her side for the past year and a half, who had been her rock and her very best friend, the love of her life. This man who had come to save her on Friday night, when she had been seconds away from dying a horrible death, this man who had literally put his own life on the line for her...

'Are you crying *again*? Stop it, I'm going to be fine.'

Adam opened one eye and squinted at her, then opened the other too.

'I'm still freezing though. Can you find a nurse, ask someone to turn up the heat a bit?'

His voice was weak, but her Adam was still there, Cora thought, as she wiped her eyes for at least the sixth time that day and smiled at him.

'In a minute. Just let me look at you a bit longer first. I can't believe... I just can't believe you're alive, and going to be OK. I thought... I thought...'

The tears sprang to her eyes again, and she grabbed another tissue as Adam groaned, feebly but still impressively theatrically for a man with a bullet hole in his chest. All weekend, she'd been told by the doctors to prepare for the worst, that someone with Adam's injuries, somebody who'd lost as much blood as he had, was unlikely to survive. But remarkably, somehow, he was now not just alive, but alive and talking and telling her off, and Cora felt as if she was going to explode with joy, if she could only stop crying for long enough.

The bullet which John had fired into Adam's chest had, it emerged, fractured a rib, bounced into a lung and punctured it, then ripped through his shoulder blade on exit. He would be in recovery for a long time, but he *would* recover, the doctors seemed pretty sure about that now.

The police had been in touch too, to let her know that over the weekend John Smith had made a full and frank confession, admitting to the murder of Leanne Brimley. Leanne, who had done such a brilliant job of uncovering so much sleaze, and paid for it with her life. The more Cora thought about it, the greater her admiration for this young girl, and all she had done. OK, maybe it hadn't been very nice of her to threaten John, to try to blackmail him like that, but clearly she'd been desperate. She'd played dirty, yes, towards the end of her campaign. But no matter what she'd done, she still didn't deserve to die. It was still hard to come to terms with the fact that she'd been murdered, but Cora hoped the news would bring some sort of closure for Liam and his mother. She would go and see them, she had decided, as soon as she could bear to leave Adam's side. She knew that all this would take time to get over; the horror of Friday night was still fresh in her mind, memories of her fear for her own life and her anguish at seeing Adam in a pool of blood haunting her whether she was awake or asleep. She was trying to concentrate on the positives, that Adam was alive and that John would be locked up for a long time, not just for what he'd done to Leanne but also for what he'd done to her and Adam, but she was still feeling very fragile. Oddly, she'd found herself worrying too about

293

what would happen to John's sister Maisie now, and vowed to find out about that as soon as she could.

Joanne Kennedy, the police family liaison officer who had come to see them both in the hospital earlier today, had also shared another interesting piece of news. Dougie Granley, the manager of Midnight Diamonds, was in police custody. Cora had at first assumed that Sam had decided to go ahead and report the club, but was surprised when Joanne confided that it had actually been Randall Greythorpe who had made the call.

'He thinks Granley might have given John Smith the gun,' she said. 'And he's also asked us to look into allegations that Granley is employing underage girls. Sounds like the guy's a pretty unpleasant piece of work.'

'Wow.' Cora's view of Randall Greythorpe suddenly changed. He probably *had* been genuine then, when she'd asked him about Midnight Diamonds and he'd claimed to know nothing about what was going on there. And clearly, he hadn't known anything about how Leanne Brimley died either - John had told her that. She suddenly felt a little guilty about thinking so badly of Greythorpe. Maybe she'd have to pop in and see him too, when she visited the Brimleys. Then she thought about walking into the site office again, and shuddered. No, she couldn't do that. She couldn't go back into that room, not after what had happened there. Maybe a phone call then, that would be enough. She might pop in and see old Arthur Everton though, the neighbour who thought of Leanne as a granddaughter, and who had been so shocked by the thought that she had taken her own life. She wondered if they would ever find out who had written the hate mail, the threatening letters Leanne had received. It didn't really matter now, she supposed. They had, after all, had no part to play in the girl's death. Nobody had, except

John Smith.

The final piece of news had been that DCI Gordon Gregory was also in trouble again, being questioned about his connections with the strip club too. Cora thought about Sofia, the young girl who seemed to be so scared of the police officer. She might give her a call, tell her he'd been arrested. Maybe she would speak out, tell somebody why she was so frightened. Maybe Cora could help her somehow. She wondered what Gregory had been up to. No doubt she'd find out, in time. That didn't really matter now either, though. Nothing mattered, except that Adam was alive. She sniffed again, and reached for yet another tissue, smiling at him through her tears.

On the other side of the private room, Harry looked up from his games console and grinned at Cora.

'You'd stop crying if you knew what Daddy had got you for Christmas, wouldn't she, Daddy?'

'Shhh, Harry!' Adam hissed, slowly and painfully turning his head to look at his son. 'It's not Christmas Day until tomorrow. She can't have it until then.'

'But Daddy, I won't be here tomorrow now, will I? Because I'll be at Mummy's instead of in London with you, because you got shot. And that means I won't *see* you giving it to her, will I? And that's not fair. It's Christmas Eve, it's *nearly* proper Christmas. Please, give it to her now. Pleeeeeeease!'

Intrigued, Cora looked from father to son.

'Well, I kind of want it now, too, if Harry's so excited about it. But Harry, all the presents are around the tree in Daddy's flat, remember? So we'll have to wait. Daddy might be moved to a London hospital in a few days, so we could open it then…'

'Not all of them! This one's special, and it's here. Daddy's been carrying it around with him, in case you found it in the flat and looked! He said he knows what you're like. Hang on, I'll show you!'

Pretending not to hear a warning moan from his father, Harry leapt from his chair with a gleeful expression and Cora watched, puzzled, as he started rooting in Adam's overnight bag, the one he'd had in the car ready for his weekend with her in Cheltenham and which the police had delivered to the hospital for him after the shooting.

'Harry, don't... oh, sod it. Go on then. Now's as good a time as any, I suppose. Didn't exactly plan it like this, though.'

Adam's voice wasn't much more than a croaky whisper now, but he shifted himself a little higher on his pillows and there was a sudden gleam in his eye as Harry approached the bed, a small blue box not quite hidden in his palm. Cora's eyes widened as the little boy handed the box to his father. Oh my goodness. That wasn't... he wasn't about to... *was he*?

'Come here, Cora. Hold my hand for a minute, will you?'

She edged closer to the bed, her heart suddenly beating so fast she felt a little faint, and gently picked up his spare hand.

'OK. What... what's going on?' she said.

'What's going on, Cora Baxter, is that I love you. I love you despite all the ludicrous situations you get yourself, and me, into. I love your passion, and your loyalty, and your determination. I love you with all my heart, totally and unconditionally, and there is nobody else in this world I would rather spend my time with. And as the past few days have shown us rather too clearly, life is short, and there's no point in putting things off when you can do them today, right now. So what's going on, Cora, is that I'm asking you to marry me.'

She was crying again now, the tears flowing freely down her cheeks, her hands trembling as Adam pushed the little box into her fingers. Somehow, she managed to open it, knowing that she didn't care if the ring inside was made of plastic. All that mattered was that Adam was alive, and that he wanted to be with her, and that everything was going to be alright. It wasn't plastic, of course, and she gasped as the stunning solitaire diamond set into a twisted rose gold band glittered against the blue velvet. She looked back at Adam, who was watching her expectantly.

'Yes, of course I'll bloody marry you, you gorgeous, wonderful man,' she said quietly, the tears suddenly subsiding. 'I love you so much. Thank you, so much, for loving me too, despite... well, despite everything.'

She leaned in and kissed him gently on the lips, and he lifted a hand and pulled her closer, his grip on her neck surprisingly strong.

'Hooray! Hooray!'

Harry, who'd been watching quietly, hands clasped to his mouth and eyes wide, suddenly started jumping up and down like an excited monkey, and Cora and Adam let go of each other and grinned.

'Looks like I'm going to officially be your stepmother then, Harry!'

Cora took a step towards him and he stopped jumping and leapt into her arms.

'Wicked!' he said. 'Oh, hahaha, wicked stepmother! That's funny!'

They all laughed, just as the door opened and, to Cora's enormous surprise, Nathan, Rodney and Scott filed in, closely followed by Rosie and Nicole.

'What are you all doing here?' she asked.

'Well, we've been covering the story about John Smith

and his shenanigans this morning for the show, so we thought we'd pop in, see how you're both doing. And we met these two reprobates in the car park,' Nathan said, and pointed at Rosie and Nicole, who Cora now noticed were laden with bags which they'd begun unpacking.

'Sam and Wendy are coming down from London to see you both later this afternoon, Sam rang me this morning. So we thought the place might need cheering up, seeing as it's Christmas Eve and everything,' Nicole announced, pulling a long strand of battery-operated fairy lights out of one of the bags and looking around the room for somewhere to hang them.

'And we also had rather a lot of food to use up, after our nice "pretend Christmas" weekend was so inconveniently cancelled. So we thought we'd have a party here instead, seeing as Adam isn't dead or anything now,' Rosie added. She had a box of dark chocolates in one hand and what looked like a Christmas pudding in a bowl in the other.

'Errr... right. Well, not sure what the staff are going to say, but feel free,' Cora said. She looked at Adam, who was watching everyone with an amused expression. He raised his eyebrows and nodded towards Cora's left hand, on which the beautiful ring was now sparkling.

'Go on,' he whispered.

She grinned. 'OK,' she whispered back. She turned back to the others, but just as she was about to speak Rosie let out a shriek.

'CORA! What is that on your left hand? Is that... is that an *engagement ring*?'

Cora held her hand in the air, palm facing towards her, and smiled.

'Might be,' she said.

The room erupted, Rosie and Nicole hugging first each

other and then Cora, the boys high-fiving each other and then rushing to the bed to - carefully - take turns doing the same to Adam, Harry running around them all in excited circles like a collie trying to control a pack of unruly sheep. When everyone finally calmed down, Adam put a hand to his chest.

'Mozzarella,' he said quietly, his eyes fixed on Cora.

She looked at him with alarm, as everyone else stared.

'Huh?' said Rodney. 'You alright, Adam?'

'I'm so sorry, we have Brie, Cheddar and some blue, but no mozzarella.' Rosie studied the table she'd laid the food out on with a worried look.

'But I can pop out and get some, if you really fancy it, Adam...'

'No, no, he doesn't want cheese!'

Cora was standing over Adam now, anxiety rippling through her.

'What is it? Are you in pain? Do you want me to call a doctor?'

He shook his head, then reached out a hand and pulled her to him again.

'It's just that I think my heart might be about to burst. With happiness. Did you really just agree to marry me, Cora Baxter?'

She sighed. 'Bloody hell, don't do that to me. Yes, I did. And it's too late to back out now. You're stuck with me, DCI Bradberry.'

She kissed him, then stood up.

'Right, shall we eat? I'm starving, all of a sudden.'

'What's the mozzarella thing, though? I don't get it,' asked Nathan.

Cora and Adam exchanged looks, and smiled.

'It's a long story, Nath,' she said. 'But one day soon, I'll tell you all how mozzarella saved my life.'

'And how it nearly bloody killed me,' Adam added drily.

'Errrm… OK then,' said Nathan. 'Well, food then? Can you manage anything, Adam?'

'I'll feed you, Adam. We can share,' Cora said, picking up a paper plate from the stack Nicole had balanced on the bedside table.

'Thank you,' he said softly.

She reached out a finger and gently stroked his cheek.

'And do you think we can try never, ever to say the M word again, as long as we live?'

'Mozzarella? Whoops, sorry. Deal,' he said.

'Thank you, husband to be,' she said. 'I love you. Love you now, love you always.'

'I know. You crazy lady. Right back at ya.'

She blew him a kiss, and went to fill their plate.

THE END